Unexpected

Viator Legacy Series: Book One

Erin Lausten

Drago Fortuna Publishing

For my husband, without you my dreams would be unrealized

To the Beta Babes Eliza, Mindy and Kelly, you make me a better writer

To Emma, your hawk eyes made this possible

1

White. Why had she worn white? Hailey McIntyre grabbed a napkin and dipped it into her glass of water then scrubbed viciously at her shirt. The orange stain faded but she was left with a giant wet spot across her chest that would take an hour to dry. She sighed, gave it up for lost and returned her attention to lunch.

Jason smirked at her from across the table. She responded with a middle finger salute then laughed as her heart warmed. He was the brother she'd never had and those were the best kind. They never fought over parental approval or premium bedroom spaces. Their affection could be real without the history and it was absolutely perfect.

The wax paper crinkled as she wrapped her fingers around the special sauce soaked sandwich. Grease and caffeine had been just the thing to stop the incessant pounding in her head. She really needed to rethink the wisdom of going out to the bar on a work night. Casting a glare at Jason she wondered how he managed to always wake up no worse the wear from a night out. The man had to have some kind of party man super power.

Based on the sappy grin he'd shared when he passed her cubical that morning he'd gotten lucky the night before too.

She said, "So, how do you do it? How do you walk out of the bar every night with a different man on your arm?"

He waggled his eyebrows and leaned against the back of the thin plastic yard chair that lent that special seedy ambiance to Rizzo's Super Subs. His hands patted his belly. A black cotton t-shirt clung to his slight paunch. Black might be slimming, but it didn't hide it all. "It's the power of smokin' hot abs, babe. I can turn a man on fire at fifty paces."

Hailey rolled her eyes. "You are a piece of work."

"A work of art, sweet heart. A work of art," he said. The chair, fed up with the ill use, folded back on itself. Jason lunged forward, knocking the table several inches toward her. Swift hands saved her Diet Coke from tipping over onto her half-eaten pastrami-on-rye: The best damn sandwich in Los Angeles County.

"I wish I could turn a man on fire at fifty paces." She replied placing her soda back onto the plastic checkered table cloth.

"Girlfriend, you turn men on fire with that caustic wit of yours. There's just nothing left of them to walk out of the bar with," Jason said.

Hailey snorted and cracked a grin. He was right. She probably could have a guy on her arm with relative ease. The trouble started when she got bored. And she always got bored. If they weren't talking about the drunkfest the night before they were bragging about their recent material acquisition. The winner last night had bought himself a brand new, hot off the presses, smart phone. Then spent three hours showing her every feature, every app—every stupid little thing until she wanted to dump the slim silver gadget into her pint of Sam Adams.

Her beer survived—enough for her to finish it. The poor sap hadn't been so lucky. As each agonizing minute progressed her remarks went from witty to scathing until she reduced him to a withering weed at her feet. She left the bar with glares pounding her back, convinced that at thirty she was well on her way to spending her life as the crabby spinster that lived in the corner house waiting for the opportunity to turn the hose on the neighborhood kids.

The candy red plastic lunch baskets sat among the balled up napkins and grease covered wax paper like eighteen wheelers in a twenty car pile-up. The clock on her phone flashed the time and her shoulders sunk. Ten minutes until she needed to be back at her desk, plunging back into the mess that was the marketing proposal. Ten minutes that would feel like half a gasp. The four hours left in the work day would no doubt feel like fifty years.

"Dude, we have to go," she said.

Jason tipped his head back and drained the last of his full octane Mountain Dew. Then stood and brushed the crumbs off his lap. He held out his elbow and she slid her fingers into the crook of his arm. It was nice having a man treat her like a lady. It was too bad he wasn't her type. Or that she failed to have the correct anatomy for him.

"So, you're going to love this." He pushed open the door to Rizzo's, letting in the ozone rich Los Angeles air. "McDermott is preggers."

"Dude! Shut up!" She stopped and slapped him on the arm. "She's what, like fifty?"

"Forty-five."

"Wow." She hugged her arms around her chest. Karen McDermott, their manager and all around crazy lady, was pregnant. The woman had mood swings as a rule. Add

3

hormones and the office might go up in flames before she reached full term. Terrifying was the only word for it. "Who would marry her? The man must want to kill himself."

"It's Ron in operations." Jason started down the three crumbling cement steps that led toward the tiny back parking lot.

Once she pulled her lip off the ground she ran after him. "Ron? Little Ron, the one with the crooked teeth that won't look anyone in the eye?"

"That's him."

"Oh my god. That is too much," Hailey said. Her beat-up grey Civic waited pitifully beside the alley trash bin. When they'd arrived the lunch rush just hit, leaving the sliver of land as the only option. Now, the lot was empty save for the three cars that belonged to the staff. Flies buzzed around her head and she held her breath against the stench as she slid along the car to the driver's side.

Hailey rifled through her purse for the keys as a scrawny man approached them. His saggy pants and over large shirt swallowed him up in un-mastered ghetto style. The glazed eyes of the eternally stoned peered out from beneath a beat-up baseball hat pitched precariously on stringy hair.

Jason watched him with shoulders tense and lips thinned. Cursing her choice in handbags, Hailey's fingers swam through the mass of receipts, makeup and gum wrappers. The keys and her cell phone had sunk to the deepest recesses and neither cooperated with her desperate search.

"Hey man, what's up?" Jason kept his voice cool and relaxed, but his stance remained wary. The druggie stopped five feet from the car and glanced furtively to the side, his jittery reflexes sent waves of warning flowing through her

4

head. His long-fingered hand slid into deep pockets and she held her breath in dread.

Jason threw his hands up with palms out and fingers wide. "Look dude, we don't want trouble, tell us what you want."

The man's eyes were frantic and his lip curled as he snarled, "Shut up, fag and get away from the car."

A gun flashed toward Jason as the man strode toward the driver's side. "Give me the keys, bitch."

"I...I can't find them," Hailey stammered. The world shrunk around her and time trickled to a creep. Blood rushed past her ears in a deafening roar and the hairs along her arms tickled in anticipation.

"I said give me the keys!" The man's yellowing teeth bared and his fingers clenched the handle of the gun. Hailey squeaked, praying he wouldn't shoot Jason.

"I think I left them inside," she replied.

A red flush spread up the man's neck. Hailey felt it before she saw the gleam in his eyes shift from barely restrained violence to deadly intent. When the gun swung toward her, Jason's shouts were swallowed in a cotton-like fog. Fear barely registered when the gun went off. As the world around her flashed bright white she prepared for the excruciating pain of a bullet hitting her chest. Everything slowed to a crawl but her thoughts ran sharp and clear. This was a hell of a way to die, she thought just before she blacked out.

When her senses returned a wave of nausea flipped her stomach into a round of cartwheels. A headache split an arc of hot fire through her temples and her ears felt like someone had stuffed in cotton, added water, and shook. Strange, this was not what she thought getting shot would feel like.

She opened her eyes. Expecting to see the concerned faces of a couple of hot EMT's or at the very least Jason, she was surprised to find her nose inches from a giant wooden barrel. A thin iron band ran around the bottom that held together the bentwood slabs. The last time she'd seen a barrel like that was with her Aunt Sue at the Old West movie lot. She was ten and Aunt Sue was cancer free.

Flipping to her back, she closed her eyes. Nausea swamped her stomach and only after several deep breaths was she able to reopen her eyes. Through the darkness, slivers of light peeked through the cracks between the hand-hewn wooden boards that made up the ceiling. A drop of water careened from a crack and splashed on her upper lip. The cool wetness settled against her skin triggering a torrent of sensations through her body. Her ears popped open with a horrendous howl.

"Argh!" She cringed and slapped her hands against her ears. Muscles twisted and agony shot through to the bone. The suddenness of the pain and sensations crashed her system sending shockwaves through her fingers and toes. It was as if a switch turned off the morphine drip. She curled into a ball and rocked.

It was impossible to guess how long she writhed on the hard floor but it eventually subsided and everything inched toward normalcy. Little sounds outside her head crept in. the creak of wood shifting its weight echoed through the room. The soft hum of voices floated above the laboring planks.

A loud thunk slammed through the ceiling. A rush of water droplets splashed across her body, soaking her already damp shirt. She sat up and scooted back to lean against the hard plank wall. The room rolled from side to side. Nausea followed at a softer pace, but threatened her equilibrium nonetheless. If it hadn't been completely ridiculous she would have sworn she'd been dumped on a boat.

The room plummeted down and to the side then heaved back to settle into a mild rocking motion. She pressed her ear to the wall. Water sloshed against the wood. It must be some kind of hallucination. No one sailed wood boats anymore. Unless they were weird — or rich. Maybe she'd been kidnapped by a crazy rich guy. A *hot* crazy rich guy. Now that might be something she could handle.

She struggled to her feet and rested a hand against the wall. When her head stopped spinning and stomach quit rolling she scanned the room for a way out. A soft frame of light illuminated a door several feet to her right. The barrels surrounding her were bound tight with thick twisted rope to prevent shifting. Somehow she'd been stowed in the only free space large enough for a body to stretch out.

Hailey wiggled and wound her way through the barrels to the narrow walkway that ran through the middle of the room. Once she reached the door it wouldn't budge. Was she trapped accidentally? She couldn't think of a single reason someone would lock her in a place like this.

Her fists pounded at the door, but all she managed was a muffled thud. Shouts and screams it was then.

"Hey! Let me out!" The room rang but the sounds dulled before they could make it through the walls and ceiling. After several minutes she leaned in and placed her ear against the crack between the door and jamb. Nothing. "Argh!"

She slumped to the floor and banged her head against the door. Going hoarse wouldn't help the situation. She banged her head against the door again and was rewarded with a sharp pain through her temple. Beating herself senseless wouldn't help either.

The heavy moisture seeped into her pores. A couple hours in this place and she'd have fingers like a Shar-pei's face. All the events that led to this moment were laid out in her mind and not a single one added up. She gave up trying to figure it out when the scenarios included fairy dust and magic wands. Closing her eyes she commanded herself not to freak out.

Metal scraping against metal woke her from an unexpected doze. She had barely enough time to scramble to her feet before the door swung open and a backlit figure stood in the hall. With his short legs and wide shoulders he looked more like a podium than a man. He took a few steps into the room before he noticed her standing there.

"Holy Mother Mary!" He jumped back several feet and grabbed the door jamb. His other hand flew to his heart. The stink of unwashed masculinity wafted to her nose and instigated a new bout of nausea. "Why are ye in 'ere boy?"

"Excuse me?" Hailey said and stepped into the light.

"Lordy! Yer a woman!" His wide eyes, gapping mouth, and gender identification issues suggested she hadn't been expected.

"Last time I checked." Hailey peered over the sweat drenched man into a dimly lit hallway. Despite the man's diminutive height, his broad shoulders and thick neck kept her wary. "Look, I'm not sure how I got here, but if you let me through I'm sure we can…"

Meaty hands shoved her back with such violence that she landed heavily on her tailbone. The door slammed shut and she heard the metallic scrape of the key turning in the lock before she caught her breath.

"Shit," she breathed. With trembling limbs she struggled to stand, adrenaline pumped her heart like a bilge. She didn't care if he was built like a bull dog; the man was going to find himself flat on his ass when she saw him again. She rubbed her tailbone. The fact that she'd never actually hit a person wasn't relevant. No one pushed her.

Shouts failed to bring him back. Several violent kicks to the door just bruised her foot. Eventually she sat and buried her head in her arms. The day was really starting to suck. After a while her butt went numb and she stood to pace. Pacing always made things better. It settled her mind and let the thoughts fall into order. It also prevented the flood of tears perched precariously at the edge of her eyelids. She hated crying.

The sound of the key in the lock barely registered. She spun around just as the door swung open and a huge shadowy man loomed in the doorway. All her false bravado fled and she took a step back as he advanced into the room.

His voice boomed, "What, Madam," he grabbed her elbow and yanked her against his chest. "Are you doing on my ship?"

2

Derian gazed across the green plain that surrounded *Santlache*. The soft breeze and peace obscured its bloody past. Memories swirled, a flash of iron, a scream of agony, the expectation of a killing blow. He'd mourned the ghosts that clung to this hill long ago, but still they curled around the ether of time.

It was always the same. The sweet peace cut into his soul like a blunt knife, the silence a harsh reminder of the fate of men. Still, he came to watch the story of this place play through his mind. He came to remember that which he could never witness again. He came to see where the Duke of Normandy took away the life and homeland he once took for granted.

Cool metal vibrated against the inside of his wrist. He lifted the leather band that hid the communicator. The tiny bead of light switched from red to green. He stood and brushed the grass from the snug denim.

The landscape coalesced into a haze and faded from view, replaced by stark white walls and utilitarian desks. Several faces peeked above modular walls as he materialized; bland indifference settled over the flashes of curiosity.

Speculation hid behind the mask of professionalism. But every soul in the room knew that when he appeared in headquarters interesting times followed.

Derian ignored the bodies that filled the rows of cubicles and stalked through the aisle to the steel door that led into the bowels of the *Domus*. A light blinked red twice then switched to green after he punched in his access code. The door clicked and Derian strode into the long winding hallway of the *castellum* that housed the highest levels of bureaucracy, top secret laboratories, and the control center for the *viators*.

The labyrinthine halls were designed specifically to funnel intruders away from the most sensitive areas; but he could slide through the halls silent and unnoticed, knowing each false turn and disguised entrance. He stole into the Magister's office and waited for his presence to be acknowledged. Two men were hunched over a heavy oak table and three chairs sat empty between the table and the matching desk. The smaller of the two men shook his head emphatically as the other pointed at the table.

It had been some time since he'd been summoned by the Magister. His recent assignments consisted of simple apprehensions warranting little concern and less communication. Derian itched for a challenge and could feel the familiar spark of anticipation for the hunt.

"Magister," Derian said.

Millard, a spindly and nervous man jumped at the voice. But the Magister merely glanced up at his top operative, unconcerned by his sudden appearance. Lucius Gratius Cossus was a tall man and dark like Derian. But where Derian was rugged and harsh, the Magister was clean-cut and staid. Neither man was quick to smile, having seen far too much in their long lives to warrant easy levity.

They partnered on several apprehensions prior to Lucius' appointment to Magister. He long ago grew accustomed to the ghost like maneuvers that made Derian a legend.

"Join us," Lucius said and motioned toward the table. A large screen lay imbedded in the wood showing pinpricks of light scattered across a digital image of the earth. Lucius slid his finger along the screen and spun the globe, tapping it to a halt when it reached the Caribbean. Several of the pinpricks in green and yellow aggregated on the islands that peppered the region. A single red light blinked a hundred miles to the east of the islands. Lucius tapped that light twice. The screen zoomed in and pulled up a box of data.

"An unregistered *viator* jumped an hour ago and landed here." Lucius pointed to the screen. Rows of null signs filled the box. The only data available were GPS coordinates and a date. That wasn't much to go on.

"A rogue?" Derian asked.

The nervous little man spoke up, beads of sweat lined his brow and he mumbled his words. Millard was one of the many that worked in the data tracking division. Had he not been a *viator* he would have been comfortably found counting pennies as an accountant. "We're not certain. Even rogues have a registered birth. This one is a complete unknown."

"A *novus*?" Derian asked and the man nodded, anxiety written clear across his face. A *novus* was a *viator* that only recently learned to jump time. Derian scowled then turned toward Lucius. "I don't babysit, you know that."

"But...but..." The blubbering data tracker was forestalled by a stony glare from the Magister.

"I am aware of that. This situation is unique," Lucius said. Derian leaned back and crossed his arms. Lucius continued undaunted, "You know all travelers are registered at birth. We've never had one just show up on the map like this."

"Then send a *praeceptor*," Derian said. All *novus* were assigned an agent to ease the transition to *viator* status. The first jump could be a painful shock and required a guide and teacher. Both skills Derian lacked. His talents lay in the hunt and apprehension of those *viator* that chose the life of a rogue. These rogues were reined in to prevent any threat to the *Domus*, Council and the *viators*. Unfortunately, as had been the case of late, many simply bristled under the limitations of the law and wanted to stretch their legs.

"Even if I were certain this was a *novus*, I couldn't do that." Lucius tapped the red light again and the picture zoomed in to an image of a Galleon with sails billowing in the wind and riding low in the water. He pointed at the date. "Our records show this ship was captured and commandeered by John Davies one week before this jump." Lucius leaned back and considered his agent. "Whoever landed here has found themselves on a ship full of pirates."

The situation intrigued him. Derian had never tangled with pirates. And this group found a way to take an entire Spanish Galleon. Lucius smiled and Derian knew the Magister hadn't missed the spark of interest he tried to hide. Lucius jumped on that knowledge and said, "There isn't a *praeceptor* with the skills to extract a *novus* from this situation."

Derian grunted. The logistics involved in the extraction were nightmarish. The *novus*—if that was what they were dealing with—would be disoriented and incapable of a second jump for days. First he would have to land on the ship unnoticed, find the *novus*, and then get them off the ship, onto dry land, and into the patient hands of a *praeceptor*. All this while pursued by irate pirates.

Derian grinned. "Let's hope the pirates have left me something to save."

"Good." Lucius nodded. "Marianne is waiting for you. She was particularly excited about dressing you for this."

"That confident I would say, yes?"

Lucius said, "Of course. Who wouldn't want to fight pirates?"

Derian put out his arm and the two men shook hands. As he walked through the door the blubbering started up again. Lucius' irritated voice faded in the distance as Derian made his escape. "Shut up Millard, no one thinks it's your fault."

***

"Dude!" The man was huge. And boy his breath was rank. Hailey raised her free hand to cover her mouth and nose before she choked on the fumes that enveloped him. She looked up into the deepest darkest blue eyes she'd ever seen. A person could swim a mile in those eyes — if they weren't spitting fire.

"How have you survived here?" he growled. "Who has assisted you?"

"How have I...What are you talking about?" Hailey asked. A muscle twitched in her captor's jaw. She tugged her arm but his fingers dug painfully into the tender elbow joint. "Let me go!"

With a snarl, he propelled her from the room out into the narrow hallway and up a thin stairway. They burst into the bright light of the afternoon sun and her eyes burned in protest. She threw her free arm over her eyes. Now would be a terrible time for him to decide to let her go. His pace kept her so off balance she could feel her toes dragging behind. She needed to catch her bearing. "Hey! Can you slow down?"

He stopped and she careened into his chest—again. This whole chest thumping thing was old. She glared up at him. "Dude! What is your problem?"

"If you would like the men to get a good look at what has been hiding below deck, then by all means, let us slow down."

Hailey shifted her angry gaze from the odious man to the surroundings. They stood in the middle of a giant ship—the kind one expected to find in an epic movie. Dozens of sweaty unwashed men dressed in ratty clothes with faces burnt to a crisp stared at her with open mouths. Were they filming *another* Pirates of the Caribbean? She could have sworn they'd finished that series already.

Confused, she turned back to get a good look at the man that hauled her around the ship like a floppy headed rag doll. He was cleaner than the others, but not by much. His sun-baked skin created a striking contrast with his blue eyes. Thin lips turned down in a scowl and a few wrinkles touched his eyes—from bad skin care no doubt.

Breeches that looked very much like canvas hugged his legs and his shirt hung open at the front. Hailey blushed when she looked up to see his eyebrow raised. She said, "Don't even think I was checking you out!"

"Madam, do you have any idea where you are?"

"No."

He straightened, shook his head, and ran his hands through his hair. His frown deepened. Concern tickled at her senses, but reality was floating off in the weird space between dreams and waking. She doubted that she had miraculously appeared on a movie set, but alternative explanations were not forthcoming.

He pivoted on his heel and hauled her toward a set of stairs that led to the back of the ship. She was pretty sure they had a name for each place on the ship. Fore, aft, port, starboard—whatever, she'd never learned them. All she wanted was to get off and find out how the hell she'd gotten out of Rizzo's parking lot.

His stride was a little more restrained, but she was still huffing when he led her through a heavy oak door. Two steps into the room he released her and slammed the door. She scuttled across the room and stood behind a tall back chair. The room was huge. Ships were supposed to have tiny rooms, not ones bigger than her apartment. Windows lined the far wall and beyond was the infinite blue of sky and sea.

"Please tell me there is land on the other side of this boat," Hailey said.

"Sit," he ordered and pointed at the chair. Its rich opulence had seen better days. Slashes and stains paid homage to a violent past. The manhandling irked her, but her legs were ready to give out, so she sat. She was on a gigantic ship with a bunch of mean looking stinky men and not a modern stitch of clothing on them. If it weren't crazy, she'd swear she was on an honest to god pirate ship.

"Who are you?" she asked, perching herself on the edge of the seat. The scowl remained on his face. She wouldn't be surprised if he refused to answer. He leaned a hip against a heavy dark wood desk littered with papers and various foreign instruments.

She stared out the windows and took a deep breath trying desperately to stem the panic. All the signs screamed she was not an expected guest. If that were the case how had she gotten here?

She turned back to look at the man lounging against the desk. He stared at her legs as if he'd forgotten his lunch in the fridge and someone had walked by with hamburger and fries. "Dude!"

He tore his gaze from her body to her face and his hungered expression became a scowl. She trusted the scowl more. At a serious disadvantage she figured she would have better luck against anger than lust. Playing out a scene from a romance pirate novel was not high on her to-do list at the moment.

"What are you doing on my ship?"

"I take it you weren't expecting me," she replied. He pushed himself away from the desk and started toward her. She jumped off the chair to put it between them. "So, that makes two of us wondering why I'm on your ship."

He stalked her, jump-starting her heart into fourth gear. "Madam, you grow tiresome."

He swooped around the chair and Hailey skidded to the other side. "Enough with the stomping and chasing. I want to know what's going on as bad as you do."

An iron hand snapped out at her elbow and she barely slipped out of reach. With a high-pitched squeak she ran to the opposite side of a ridiculously large bed. It wasn't until his scowl turned into a wolfish grin that she realized she was trapped between the wall and the bed. This was not good. "Shit."

The tawny haired devil braced his arms on the mattress and grinned. "I had not intended to move to the bed this quickly, but if you are offering..."

"No way, Romeo." Hailey positioned herself at the corner. If he came around she was going over the mattress.

"Perhaps you would prefer I invite my men to join us?" He leered at her. Hailey had never actually seen someone leer before. Where was a meteor when you needed one?

"Sorry, not into the kinky stuff," she said.

"Stowaways do not have a choice in their fate, Madam." He scanned her body deliberately. "Even one with delicacies such as yours."

His good looks melted away as all decency flew out the window. Now every ugly detail and mannerism turned her stomach. One eye trained on him, she scanned the room for defense options. Overpowering the man was impossible and he was a little preoccupied with carnal activities to be open to negotiations. She needed something to neutralize the situation. "I'm not a stowaway."

"What would you be then?" he drawled. Condescension dripped from the words.

"Lost," she said.

He shifted from one foot to the other. A small dagger swung at his hip. An idea percolated. She pulled her lip between her teeth and waited for his next move.

He growled and darted around the side of the bed. Hailey hopped onto the bed and was about to go over the side when her ankles were trapped in a vise-like grip and yanked out from beneath her. He pulled and she rolled, hauling the blanket over her body. It was a poor shield against a lust-filled lunatic, but she would take anything that would slow the inevitable rape.

Landing heavily on her, he crushed the air from her chest. Her response was breathy, "Get off me, asshole!"

His hands grabbed at her, ripping at the blanket that separated them. Hailey shoved and grunted. The hard length of his erection prodded into her thigh. The reality of the nightmare seared into her mind.

The maniac tore the blanket from her fingers and flung it aside. His claw-like fingers ripped her blouse open. He stopped moving and raised an eyebrow. "Your un-mentionables are as strange as the rest."

For the moment he was confounded by her bra and how to remove it. This gave Hailey a much needed second to catch her breath. "Please don't do this."

He cupped her breast through the soft cotton fabric. Her throat closed in revulsion and she could feel tears building at the corner of her eyes. All women lived knowing that rape was possible, but she never really believed it would happen to her.

His hips ground against her and she hiccupped in anxiety-filled frustration. He braced an arm across her chest, and lifted himself to yank the rest of the blanket from between them. She pummeled her fists against his chest. He trapped one of her hands in his fingers and squeezed. Knuckles ground against each other and pain shot through her wrist. The bed creaked as they rolled and struggled.

Hard cool metal grazed her free hand as the dagger fell within reach. Letting her body go limp she stared blankly up at the ceiling. He chuckled, taking her lax body as a signal of acceptance and rifled around his waist to wrestle with the ties of his breeches. He was braced heavy and unbalanced on top of her chest.

Her elbow was pinned against the bed but her hand was free. She wrapped her fingers around the dagger and waited for him to move. He shifted, leaving her enough room to pull the blade from its sheath. His eyes met hers as he moved his efforts to removing her pants. He looked down when his fingers found the zipper.

Hailey drew in a breath and slashed. He roared as the metal sliced through skin. Instinct made him move his body from hers and she rolled with the advantage. Their limbs flopped in a frantic dance for control.

She grunted, kicked and slashed. He'd win the fight but she'd be damned if she'd give it to him free. A heavy hand landed across her face, snapping her head to the side and she saw stars. When she could see clearly again there was murder in his eyes.

3

Luck was a *viator's* greatest friend or most devious enemy during a jump. Control for the exact time and location was a difficult skill to perfect. A thousand years of practice taught Derian to be good, but even he couldn't be sure where on the Galleon he would land or who would see him blink into existence.

Most landings he planned in uninhabited areas and he would then walk toward civilization to prevent unnecessary complications. However, Lucius had nailed it, this was a special circumstance and his adrenaline ran hot. He arrived in a defensive crouch, his knives flashing in the sunlight, ready for attack. Knives always proved the most effective defensive weapon. Quick reflexes allowed him to act with split second accuracy and control he couldn't be sure of with firearms. He brought his Glock, but it was tucked safely in his shoulder holster for the moment it was needed.

Luck proved sweet and landed him in a hidden corner of the deck. He could see a dozen sailors, their backs to him, distracted by a commotion at the stern of the ship. A hushed murmur rumbled across the deck. His stomach clenched. Apparently the *novus* had been discovered. A door slammed and the murmur intensified into a speculative roar.

Derian needed to get to that door. He hoped the discovery of an unexpected guest would distract the crew from an additional intruder. Dressed in the same baggy breeches and loose fitting linen shirt as the men on the ship he felt relatively confident he could slip in unnoticed. He cocked his head away from the crowd and strode across the deck as if he had every right to be there.

The route to the second deck was blocked by twenty of the nastier looking sailors. The crews of pirate ships were often made up of men given a choice of joining the ranks or going down with a captured ship. They were victims of circumstance. But those standing before him exhibited the look of veteran piracy. These men looked like they enjoyed their occupation.

He slowed. He didn't trust his disguise enough to infiltrate that group. The wall that ran the width of the deck would be an easy climb, if he could ascend without being observed.

A pile of rope at the far end of the deck could serve as a suitable boost, but it was exposed. He wandered over and leaned against the rail. A diversion would have to be created to enable his climb. Tucked beneath his shirt was a form fitted utility vest filled with various aids, including a number of explosives. Carefully placed, they could provide the cover he needed to retrieve the *novus*. But it was risky and he didn't have his exit strategy figured out quite yet.

He scanned the deck and spotted a small dingy. If the *novus* could hold out until night, they might be able to steal away in the darkness. It was a weak plan, and needed revising.

A masculine shout roared from the deck above. All eyes were on the stairs as several men ran up them. Derian jumped on the opportunity.

He pulled himself up then swung his body over the rail. Landing in a crouch he watched to see if he had been noticed. The terrified shouts of a woman added to the cacophony of sound. The hairs at the nape of his neck rose and adrenaline rushed through his system. The *novus* was a woman and now she was at the mercy of a ruthless pirate. Derian knew exactly what he would encounter when he entered the cabin.

Men were banging on the door with their fists. "Cap 'in!"

It swung open with a furious force and the woman was shoved out the door and onto her knees. She stood quickly with fists clenched. Chin length sandy blond hair stuck out frizzed and knotted. Her baby blue blouse hung open in testament to a violent rip and one of her rage filled eyes swelled puffy and red.

Ten men stood gaping at the woman and her exposed breasts. Shoulders heaved in anger and humiliation, her stance was bent-kneed and ready for action. When an arm reached toward her she lashed out and knocked it away. Her movements were untutored but quick and with proper training she might have had a fighting chance. As it were, it would be a matter of seconds before she was overpowered.

The captain stomped out of the cabin, a bloody stain soaked his shirt just above his hip. He grabbed her arm, dragged her across the deck and down the stairs. Had the situation not been so dire, Derian would have smiled at the ease at which she lashed out with expletives, even a few of the pirates appeared impressed.

The captain's voice boomed over her invectives, "We have a wench that needs punishing! Wyatt!"

A stocky man with a missing hand scuttled across the lower deck. The captain approached the mast and a rope was produced by one of the other pirates. Derian cursed. He couldn't stand and watch the fierce little woman whipped, but his options were extremely limited. Knives would be ineffective against so many men. Derian moved toward the stairs, watching for an opportunity.

The one-handed man produced a whip. Even from the deck above he could see her blanch. Her struggles intensified, but were ineffective. The remains of her shirt were ripped off her body and an appreciative murmur went up from the crowd of leering men. She screeched exactly what she thought of each and every one of them.

Derian refused to stand by and watch anymore. He pulled his gun and pointed it at her captors. The woman spotted him at the rail just as he pulled the trigger. Her eyes opened wide in surprise and her mouth flapped open then shut. The bullet whizzed past the captain's head and lodged into the mast. The surprise from the bullet forced him to drop her arms. He spun around and Derian pointed the Glock square at the man's torso.

With all attention trained on the shooter she ran and the small crowd split with ease as they stood dumbfounded. She sprinted up the stairs to the next deck, past him and into the cabin. Derian didn't wait for the pirates to recover from their shock before he too ran toward the cabin. The captain's furious shouts pressed the pirates into action. Derian let loose several more shots to slow their attack.

He swung the door shut just as the first pursuer reached the top of the stairs. Bracing his body against the door he found the woman furiously trying to haul a heavy oak desk in front of the door.

"It is probably secured to the floor," Derian said.

"Damn it!" she shouted then kicked the desk. "Any ideas?"

"At the moment?" Derian felt a body hit the door. "No."

She ran to an open window and stuck her head out then turned back to him. "So, do they have escape boats on this thing?"

"On deck," Derian said.

"Crap." She ran to a large chest and rifled through the contents. Her position gave him an excellent view of an exquisite round ass that wiggled a little as she scrounged. He had always been partial to a nice ass.

A second body hit the door. A chirp of victory came from the woman and he saw her pull out two shiny daggers. Then she pulled out a shirt and threw it over her head. "If I'm going down, it's not with my ya-yas hanging out."

He couldn't help but laugh. "What's your name?"

"Hailey. Yours?" She stood brandishing the two daggers in tight fists.

"Derian." He smiled at her courage. She was short, her head would be lucky to reach his chin, but she stood like she was in command. Her cheeks flushed and her lips were slightly parted. The soft linen shirt covered the wonderfully full breasts he'd caught a glimpse of on deck.

When Derian first landed he had expected to finesse the situation; not run through with his guns blazing. Their only chance for escape was the little boat on the other side of a mob of angry pirates. He did not relish taking on a ship full of battle ready men. His supplies consisted of his Glock, knives and the few small explosives. The odds were against them and they were running out of time.

Splintering wood told him exactly how little time remained. The pirates had brought axes and were hacking through the door. It wasn't the most efficient way to get to them, but it appeared the captain wasn't quite desperate enough to turn one of the cannons on the uninvited guests.

Derian lifted his shirt to pull out one of the explosives from the utility vest. When he looked up the color on her face faded to a sickly pale. She shimmered briefly and then disappeared.

He stared at the empty space where she once stood. New *viators* took days to recover from a landing. There was no way she could have done what he just saw her do. But if she were a veteran why hadn't she jumped as soon as things got hairy? His interest perked and he returned the explosive to his pocket. The woman with her steely courage and sharp tongue was an enigma. She owed him answers but first he needed to get off this ship and report back to Lucius. The Magister would be quite interested in this new development.

***

Hailey woke up soggy. Face down in thick grass she opened her eyes and met the beady eyes of a disgruntled beetle. The headache pounded, her muscles ached, her stomach rolled, and the numbness of her senses returned. But the agony was blissfully absent.

A thick stand of bushy trees stood directly in front of her. She sat up on her knees to examine the landscape. Three rows of overgrown hedges surrounded the boggy green field where she found herself. At the far end of the field stood a small cottage with a faint billow of smoke curling out of its stone chimney.

She looked down. The thick morning dew had soaked into her thin linen shirt and it clung to her body like cheap plastic wrap. Luckily there weren't any psycho pirates around. Unfortunately, neither was the handsome hero with his blazing guns. The memory of his fortuitous entrance tickled her heart. If she had been the type to catch the vapors she would have right then. But she wasn't. In general she preferred to fight her own battles, though she didn't have a problem allowing him a shot at a few.

But, he was gone; and she had no idea how she had teleported from the ship to a wet green field. If things hadn't already been surreal she might have gotten worried. However, things seemed to be progressing consistently. Any minute now she expected to see winged monkeys or a yellow brick road.

The two highly-shined daggers lay beside her. She grabbed them, stood and brushed the grass and dirt from her clothes. Determined to find civilization and possibly answers to her predicament she headed across the field to the small cottage. She eyed the foundations for striped socks and ruby slippers.

Suddenly, her ears popped with a loud *fwump*. A projectile hit the cottage and a tempest of fractured wood and glass flew through the air. Half of the building lay in rubble across the field.

Several figures stumbled out clutching at the bloody remains of their bodies. Screams of agony and gunfire filled the air.

"Oh my God!"

She threw herself down and belly crawled to the nearest stand of hedges. Gunfire exchanged between the house of rubble and the opposite cover of vegetation. Thanking heaven she landed far enough away from the combatants to go unnoticed, she slithered under the nearest hedge.

A second projectile exploded. A few more shots peppered the air then a frightening silence followed. She shook from head to toe and her heart ran like a rabbit chased by a pack of dogs. She peered between branches as several men sprinted from the cottage into another stand of trees.

After a few moments five men walked out from hiding in the hedges and tramped toward the cottage. They wore green coats and slacks with tall black boots. Each sported a hard metal helmet and held their rifles ready. Harsh words floated across the field to her ears. It sounded German. What the hell was she doing in Germany?

The ground rumbled beneath her. The sound of grinding gears and crunch of a road pummeled by extreme weight came from beyond her damp hiding spot. Without rustling the branches, she shifted her body to peer out beneath the rich green leaves.

A hard packed dirt road lay between her and another line of hedges. Far to the right a tank swiveled onto the road. Several soldiers in the same green uniforms as the men she witnessed earlier walked beside it, rifles drawn and pointed at the surrounding cover. She'd seen enough war movies to know these weren't just German soldiers. They were honest to god Nazis.

Hailey cursed as the tank continued its crawl toward her spot. The white linen would shine through the underbrush like a strobe light and draw the attention of the hyper alert soldiers. The five soldiers were still in the field behind her and no matter how deep she sunk into the brush the passing foot soldiers were sure to spot her.

Could she use the daggers as defense? It seemed ridiculous to even consider. She wasn't exactly a couch potato; she did her weekly guilt-fed run around the block, but she was no action star. A single self-defense class was her only experience with fighting and those lessons proved unsuccessful against the pirate captain. Taking on a bunch of trained soldiers would end the same and probably worse. If her dark haired hero from the ship intended to follow her, now would be the best time. She might even propose marriage if he did show up.

The tank and patrolling soldiers approached from twenty feet away. She clenched her fists around the daggers. Each step the men took shot a shiver through her nerves. Maybe she would disappear again. That would be extremely convenient.

Her adrenaline reached its peak when a barrage of gunfire scrambled the tank infantry. A projectile exploded at the nose of the growling machine, deafening her momentarily and sending dirt and rock ricocheting through her cover.

"Shit!" she breathed. All attention focused at the opposite side of the road. She shimmied around to see the five soldiers run through the field to join their comrades in battle. Once they passed from view she crawled out into the field to search out a safer location to hide.

She plastered her body to the ground and slithered away from the shouts and gunfire. Another stand of trees stood perpendicular to the one she just left, an agonizing forty feet away. Time must have stopped because it took forever for her to pull her body across the field. She considered standing, but preferred to keep her body plastered to the ground. Her heart beat started to slow when she realized she was only a few body lengths away from her new hiding spot.

A heavy hand landed on her shoulder. A dirty palm across her mouth muffled her scream and lips brushed against her left ear. He said, "Mademoiselle, restez tranquille."

Hailey sighed in relief at the French. She didn't understand what he said, but nodded anyway. The palm fell away from her lips and she twisted around. The dirt streaked face of a soldier greeted her, his tan uniform covered in mud.

"Oh my god. Tell me you're one of the good guys."

His eyebrows shot straight up. "You're American!" he whispered.

"Yes."

"What are you—" He turned his head toward the gunfire and pursed his lips. Grabbing her arm, he pulled her to her feet and led her hurriedly along the edge of the hedge. Every ten feet he would pause in a crouch, scanning the area around them and then continue on.

They entered another stand of hedges, and sat to catch their breath. When Hailey began to speak, he raised a finger to his lips and shook his head. She was happy to have someone take the lead, but her heart cringed at his youth. He couldn't be more than twenty. At twenty she'd been busy drinking, partying and dating boys just like this. None of those boys knew anything about what it was like to slog through muddy fields while facing death at the hands of a Nazi soldier.

A break in the gunfire served as an eerie companion as they waited. Ten minutes passed and all she could hear was the throbbing blood running through her veins. Still they waited. She never listened so hard in her life. Not a sound came from behind them. When birds started to chirp she felt a rush of relief as if their voices rang out in good omen. Still, the young soldier made them wait.

She sprawled on her belly with her head resting on her hands. Sleep hit her without warning. And when an insistent hand shook her shoulder she nearly swallowed her tongue. Dusk settled and the soft sepia colored light played with the shadows of darkness. Her rescuer motioned for her to follow him and they moved back into the field.

They walked without rest. She was grateful for the activity but it took nearly all her available brain power to not stumble over the landscape. At least it kept thoughts about the past several hours at bay. She needed to think about the last half day and how she ended up with a young American soldier hiding from Nazis. But not now. She didn't want to think about it right now.

Darkness enshrouded the trail when they approached a small village. They slowed and the soldier trilled out a bird call. He kept a hand on her arm and waited until another responded in kind.

He smiled and led her into the village.

4

Lucius prowled the room. The hunter's instinct hit with an undeniable force. Derian felt it and the Magister suffered under the same compulsion.

At least Derian still retained an outlet for the hunt. Lucius was trapped in a cage of bureaucracy that no operative would envy. His experience and strategic talent made him the strongest leader the *Domus* had for the two centuries it had been in existence, but given the choice, he would be working alongside Derian.

"You are certain she's a *novus*?" Lucius asked.

"Yes," Derian said.

He sat in one of the upholstered chairs added to the office by an assistant in an effort to make Lucius appear more "approachable". It failed. The assistant was a sweet woman, and Derian would never tell her that not even white daisies and puppies could make Lucius more approachable.

"Yet she jumped after only a few hours." Lucius paused his feline prowl and turned his eye to Derian. When the door opened and Millard from the data tracking division entered, Lucius motioned for the man to sit at the command table.

"She had no idea what she was doing. If she had, she would have jumped long before I got there," Derian said. Hailey's anxiety riddled face flashed in his memory. What must the young *novus* be thinking now that she'd jumped through time twice? Had her parents prepared her?

"It could be a ruse," Lucius said.

Derian looked up at his friend. Something beyond an unregistered *viator* bothered the staid man.

"What is it?" Derian said.

Lucius knew why he asked, they'd communicated without words for as long as they'd known each other. They could read the shift of thought as easily as they wielded a weapon. And both had been warriors long before they jumped the first time.

"I don't know," Lucius said as he slid his palm across his forehead then over his military style hair. Strain put a glassy sheen in his eyes. "A number of *viators* have fallen off the map." He glanced at Millard. "And we have had two *venators* turn up dead."

Derian sat up. *Venators* were the elite of the *viators*. They functioned much like military Special Forces and rogue apprehension was only one of the many services they provided the *Domus*. It was a dangerous life. They landed in unknown situations, always with the possibility that it could turn deadly. But two dead? The last death prior to these happened nearly a century before and that had been an accident.

"Were they on a case?" Derian asked.

"No. Both were on leave, different places, different times," Lucius replied. "We are still waiting on the autopsy reports."

"Do you believe there is a connection between the deaths and the *novus*?" Years in the field chasing rogues provided Derian extensive experience with deceit and treachery. He could have been wrong about the woman. Her shocked expression as she jumped could have been the repertoire of a skilled actress. But his instincts told him otherwise and he rarely had to question his instincts.

"I don't know. Whatever is going on, I don't like it." Lucius stopped at the command table and looked down at the screen the data tracker manipulated.

"Let me go after her." Derian joined them at the table. Several layers flipped past on the screen at high speed. Without Hailey's stats inputted in the database they couldn't simply pull up her location. The scan, though swift, took time.

"If she is a *novus*, she will need a *praeceptor*," Lucius said. His eyes shot up when Derian nodded. "Are you certain?"

Derian shrugged. "It's time I tried it, don't you think?"

Lucius considered him for a moment without a word. For hundreds of years Derian staunchly refused taking the mantle of a *praeceptor*. Why he decided now was the time to change his mind warranted thought. Either the fact that he'd been unable to protect her had him foolishly trying to rectify the situation or he wanted a closer look at the white cotton bra he'd glimpsed on the ship. Neither were sound reasons to establish a lifelong bond, but he wasn't in the mood to reflect.

"Have you found her?" Derian's gruff query made Millard jump.

"It's still scanning," Millard said.

Derian spun away from the table in frustration. With the decision made to pursue Hailey, eagerness compelled him to begin right away

Lucius leaned against his desk, his arms crossed against his chest. Derian rested his hip against one of the chairs. "Any theories on why she isn't registered?"

"We investigated the possibility of a *viator* and human mating. But none have ever been able to jump. This would be a first." Lucius didn't look convinced by his hypothesis. "Or, it was an unregistered pregnancy."

Derian raised a brow. Pregnancy in *viator* women was rare and usually a publicized event for the community. The population had experienced significant growth over the last thousand years, but the possibility of a pregnant *viator* going unnoticed was suspect. "Why would the parents hide the birth?"

Lucius shrugged. Whatever the reason, the key to discovery lay in the blond woman lost in time. A quiet yip of success escaped from Millard and was quickly followed by a gasp.

Derian stalked to the table and looked down at the screen. A single red pin light blinked on the map, the surrounding country was surprisingly empty of *viators*. His heart skipped when he saw the familiar coastline. "Normandy?"

Millard nodded. Derian glanced at the date and said, "Tell me she's not there when I think she is."

The timid little man lost all the color in his face. He looked at Lucius and said, "June 11th, 1944."

Lucius and Derian both swore. Derian strode toward the door. The woman had landed in the middle of the D-Day Invasion.

"Wait! Sir! There's more!" Millard called out.

Derian froze and swung back to table where the data tracker wrung his hands. Millard said, "She's in Graignes."

Derian sucked in a shuddering breath and forced himself not to shake the details from the stuttering data tracker.

"American paratroopers are barricaded in the village. They have probably engaged with the Germans already. In the next two days many will be murdered by the SS and the village will be burned."

Derian went cold. He needed to get to Hailey before she was discovered by the Germans or became collateral in the looming battle. He looked to Lucius, "I am going to need some phenomenal clothing."

***

The church stank of too many bodies and too little hygiene. Several injured service men lay on the hard ground tended by local woman. Hailey couldn't help the shivers of premonition as she looked into the fresh faces from her homeland. The pain painted their eyes with fear. Compassion was all that could brush strokes of hope against the terror. The women spoke French, the men English, but the language didn't matter. They were all the same in this place.

She slumped into a pew and leaned her head against its hard back. Somehow she'd found her way to Normandy during the Second World War.

There hadn't been much time to think about it when she'd been fighting with pirates and hiding from Nazis. Now she had the time and she wished she didn't. Only two answers made sense. Either she was stuck in a coma after being shot by that damn druggie or she really could travel through time.

The biggest problem with the coma theory was it required her creativity to be through the roof. Who dreamt they could hop from a pirate ship to German occupied France? And then there was Derian. Jason would say her subconscious was telling her she needed to get laid. Her lips turned up at the thought.

The two daggers flashed in her hands as she fiddled with them. A loud groan echoed through the room followed by the muffled cooing of a nurse. According to what she'd gathered from the hushed conversations, the village had suffered three assaults that day; the last ending only an hour before John escorted her to the church.

She glanced across the pews to where he sat speaking with one of the local villagers. John was only nineteen. He'd enlisted in the army six months ago, had a mother, two sisters and a sweetheart left back home in Illinois. He was a good kid caught up in the insanity of the world stage. It made her stomach queasy. If she could travel through time and this really was World War II, there was a good chance many of the men in the room would never return home. A shudder wracked her body.

History made her break out in hives. She never studied so she had failed every test from elementary school to college. She'd been too busy planning social events and running for school office. Who would have thought history class would have this kind of relevance?

A young woman shuffled by, her eyes lowered before they met Hailey's. No one knew quite what to make of strange American woman with no idea where she was or how she'd gotten there. Several of the officers cast suspicious looks at her and she didn't blame them. In her opinion, an American woman with amnesia was a weak excuse for a spy, but they needed to be vigilant. It was war after all.

John hadn't been suspicious though. With a ready smile he brought her food, water, and found her clothes to replace what the mud ruined.

She sighed. Options were limited. She was stuck in this church in the middle of a war. Running off into the French countryside would be stupid. Trying to get back to America would be useless. What would she find in 1940s America?

And if she were dreaming, no amount of pinching was waking her up. It frustrated her that she had no idea what was happening. Derian, with his very modern gun, might have the answer. But he wasn't here.

A man entered her periphery. She looked up into kind eyes when he spoke to her, "Madamoiselle." Hailey smiled. It was the local priest. He continued, "You come with me? We have a place for you to sleep."

She nodded and pulled on the pew in front to get to her feet. Sheer exhaustion paraded to the forefront of her mind. Perhaps after she slept everything would make sense.

Hailey woke to the rustle of nervous preparation. The cold seeped through the thin pile of blankets. Everything ached but most of her exhaustion had dissipated in the night. She rolled to her side to peer through the ethereal shadows of dawn dancing through the church. Several bodies lay to her left, the late shift Watch trying to catch a few more moments of rest before they were called back to action.

She got to her feet and slunk through the church in search of a bathroom. The conditions weren't exactly medieval but her nose still pinched at the smell and lack of hygiene. She had never been one of those romantics that thought things had been better back in the day. And she had even more reason not to be now. Traffic and smog were fine as long as she got her flush toilet and hot water.

Sometime in the night the village woman had been sent away. A few of the French men stayed behind with the paratroopers, but she was pretty sure they expected the assault to start up again. Reports of the Germans surrounding the village skipped through the room.

She shook off the shiver of trepidation that ran up her spine. If this were a dream, then she had nothing to worry about. Of course, if it wasn't a dream…

John called to her from across the church. He waved to her high above the heads of the scrambling service men. She weaved through the pews and men to join him. An officer spoke emphatically with him and an older French couple. Every few words he would look over at her. When the French gentleman nodded the officer reached out and shook his hand.

John smiled, and turned to introduce her. "This is Antoine and Elodie. They have agreed to take you with them. You'll be disguised as their daughter. If you are stopped by the Germans don't say anything. They are going to pretend you're deaf."

"John, I…" This young man had protected her without a thought. His soft brown eyes were kind and generous. If only she knew what would happen here today. All she could think to say was, "Thank you."

As they were about to leave, Hailey turned and placed a kiss on John's cheek. "Take care of yourself. I want you to go home to your girl and have lots of babies."

John laughed, "So do I. Good luck, Hailey."

The percheron ambled along the lane. It pulled the small cart and its three passengers as if the threat of death were the last thing on its mind. Hailey glanced at the burly horse. It probably had no idea that Nazis were running around the countryside like roaches after dark. It shook its mane and let out a snort. She envied the big dumb animal.

Elodie and Antoine sat together on the narrow bench, the reins in Antoine's expert hands. Every quarter mile Elodie would twist in her seat to give Hailey a reassuring smile. Neither she nor Antoine spoke a lick of English but kindness was a language of the heart, so it really didn't matter.

A never-ending line of hedgerows lined each side of the lane. After the first mile she stopped jumping at every sound, but her nerves wouldn't settle. It was far too easy to hide in this landscape. She huddled in the back and massaged her temples, the dull headache made it hard to focus and the persistent creak of the cart only intensified the pain.

The dawn haze lost its grip on the day and the full morning sun eradicated the shadows as they approached a blind turn. Antoine's soft murmurs soothed the animal to a slow walk. The tension in the shoulders of the French couple was palpable.

They made the turn. A cautious sigh escaped Hailey when the road before them stood empty. The reigns snapped against the horse's neck and they continued on. She let out a sharp laugh and Elodie reached back to grab her hand. The two shared their relief in voiceless companionship.

Hailey relaxed against the side. Surely the Germans would be primarily focused on the American troops. Why would they stop an old husband and wife and their poor deaf daughter? A breeze lifted her hair and tickled it against her nose. She sneezed then closed her eyes. It could have been a spring day in California — except for the lack of ozone and heavy particulates.

A shot punctured the air. Her eyes flew open and the cart groaned to a stop. Elodie held a hand on her shoulder but Hailey needed to see. She popped over the side as three German soldiers emerged from behind a small copse of trees. A laugh barked from behind her and she spun around as two more soldiers approached the back of the cart. Hailey hugged her knees to her chest.

Rifles ready, they smirked. Hailey glared. Out of the corner of her eye she saw another approach Antoine. Hailey wanted to turn her head to look at the exchange, but then Elodie reached over to grab her chin and brush a hand across her ears.

Hailey frowned and remembered their ruse. Memories of the rough and insistent hands of the pirate captain's hands made her stomach turn inside out. Could she survive being manhandled by another terrifying man? Would these men be just as cruel as the pirates? Or were they like so many Germans and just caught up in the wrong country at the wrong time?

Hailey snuck a glance at the German chewing out Antoine. The infamous double S lightning bolt insignia flashed in the light. Her nose flared in recognition. Not exactly a run of the mill German soldier. She closed her eyes and took a deep breath. Crappy luck appeared to be the thing for her lately.

The tiny hairs lifted away from her neck. When she peeked through her lashes the two soldiers at the back were staring at her with narrowed eyes.

"Frauline," a voice said to her right. Hailey didn't move a muscle. A bead of sweat trickled down her back. The SS officer rapped against the cart. He tried a different language. "Mademoiselle!"

A leather riding crop swatted her arm. Hailey whirled around. Her assailant's pale blue eyes flared and his lips turned in a cruel twist. He spoke emphatically in French. She ignored the language but imagined she could whither him with her glare. In her mind she watched his head shrivel into a raisin. It was enough to distract her from his voice.

The barrage of noise ceased. He squinted and turned away in disgust, then spat a command at his comrades. They moved aside and he motioned for the cart to go on ahead. She closed her eyes in relief as the cart lunged forward, but a second later a shot punched the air to her left. Her eyes fluttered open and her head swung toward the sound.

The SS officer leered at her. Hailey looked up at the French couple, their stricken expressions trained on the evil looking man. When she returned her gaze the cool glint of a gun shined from the hand of the German. He waved her toward the end of the cart. She complied, keeping watch on the man and the gun. Rough hands grabbed her and pulled her onto the road.

The French husband and wife were hauled from their seats as well. Hailey started forward. "No!"

Strong arms wrapped around her and lifted her feet off the ground. Hailey kicked and screamed in frustration. She was tired of being yanked, grappled with and pushed around. She shouted, "Get your sleazy hands off of me!"

"Sie ist Amerikanisch!" her captor shouted at the head SS Officer.

He stomped toward them and grabbed her chin in stiff fingers and said, "Sie sind nicht taub und sie sind ein Amerikaner."

"Go to hell," Hailey spat out.

With a sneer, he patted her sharply on the cheek. He shouted an order and she was dragged toward a black sedan hidden from view several feet from the cart. Her shirt tore as she frantically struggled. They pushed her head down and shoved her into the backseat. The door slammed. Hailey plastered her face against the glass and watched in horror as they led the French couple into an adjacent field.

"No! Let them go! Please!"Hailey pleaded, but they laughed at her through the window. A driver and the SS officer slid into the front seats and they pulled onto the road. She switched to the back window and strained to see but they turned and she lost sight of the kind people that risked everything to help her.

5

The black sedan rolled past Derian as he stood in the shadows of the hedgerow. The heavily overgrown stands of trees and bush that had proved such an obstacle in the war now provided him ample coverage. The Nazis had no idea that the exchange with the French couple and Hailey had been observed.

The cart had just reached the blind turn when he'd caught up with them. Out of consideration he'd waited to appear, not wanting to startle them. But then the SS emerged from hiding and he'd had to slide into the shadows to watch.

He'd been relieved when the cart had been sent along its way but then the deception fell to pieces, and now he faced a difficult choice. A glimpse of Hailey's tortured expression caught his eye as she peered out the back window of the retreating vehicle. His mind was made up.

The shine of his polished boots reflected the harsh late morning sun as he marched across the field to where the soldiers escorted the elderly couple. There was no reason for such a trek, unless they planned to execute the husband and wife. Battle scarred fingers buttoned his greatcoat and straightened his hat. Ready, he made his entrance.

The couple held each other close as the five men maneuvered around them in quick efficient preparation. The constant confrontation between good and evil fascinated Derian. Philosophers spent millennia hypothesizing and pontificating the issue to death. People lived and died in this paradox and he had seen it played many times before.

The woman was the first to notice him. It wasn't philosophy that could answer the questions in her eyes.

"Halt!" he ordered. The soldiers swung around, rifles ready. Derian said, "Was tun Sie?"

Their backs straightened and rifles relaxed as they realized who approached. Prior to his jump he'd debated with Lucius over the most effective disguise for this mission. Lucius insisted he would have better luck infiltrating the situation as Gestapo then as any other player in the war. The Magister's opinion held true, but only because luck intervened and Hailey hadn't been sequestered in the American camp for long. Now, it was up to him to ensure the gambit worked.

A young man with blue eyes that had witnessed far more than any one should see in a lifetime replied to Derian's question, "Diese Leute wurden einem amerikanischen Spion helfend verfangen."

Derian cringed. The Germans had mistaken Hailey for a spy. He said with derision, "Ein Spion!" His expression dripped menace as he glared at the Frenchman and his wife. Their faces blanched and the woman's fingers tightened in her husband's coat. Derian felt a twinge of regret at the fear he created, but there was nothing for it. "Und Sie waren im Begriff, sie zu schießen? Heir?"

When the men shifted from foot to foot under his scrutiny he knew he owned the upper hand. It was essential that they leave the French couple with him. He said, "Nein. Ich nehme sie."

They nodded and left as he'd ordered. He shouted across the field before the last man entered the hedgerow that led back to the road. "Wo ist der Spion genommen worden?"

The officer replied and then disappeared. Derian turned back to the couple. They were his only hope in tracking down Hailey. The officer had told him of a cottage down the lane where the SS had set up a command center.

Derian smiled and explained, "Je ne suis pas allemand." The frightened couple's eyes widened with shock. He glanced back toward the hedgerow. The Nazis may have followed his orders, but a smart man would double check to make sure. He put on a fierce mask in case suspicious eyes observed from behind the leafy screen.

He explained his cover story. When he asked for their help the enthusiastic response nearly betrayed the game. A sharp command from him tempered their reactions. They were all actors now; their lives depended on it.

***

The solid-core door was locked. Hailey rattled the knob just for kicks, and then punched the unforgiving wood. The pain was welcomed. It stopped the tears from flowing. The last few days had been so terror-ridden that her adrenaline ran simply on fumes, her body left with next to nothing in reserve. A hollow feeling filled her stomach, her head pounded, and her joints ached.

Gruff laughter seeped in under the door and she shivered. Were they contemplating her demise? The atrocities of *Shindler's List* flashed across her mind from her memory. What would be worse, a bullet to the back of the head or death in a gas chamber? She punched the door again. They would have to take her down kicking and screaming bloody murder.

The tiny room was bare. A single chair with legs that looked like they would split in two if someone breathed on it sat in a corner. A metal bed stood forlornly as the only other furniture in the room. Its mattress sagged in the middle and she figured she'd end up sleeping on the floor — if she slept at all.

A small single pane window over the bed was her only hope for escape and it was painted shut. She glanced at the door. The sound of breaking glass would definitely alert the men milling in the front room.

She slumped onto the bed, then grabbed the headboard to keep from sinking in. How had her life gone from mind numbing boredom to frantic bouts of terror? At this point the possibility that everything was part of a sick and twisted dream grew painfully slim. She was definitely not this creative.

Her fingers fiddled with the two daggers from her pirate escapade tucked in her skirts. Why hadn't the Germans searched for weapons? She shook her head in consternation, but wouldn't reject a gift of fate.

A belly laugh from beyond the door rattled her teeth. If she didn't get out of here she was going to go nuts listening to the bastards.

Determined to do something about her situation she stood and pulled out one of the daggers. Wrapping it in her skirt to mute the sound and protect her hand from the blade, she raised her fist to strike the window. Closing her eyes she let out a slow breath, there would be no going back.

Just as she was about to bring the solid pommel down a commotion broke out in the front room. Harsh voices rose and fell in agitation. She returned the dagger to her skirt and sat a split second before the door crashed open.

Derian stalked into the room. If she had been standing she might have swooned. Instead, she blushed. In order not to fling her body into his arms in frantic relief she gripped the mattress with white knuckles. He looked mean, ready for a fight and was perhaps the most beautiful thing she'd ever seen.

The tight aggression that flowed like waves off his shoulders softened with concern when their eyes met. He swung back around to face the men that had followed on his heels and pointed a finger at her. The German soldiers held expressions of awe and anticipation.

Except for the SS officer that had captured her, his jaw flexed and his fists clenched. That man was just plain pissed.

The air, heavy with hostility, made her lightheaded. The small room tightened with the heady testosterone. Derian grabbed her wrist and yanked her to her feet. The daggers nearly slipped from under her skirts as he hauled her from the room and past the stupefied soldiers. The bright sunshine glared when she tripped down the steps toward the black sedan that brought her to the small, commandeered cottage in the first place. The gentle hand that encouraged her into the backseat contrasted against the rest of his steely manner.

When she settled in the seat he slammed the door. His angry tirade continued as he walked around the vehicle. Hailey glanced out the window. A row of soldiers stood at the door, their mouths hung open. They weren't laughing now, the bastards. She restrained herself from giving them the bird.

Derian ducked into the driver's seat and they drove away. She took one final look out the back window. Irritation seemed to billow out of the SS officer's ears. She hoped she never got the chance to meet him again. Something told her a second escape would not be so simple.

They drove for several miles before Derian spoke. "Are you alright?"

"Yeh. Thanks."

He turned his head to check on her. What he saw made him frown and he pulled to the side of the road.

"What are you doing?" Her voice cracked, "We need to keep going!" The trunk popped open and she could hear him rustling in the back. The trunk lid slammed and he came around to her door and threw a blanket over her. "I'm not cold."

Derian tucked it in and up around her chin. He placed a hand against her cheek. "You are going into shock."

"I'm just a little freaked out," she said. His hand was soft and warm against her skin. If she leaned to the side she could probably fall asleep in his palm. "And tired."

"Same thing." His response abrupt, he removed his hand like she had the plague. The man went from hot to cold so fast she didn't know what to think. Instinct told her to trust him. Experience told her that was stupid. She hunkered down into the blanket. She'd worry about trusting him later. He wasn't a Nazi and that's all she cared about.

After a while she stopped looking at the countryside. The monotony of green hedge after green hedge lulled her into a stupor. She closed her eyes and leaned against the window. For the first time since this fiasco started she felt safe.

The jerk of shifting gears and the slowing of the sedan interrupted her from the light doze. Derian looked back. "Don't worry, this will only be a moment."

Wide awake, she watched him walk into a grove of trees. When he returned Antoine and Elodie walked by his side. Elodie slid into the seat beside her and her husband joined Derian in the front. Tears shined in Hailey's eyes as she reached over to grab the French woman's hand. "I am so glad you are alright!"

Hailey hated to cry. But this time it was ok. These were happy tears.

***

He dropped them off at a cottage hidden deep in the countryside then drove away to hide the vehicle. The French couple claimed the old farmhouse had yet to be discovered by roaming German troops. Tucked far enough away from the main road it would not to be of much immediate interest to the participants in the war — for the time being.

He piled branches and brush high enough to obscure the vehicle, then he stood back to inspect the job. With luck no one would catch sight of the black sedan or any other indication that people hid in the vicinity. His focus needed to be on Hailey and her newly discovered talents.

He hiked toward the farmhouse, eager to get back. The resilient *novus* had been through a lot and handled it all very well. Horror stories ran rampant through the *Domus* of hysterical *novus'* that needed to be handled with kid gloves. His first encounter with her on the ship proved she was not prone to hysteria. So far, her reactions had been relatively impressive, despite her prickly attitude after escaping the

Nazis. After what she'd gone through since her first jump, she must have a constitution of solid rock.

Smoke already curled from the chimney. He knocked quietly to warn them of his arrival and entered. Antoine bent over the fire, feeding it more wood. Derian asked, "Comment va-t-elle ?"

"Elle va plus ou moins bien," Antoine replied.

Derian slumped into a small wooden chair. According to Antoine, Hailey was doing fine and Elodie had taken her to rest. Now the fatigue crept up on him. He laid his head on his arms; the warmth from the hearth soothed the tension from his body.

A steaming bowl of soup slid in front of his nose, startling him from the unexpected doze. Elodie sat beside him and chuckled. Sleep had taken a second seat over the last couple of days, and as his stomach grumbled, he realized so had food. "Merci."

After a second bowl, He stood, intent to scout the area for roaming soldiers, but Elodie hustled him into a second bedroom and pushed him toward the soft mattress. He gave in under her persistence. It had been a long couple of days.

Alarm raced through him when he woke to hushed voices penetrating the thin walls. He tiptoed to the door and cracked it open to peer into the kitchen. A small group of men whispered around the small table. Antoine noticed the open door and motioned for Derian to join them.

Two American officers watched him with hooded expressions, their shoulders stiff in wary consideration. Mud caked their uniforms and glassy eyes betrayed long hours without rest. A young man in civilian garb sat beside them sipping at a small cracked glass.

One of the officers spoke, "They say you are American."

Derian took a seat beside Antoine. "British, actually. My fiancé is American."

The officer sat back and crossed his arms. Derian slipped easily into the cultured speech of the British Isle. His homeland had experienced significant changes in speech patterns but it was still the most comfortable accent for him to adopt.

"What are you doing in France?" the same man asked. They were understandably concerned about strangers in the area. He found no fault with their suspicion. His arms hung at his side and he softened the tension in his shoulders to reduce any impression of threat.

"I was a visiting professor at The University of Caen Lower Normandy. We have not been able to leave France since the invasion."

"Do you have proof?"

Derian shook his head. "No, but I have names you can attempt to contact. I want nothing more than to keep my fiancé safe."

"Derian?"

Five heads swung toward the soft voice. Hailey stood just inside the door to her room. The glow of the firelight reflected in her hazel eyes. With fists clenched and lips thinned she reminded him of the great Celtic warriors, ready and willing to defend what must be protected.

The men at the table sat transfixed. Her timeless beauty called toward their protective instinct and Derian could see it reflected in each of them. Not one of them would approach the fierce woman. Not as long as he lived and breathed. The proprietary emotion slammed against his chest. It was foreign and took him by surprise.

He stalked across the room and wrapped his arm around her shoulder. A strong arm guided her back into the room. "Darling, you should rest."

She stalled against his insistence. "Darling?" she ground out between clenched teeth.

"Please." He tucked a soft curl behind her ear. Placing a soft kiss against her temple he whispered, "Trust me."

"I want to know what's going on." The strength of her voice carried across the room. Every eye trained on them.

"I know. After they leave, we will talk," he answered. She considered him a moment, her thoughts flashed like rapid fire. But she acquiesced and he turned back to the men at the table. "Gentlemen, all of this has been quite distressing for my fiancé."

The civilian and one of the officers stood to leave, but the third remained stubbornly in place. No longer in the mood to cater to the servicemen, Derian crossed his arms and lifted his chin. "I do not know how I can prove to you we are no threat, but I harbor no sympathies for the German cause."

Antoine spoke in rapid assertive French and the civilian translated, "He reminds you that this man saved his and his wife's life."

Unconvinced, the officer said, "You must speak very good German to fool them like you did."

"I do. I also speak French, Russian, Greek, Latin, Italian, and Japanese. Would you like me to demonstrate?"

"I don't trust you. Something stinks about you." The thick southern drawl dripped like molasses as the officer stood. "I can't do anything about it now, but if I catch you snooping around outside this area, I will find a way to lock you up."

"As long as it is safe to do so — we will stay here." Derian stood at the door as the men piled into a beat up sedan. The translator jumped into the driver's seat and a puff of smoke billowed out of the exhaust as they drove away.

Ultimately, the campaign against the Germans would prove successful, but the loss of life and terror that surrounded them was heavy and desperate. How many times had he and Lucius debated the responsibility that the *viator* had to humanity? How many times had he watched men go off to their deaths knowing full well what their fate held?

Antoine stood beside him and his shoulders slumped with exhaustion. Derian took pity on the man and encouraged him to find his rest. "Disparaissent le sommeil mon ami."

Antoine nodded then went to retrieve his wife. A loaf of bread sat on the kitchen table and Derian grabbed it on his way to Hailey's room.

She sat with her back against the headboard and her knees pulled up beneath her chin. "What the hell is going on?"

"You need to eat," Derian said and settled at the foot of the bed, offering up the crusty loaf. Her slim fingers reached out and ripped off a healthy chunk. Her skin was pale and her gaze fatigued, but she was alert and from the way she glared at him, cranky.

After she finished chewing a small piece she asked, "So, are you going to tell me what the hell is going on?"

He ripped off a piece of bread for himself and took a bite before responding. Silence enveloped the room. She didn't move, not even a tick of impatience, just cool scrutiny.

He finished chewing then leaned back against the footboard. "They were American officers wondering why we were here. They shouldn't bother us again."

Irritation flared and she said, "Dude, I'm not worried about them. I'm talking about the time travel shit."

Amused by her directness he got to the point. "How much do you know?"

"Not a damn thing."

This surprised him. In general *novus* had at least an introduction to what would happen to them. Most were assigned a *praeceptor* long before the first jump. "Didn't you're parents tell you about this?"

Her expression darkened. "No. I don't know them."

That explained quite a bit. Lucius would be relieved. An orphaned *viator* was unusual, but not likely to be related to a plot to assassinate *Domus* agents. "Who raised you?" he asked.

"My aunt."

"And she didn't tell you about it?"

"No." She leaned forward and looked him straight in the eye. "What's with the personal questions?"

Her prickly attitude boded well for her. A *novus* with shot nerves and a passive character would irritate him after a few days. A strong constitution would make the transition easier and his job quite a bit as well. "The ability to time travel is hereditary. I am just surprised your family didn't tell you about it."

"Well, she didn't"

"Are you sure she is your aunt?"

"What the hell do you mean by that?"

"Is she your biological aunt?"Derian asked. If her eyes could shoot fire he'd be ash. He decided to try a different tactic.

"You are what is called a *viator*." When she opened her mouth to reply he held up a hand. "As you have discovered, *viators* have the ability to jump through time. Most know about this long before they jump the first time. Unfortunately, it seems you were not so lucky."

She grimaced. "Great. A super power. Just what I always wanted."

6

It took less time for her to digest the news then he'd expected. According to experience, a sudden jump with no prior knowledge of the possibility was traumatic. But she nodded as he filled her in on a few of the more pertinent details.

"So there is a super-secret society of time travelers that normal people don't know anything about. How exactly have you kept it a secret?" Hailey asked.

He stood and walked toward the small single pane window. Dawn would be coming soon and neither of them had taken much rest. He should encourage her to sleep. But her insistent questions couldn't be put off; she had a right to know. There was just so much to explain.

"We have been around a very long time," he said. When he turned, she had stretched out like a content cat on the bed. Her head sat cradled in her hand, her combativeness significantly reduced. A pull gripped his belly. Something about this woman made him want to stand closer, to reach out. Reaching out was not something he did. He was a loner. A lone wolf. His relationships were limited in time and scope. There was nothing here for him. So why the incessant need to be near her?

"There are a number of safeguards that have been in place for thousands of years to prevent our people's existence from becoming common knowledge. You will learn more about these as time goes by. Plus, when we can get you to the *Domus* there is a number of other *viator* that can help explain."

"The *Domus*? Is this your headquarters or something?"

"Yes, more or less. It is a centralized agency for the *viator*. The current location is relatively new, but the *Domus* as an agency has been around for nearly two thousand years."

Hailey narrowed her eyes. "So, how long have you been doing this? Are you from the future too?"

He sighed. He'd never actually had to explain the *viator* to anyone before. The complicated nature of their existence had become second nature to him. He tried to remember what it had been like when he knew nothing. "No, the past. I was born in 1041."

Her eyes grew wide as a pocket watch and she breathed, "Wow. You're ancient. You look really good for your age."

He laughed, "Yes."

She sat up and perched on the edge of the bed the springs groaning beneath her weight. A wrinkle line formed between her brows and she pursed her lips as she continued her questions, "So what does that mean? We don't age? Are we, like, immortal?" The last word came out in a hushed awe.

"Immortal? No. We grow old. Just not very fast. I have aged only ten years since I first jumped. Once you make your first jump you stop aging like a normal human."

"Dude." She sat in stunned silence. Everyone had a limit to what they could process; he figured she had reached that point. A distraction would help and he needed to get something out of the way. He couldn't afford to lose her in time again.

"There is quite a bit for you to learn, it will take some time," Derian said as he walked from the room to find the small bag he had brought from the *Domus*. When he returned he pulled out a set of syringes, mixing dishes and a small bottle of clear viscous liquid.

"What's with the doctor set?" she asked as she eyed the supplies warily.

Derian placed the syringes and bottle on the bed beside Hailey. She would have to trust him and he figured putting everything on the table was the only way she would. "You will have to learn how to control your jumps. It takes time and practice. But I can't follow you unless we do this."

"You can't follow me? I don't understand. Can't you just hold my hand and say *beam me up Scotty*?" Her eyes sparkled and she separated her fingers into the 'live long and prosper' hand signal, making him laugh.

"No, it doesn't work that way. It is impossible to jump with another person," Derian said.

Hailey nodded toward the syringes. "You brought those from wherever you came from."

"Jumping with anything physical, beyond the clothes on your back, can take years to learn how to do successfully. But it is limited, and people are too complex to take with you."

"Really?" Hailey pulled the two daggers out from under her skirt. "I brought these with me from the ship."

Derian's eyes widened in surprise. "That is unusual." Multiple jumps and transporting complex materials, her abilities were impossibly advanced for a *novus*. He narrowed his eyes in suspicion and he said, "Tell me about your first jump."

She shrugged. "Well, at the time I thought it was the scariest moment of my life. Not so much now. What with having pirates and Nazis after me."

Derian nodded, silently encouraging her to go on. She said, "This stupid drugged out jackass wanted my car and I couldn't find my keys. He shot at me and the next thing I know I'm on a ship with a nasty headache and the worst stomach ache I've ever had."

He watched her closely, but there were none of the tell-tale signs of deceit. How could a *novus* have skills this advanced? "The ability to jump time is connected to the fight or flight response in your brain. Most first jumps happen unexpectedly, just like yours. Though most *novus* know it will happen eventually. Some even put themselves in dangerous situations to encourage the response."

"Dude, that's nuts."

"Not everyone is patient."

She leaned toward him; her eyes latched onto his with a gaze that brokered no escape. He shifted uncomfortably and looked away. Those eyes asked for far too much.

"Did you know it was going to happen?" she asked.

"No. My parents died before I was old enough to understand."

"Oh! I am so sorry!" Hailey placed her hand over his, compassion flowed through her fingers, sending an unsettling comfort through him. "That really sucks. I never knew my parents but I do know how hard it is to lose someone you love."

Derian turned his hand and griped hers. It was soft and delicate in contrast to his large callus covered palm. "With time it fades, and that was a very long time ago."

"Fades, but never goes away."

"True." Derian let her had slip from his. How had the conversation switched to his life?

The soft blanket of night lifted under the rays of dawn. In the distance they heard a spattering of gunfire reminding them of the war that surrounded the oasis they had made of the small farmhouse.

"Do you think we're safe here?" Hailey asked.

"I don't know for how long. The easiest way for us to get to safety is to jump time."

"What about, Antoine and Elodie? Is there anything we can do to help them?"

"They will be leaving later this morning. They have family who will help them." Derian grabbed her hand again. It felt good there. "We have to focus on getting you out of this time."

Pulling her hand free, she jumped off the bed. The curtains moved easily beneath her fingers as she peered out the window. The soft light cast shadows across her face smudging the lines of dirt and bruising until they were barely visible. "Ok, fine. Let's do it now."

"It's not that simple." He took a small knife and pricked his finger. The pain was fleeting as he pressed his thumb against the skin to work several drops of vibrant red onto the clear glass.

She threw up her arms and walked away from the window. "Of course not, why would any of this be simple??" When she glanced at him her gaze settled on the blood he had squeezed onto the mixing dish. "What are you doing?"

He opened the small bottle and added half of the contents to the blood. "When a *novus* jumps they are assigned a *praeceptor* who will teach and guide them through the transition from Original Time to *Viator* time." He set the disk to the side. It had to sit for the blood and the liquid to bond.

"Ok, there's not a thing you just said that made any sense." She stood with one knee bent, jutting one hip up and out. Her arms framed her hourglass body as she set them on each hip. Despite the frumpy dress, her curves were soft and sensuous. Derian had to focus; her desirability was an inconvenient distraction.

She kneeled beside the bed and peered into the dish. "Just tell me what this is supposed to do."

"The blood will bond with the mixture. When it is injected into your blood stream you will be able to find me in time. I will do the same with you."

She raised an eyebrow. "It's a leash."

"In a way. Without it, if you jump time, I have to go back to the *Domus* and have the data analysts search for you. It takes time," he replied. A wisp of hair fell into her eyes. Derian reached down and brushed it from her face and continued, "With you jumping from one dangerous situation to the next, it would help if I could get to you sooner."

"Ah. I could see how that would be useful." She reached over and picked up the half filled bottle and brought it up into the rays of the morning sun. The light refracted through the sparkling contents. "How long does it last?"

"It's permanent."

"Ha! Right." She dropped the bottle and stood up. "I like you, but that's a big commitment, don't you think?"

Derian stood and gripped her shoulders. She was wary and a little frightened. Any thought that she might be deceiving him fled at that moment and the desire to protect her flowed through him as an irrepressible need. He'd hunted rogues for over a century. There wasn't a piece of his skill or intuition that thought she wasn't exactly as she seemed to be.

"I have saved you from pirates and Nazis. What if next time I can't get to you in time?" He reached his hand up and traced her jaw bone with his thumb.

Her eyes widened with uncertainty. "I, uh—damn it." She tore herself from his grasp. "Ok, wait. Can you just give me a minute? I need a minute."

She fled the room, leaving him in an unaccustomed dilemma. Each moment they stayed in German occupied France increased the danger of the situation. How could he convince the skittish *novus* to trust him? He glanced down at the waiting syringe. Perhaps he could just tie her down and—no, that would not work out well at all.

***

Hailey flew through the farmhouse door and kept on going. Soft dew blanketed the grass and the dawn passed away beneath the bright morning sun. A small barn rose as a promise of solitude and she made a beeline for its ancient double doors.

The interior smelled of summer and rustic animals that had long since left with the previous occupants fleeing in the shadow of invasion. Everything was just so strange. She grew up in the middle of three million people. She'd never been in a barn. Actually, she'd never left southern California. Now she was in France. She banged her head against one of the wood poles supporting the loft, then rubbed her forehead in response to the pain.

In general, she thought she could roll with the punches pretty well. But anyone would lose it after pirates, Nazis, and time travelers. Right?

Sure, for her whole life she felt as if she were waiting for something. But she figured it was a dream job or the love of her life, not the ability to hop through time like mutant meerkats on a space-time Serengeti. Take away the pirates and the Nazis and it was kind of cool. But what about all the risks? Would her next jump be into the Roman Coliseum? The Russian Revolution? For crying out loud, she could jump into the middle of the L.A. Freeway during rush hour!

There had to be a way to end up somewhere normal and safe. She kicked the pole. Derian knew how. But they would have to do that weird blood ritual thing, and that was just creepy. Her heart started to patter against her ribs. Ok, so being attached to the dark and handsome time traveler wasn't so much creepy as.... Oh, who was she kidding, he was definitely yummy; the way out of her league kind of yummy. Being connected to him for life did have a potential upside.

But it was permanent! Even marriage wasn't permanent! Well, at least not in 21st Century America. Hailey walked back to the double doors and looked out toward the small house. It was a big risk; she didn't know anything about him. But then again, it wasn't like she had many options.

In the distance Hailey heard the deep rumble of aircraft and the reality of her situation slammed back to the forefront. World War II surrounded her. With her luck she'd be captured again and paraded through the streets of Berlin if she didn't make a decision soon. With a deep seated sigh she threw out her concerns. After all, it was only forever. What could possibly go wrong?

When she returned to the farmhouse she found Derian stretched out on the bed, his head propped against the headboard. His chest rose in a gentle rhythm. She crept toward him. The hard masculine lines of his face were softened by sleep. A faint line of stubble lay as a shadow along his jaw. She whispered, "Derian?"

His lids lifted and he smiled silently. Had he been sleeping at all?

"Ok, we can do this." At her words he sat forward. "But, you have to teach me everything."

"I will teach you everything you need to know."

"Oh yeh? And who decides what I need to know?" Hailey crossed her arms against her chest. "I want to learn everything, that includes the How and Why and all that jazz."

He narrowed his eyes. "Are you going to be difficult?"

"More than likely." She sat on the bed and pulled one of the daggers from her skirt. "I'm assuming you're pretty good at this whole time travel thing."

"I am," he said.

She hesitated at his answer. Everything so far suggested he was extremely capable, but how could she know for sure? She blinked away the thought. There was no guarantee—but then again no risk no glory.

"Well then," she said as she sliced the tip of her forefinger, hiding the cringe of pain behind a confident smile. "Where do you want it?"

He held up a second dish and she squeezed a few drops onto the hard glass. Adding the last half of the mixture he put it aside beside the one that held his blood. She held a section of her skirt tight against the small wound and asked, "So are you worried about AIDS or anything?"

He shook his head, but kept his eyes intent on stirring the mixture. "Blood pathogens don't like *viator* blood."

"Serious?" There was so much she didn't know about this whole thing. She hated being so ignorant. "So, is it possible to get the Idiots Guide to Time Travel? I could really use a manual"

He picked up one of the syringes and filled it with the mixture he had prepared from his blood earlier. He took her arm and tied a rubber band around her bicep then waited as her vein popped from the inside of her elbow. Hailey took a deep breath. She hated needles. His deep voice rumbled against her ear, "If there is a manual, I've never seen it."

Hailey looked up into his deep verdant eyes. "A manual would have been nice. I think you should really look into having one produced. Just think how much easier it would be. You could just hand it over and wait while I read it." She was babbling like an idiot. But she really, really hated needles.

Her teeth bit into her lip and she closed her eyes as the needle slid effortlessly into a vein. She opened her eyes when the gentle pressure of his fingers pressed into her skin, stopping the bleeding before it could start. "Is that it?"

"That's it." He wrapped the syringe and dish in a cloth then dropped them both into the small bag.

"I'm glad you've done that before—it hardly hurt." Hailey gave a shaky smile.

Derian picked up the second syringe and prepared if for himself. "I've never done that before."

"Dude!" Hailey glared. "People go to school to learn how to do that!"

"You said it didn't hurt."

"Much!"

He finished with the injection and then put away the rest of the supplies. He stood and reached for Hailey's arm, trailing a finger around the small pinprick. Her skin tingled in a way that had nothing to do with needles.

"So what next?" She winced as her voice came out breathy. Perhaps he would just chalk it up to the needle. Knowing eyes gazed into hers and shattered that illusion. Hailey pulled herself from his caressing fingers.

He walked out of the room and answered from the kitchen. "We have breakfast."

Antoine and Elodie joined them at the table after Derian brought out a loaf of crusty bread and hard yellow cheese. The couple looked worn out but relieved. Hailey hoped they would find themselves safely through this war.

Breakfast passed quietly with a few words of French exchanged between them and Derian. At the end of the meal they made their farewells. Not one to cry much, a surprising moisture filled her eyes as she hugged Elodie. The older woman smiled and kissed her forehead.

Hailey stood beside Derian as the two walked across the field and out of sight beyond a stand of trees. She didn't know she'd been holding her breath until Derian reminded her to breathe.

"They will be fine," he said.

"Do you know that for sure?"

He pulled her toward the barn. "No. But I believe it."

The heavy doors stood open from when she had left earlier. The rustle of flapping wings greeted them as several pigeons were disturbed by their intrusion.

"Can't you just pop forward in time and find out?"

"It's not that simple. "

Hailey huffed, "You know, a lot of your answers suck."

Derian stopped abruptly and pulled Hailey toward him, his eyes peered intensely into hers. "This is new for me. I haven't had to answer these questions before."

"What? Don't you have to go through training or something?" Hailey was cranky. The lack of good sleep and strain on her system was getting to her. She didn't mean to take it out on Derian, though at the moment his lack of reasonable answers irritated the crap out of her.

"*Praeceptors* go through extensive training before they are assigned a *novus.* Your situation was special. It was impossible to send a *praeceptor.*" He grinned wolfishly and let her go. "You got me instead."

Hailey watched as he pulled a ladder toward the loft. She asked, "What made my situation special?"

Derian held out his hand and boosted her up the ladder. "Few *viators* can land on a moving ship. Most have a general radius they can aim for, usually about a mile wide after years of practice. You needed someone with a little more skill than that."

"Ok." Hailey swung off the ladder once she reached the top. "So, why do you think I ended up on the ship instead of the middle of the ocean?"

He joined her on the loft then stopped to watch her. Her skin flared with white heat as his gaze held her. "I don't know. There are a few things you have done that are — interesting."

The boards creaked under their weight and bits of hay fell through the cracks between the aged wood. Hailey finally realized how precarious their location was. "Why are we up here?"

"You probably won't be able to jump for another day or two. Most *novus* require several days to recover from their first jump before they can attempt another." Derian walked to the edge of the loft and looked over.

"And I'm a *novus*?"

"Yes. It is what we call those who have just recently learned to jump time." He motioned for Hailey to join him at the edge.

The freakiest thing wasn't so much that she could jump through time, it was that everything he was telling her actually made some sense — sort of. She said, "But I jumped twice already and I didn't have a couple days in between."

Derian took her hand in his. "Yes. You seem to be more advanced than the usual *novus*. It is interesting." He swung her around and grabbed both her hands. Her toes teetered on the edge and she realized a slight push would send her falling toward the hard ground.

"Shit!" Her heart thumped and she struggled to gain purchase. He leaned forward, sending her balance completely into the hands of his solid grip. "What are you doing??"

"Trust me," he said.

"Trust you?" her voice shrieked.

He stood calm and collected; his hands never wavered, but held her steady over the precipice. "What do you feel?"

She had no inclination to examine her feelings at the moment. The bastard had her completely at his mercy. One moment she was quietly trusting, the next—what had she been thinking?

"Hailey, focus," he said, his calm voice cutting through the panic.

"What the hell are you talking about?"

"What do you feel?"

"I feel pissed off!"

His lips turned up at the corners. "No. At the back of your neck. Do you feel something?"

Hailey stopped fuming for a moment and focused on the back of her neck. A prickly tingle shot through the hairs. It felt a little like a highly medicated dandruff shampoo. "It tingles."

Derian pulled her toward him and into his arms. He placed a quick kiss onto her forehead before she could push him away and said, "I am sorry. I did not want to scare you, but it was the only way I could show you how a jump works."

Hailey stepped back out of his embrace, putting several feet between them. "Ok. Explain."

"The tingle you felt was your body reacting to danger. This activates the fight or flight response and that is what allows you to jump time. To do a controlled jump, you have to teach your brain to do this even when you aren't in danger."

"How?"

Derian shrugged, "Concentration and practice."

Hailey crossed her arms and bit out, "And you couldn't tell me you were going to show me that why?"

"Would you have been scared if I had warned you?"

"No." They were both silent for a moment as Hailey processed what he had told her. His expression revealed nothing. She felt like she was in algebra class, angry at the teacher because he couldn't just put the answer in her head. Frustration was not a feeling she handled well. If they were going to get through this before she strangled him, she would have to learn quickly. "Alright, I forgive you. But don't do that again."

He smiled.

"Or anything even remotely like that!" Her bristly attitude was getting the better of her, and she knew it. If he were to run screaming from her after just a few days, she wouldn't blame him. But for some reason she couldn't pull out the nice Hailey for all she was worth.

Derian pointed toward the ladder. "We can go down now."

"You go ahead," she said, still unwilling to give him her complete trust.

"If you come down after me, I won't be able to stop myself from looking up your skirt." Her head snapped to face his, her cheeks hot with a rosy blush. As he closed the distance between them he continued, "There is nothing more I would like to do, but I have much to teach you and there is little time." He trailed a finger along her jaw line. "And you are far too distracting."

She hurried toward the ladder and scooted down the rungs. The soft rumble of his laughter followed and the heat spread down her neck and across her breast. She needed to get a grip. It wasn't like he wanted to sleep with her. That would be ridiculous—right?

As soon as she hit the floor she took off through the double doors and fled hastily to the farmhouse. Cowardice rarely reared its ugly head in her, but then again, she rarely had super sexy time travelers turn on the charm. Rarely? Ha! Never was more like it.

She ran into the little bedroom and slammed the door. Jumping onto the bed she buried her head in her arms. So she was going to be an ostrich about this and hide out. She was ok with that— really.

**

Derian stayed a while in the barn. Hailey needed time to adjust to her new life as a *viator*. And he needed time to recover from his very evident need. Hailey wasn't what he usually looked for in a lover. Her curves were in all the right places and he had no doubt she would be passionate and fiery in bed. But she was prickly and ornery instead of soft and amiable. One moment she reacted with good humor and the next with bitter frustration.

Her courage in the face of imminent danger had already impressed him, but the flickers of vulnerability and apprehension she tried desperately to hide behind her hazel eyes tore at his insides. Priorities needed to be considered. Attraction was a minor concern compared to the issues at the *Domus*. He just needed to remind his body of that— somehow.

He leaned his head against the wall and listened to the sounds in the distance. The air beside him fluctuated and thickened as molecules were displaced by an incoming *viator*. Derian stood unmoving as Lucius materialized at his side. The centurion turned an inquiring eye on his *venator*. "You're filthy."

Derian grunted, "Haven't had much chance for a shower."

Lucius cast a glance at his surroundings then returned his attention to Derian. "Where's the girl?"

"Back in the house. She's a little upset." Derian thought back to how quickly she ran from the barn. Her flight response was alive and well, which would bode well for keeping her out of trouble. If only she wasn't running from him.

"Did you do the blood transfer?" Lucius asked.

"An hour ago."

"You've been here over a day."

"We had some threats to handle," Derian answered. The close call with the SS was still a raw reminder of the danger Hailey seemed to attract. "The Nazis had her when I arrived."

Lucius turned his stoic gaze from the distant trees to Derian. "Pirates and Nazis. You've been busy."

"She has a tendency to jump into challenging situations."

The tall Roman snorted, "Let's hope she doesn't make it a habit. What do you know about her?"

Derian wasn't fooled by Lucius' calm demeanor. Something about the Hailey anomaly had his intuition humming or else he would have waited for Derian's report back at the *Domus*. She wasn't a threat, at least not as herself. But the reason behind her hidden identity could be and Derian was determined to discover it. "She wasn't raised by *viator*. She lived with an Aunt, but I am convinced the woman was human. Hailey knows nothing about jumping time or her birthright. Someone has gone to a lot of trouble to keep her hidden."

Lucius was quiet for a moment, letting the implications run through his mind. He had been appointed as Magister as much for his experience as a *venator* as it was for his ability to sniff out connections and possibilities for any situation. "You're certain she is an innocent?"

Derian nodded. Of that he was positive, perhaps foolishly so.

Lucius let out a deep sigh then said, "On that I will trust you. But it would have been easier if she weren't. What of her abilities? She jumped twice."

"And brought material—two daggers from the ship," Derian said.

Lucius' brows shot up in surprise. "Anything else the woman can do?"

"Well, she didn't land in the middle of the ocean on her first jump, but that could have been sheer luck." Both men were skeptical about such a convenient excuse. In his near thousand years as a *viator* Derian had seen his share of luck intervention, but the condition was significantly rarer than most credited. *Praeceptors* established the connection to their *novus* prior to the first jump for this very reason. A number of *novus* found themselves under water, on the edge of cliffs, and in other deadly situations. A *praeceptor* had to be ready for them all.

Except for pirates and Nazis. That was a new one. He smiled inwardly at the thought.

"Keep an eye on her. I don't like this," Lucius said.

"You've said that. What's going on with the murdered *venators*?"

Lucius' expression turned black with frustration. "We couldn't determine cause of death. Roderic thinks it may have been a poison."

"Poison? What kind of poison could work that quickly through a *viator*?" Shock and worry pulsed through Derian. Once a *viator* jumps time his internal clocks shifts from

Original Time and slows all aging processes. From what Roderic and his team of scientists had determined, a *viator* aged at a rate of one year for every hundred of Original Time. This made them poor hosts for biological disease and anything that took time to kill. Poison was an ineffective weapon. It could take hundreds of years to kill and more often than not it would have been flushed from the body before it could do any real harm.

"If a rogue has discovered a fast acting poison the *Domus* and all *viators* are threatened." Lucius pushed off the wall of the barn and stood a few feet away, his face turned toward the distance, but his expression focused inward. His friend and mentor weighed the heavy thoughts before he continued, "I am nearly certain we are dealing with an organized rebellion. There has to be someone leading this operation. It feels bigger than a single man."

Rogues were loners, unwilling to form alliances. By their very nature they shied away from strong leadership. The kind of man that could bring together an organized threat to the *Domus* should not have gone under the radar. How did they miss this? To Derian's knowledge something like this had only happened once in the history of the *Domus*. It had in fact been the reason the *Domus* had been established during the Roman era. The war that had occurred left a lasting impact on their history and it happened long before he'd jumped his first time. How could Hailey be caught up in a threat of this magnitude?

"What do you need me to do?" Derian asked.

Lucius placed a hand on his friends shoulder. "Watch the girl. I have all the *venator* on alert and Roderic is doing all he can to discover who or what we are dealing with." His head turned at the sound of a door slamming. "This girl is an outlier. I don't know if or what she has to do with this, but we have to know — and soon."

Derian nodded and gripped his friend's arms in a brother in arms handshake. Then the image of the Magister shimmered and faded from view.

A string of curses floated from the farmhouse. Hailey was apparently ready for the next round. With all he had just learned, he was more than ready himself.

7

Hailey rubbed her elbow and glared at the door jamb and its collection of splinters. She'd been so focused on getting back to Derian with more questions that she hadn't looked at where she was going. Now she couldn't remember what questions burned so hot that allowed her to run stupidly into a door. She needed to chill or she wouldn't get any of this figured out.

Derian strolled up, his face unsmiling, but a suspicious glint of humor sparkled from his eyes. At least she kept him entertained.

"Are you alright?" he asked.

"Yeh, I just hit my funny bone." She turned and reentered the house. Overwhelmed with the need to fidget, she made a beeline for the kitchen. A few cracked and dirty dishes waited beside a tiny cast iron sink and the counters needed wiping. A distraction would help to clear her head and maybe make the conversation less intense. She was getting tired of intense.

The water ran cool through her fingers as she rinsed the plates. Derian seated himself at the rugged country table. She could feel his eyes on her back and it made a flush spread from the nape of her neck to her ears. The awareness she felt toward him was making her jumpy. Either she got over it or she needed to jump his bones—and soon.

"I have a few questions," she said.

"Just a few?"

"Don't be a smart ass, I'm serious." She swung around and leaned against the sink. "I've done some thinking, so tell me if I'm wrong."

Derian motioned toward the chair opposite him. She said, "No, I think better when I stand, or walk. I pace a lot."

He didn't respond, just leaned back and watched her. Strength emanated from him, making her think of steel and steam engines. Despite all the questions, insecurities and fears, she felt safe in his presence. It might be stupid, but she trusted him.

"So my parents had to be time travelers too—*viators,* right?"

His head inclined in agreement.

She continued, "But since I never knew them, I missed out on all kinds of pre-time travel education."

"More or less."

Hailey grabbed a hand towel and wrung it into tight twists as she walked the room. "So once I get this jumping under control then I can pretty much go wherever I want? Whenever I want?" She stopped, pivoted, then walked back the opposite way. "Can I go into the future?"

"You can travel to any time that does not go beyond Original Time."

"What is Original Time?" she asked. Derian shifted as she walked passed him. Hailey knew her pacing could drive people nuts, but at the moment, she didn't care.

He answered, "Original Time is the furthest time has gotten. Right now it is 2010."

"Ok. So you can't travel to 2020."

"No. Time is like an unrolling carpet. You can go to any time that has already passed, but not to what has yet to occur."

"A carpet?" she asked.

He shrugged. So he wasn't a physicist. The explanation worked, she guessed. For nearly a year she'd been addicted to the Discovery Channel. Plenty of specials attempted to tackle the idea of time travel. But the truth was, she could never really understand the concept of time anyway, so how someone could time travel was beyond her. Just thinking about it made her brain hurt. "So why can we do it but other people can't?"

"We don't know. *Viators* have been traveling since time began and our scientists haven't been able to figure out exactly why."

"You know this all sounds like a bad science fiction movie."

"Don't they say life is stranger than fiction?" he replied, his lips unsmiling, but that sparkle still flashed at the corner of his eyes.

She placed her hands flat on the table and leaned toward him. "Ok, fine, I'll suspend my belief on that, but you said you started time traveling in 10 something or other."

"1066."

Hailey straightened her back. "1066? I know that date. Why do I know that date?"

Derian frowned and said, "The Battle of Hastings is what they call it now."

"That's right. In England. I think I saw a special on that. What did they call it then?"

"An invasion," his reply came curt and closed.

Hailey looked closely at Derian, his entire expression was hooded. He couldn't have been? Could he? "Were you there?"

"It was where I first jumped time."

Hailey slumped into the rickety table chair across from him. "Wow."

He didn't offer more and she got the distinct impression he didn't like to talk about it. A story hid in his expression. Maybe someday he'd tell her about it. But she couldn't blame him for not wanting to share his past. The past could hurt like hell and who wanted to relive that?

Hailey threw down the towel. "Ok, I think I've had enough. Let's work on getting us out of here."

***

Hailey snarled at Derian, "You said this would be easy!"

Derian let out a long tortured sigh that would have made an old-country grandmother proud. "I did not say it was easy, I said this would be easier."

Her head pounded against her temples and the strain on her eyes felt like sand against a bare-bottom. They had spent three hours trying to jump time. At first it was a lot like the meditation exercises that had been so popular in the 90s. Visualize. She just had to visualize.

As the frustration intensified she started to grimace and stiffen her neck muscles. Nothing worked and now she just wanted to curl up into a self-medicating ball of misery. "I'm never going to get this."

Derian walked up behind her and started to massage the strained muscles in her neck and shoulders. She moaned and leaned into his fingers. His voice soothed, "You have only been trying for a little while, *léof.* It will come."

"Hmm." Hailey let herself drift from the insanity of the moment. His scent caressed her like the crisp autumn air, earthy and sweet. Little butterflies flittered through her belly as his fingers trailed up behind her ears and then around to her temples. As the moments passed heat rose across her breast and up into her cheeks.

"Ah, Derian." His fingers stilled then continued rubbing the tension from her scalp. "Is there some kind of side effect to that blood thing we did?"

"Side effect?"

"You know..." How did one ask this? She shifted uncomfortably the chair creaked dangerously beneath her thighs. "Does it make you feel attracted to the other person or anything?"

He lifted his hands from his ministrations and she cursed herself for bringing it up. Now she'd done it. Could someone actually die from embarrassment?

His arms came around her and braced themselves against the table. She felt the soft breath from his lips beside her ear. "No, *léof*. That is just between us."

Hailey shivered as goose bumps popped up all over her arms and neck. He pushed himself away and walked to the sink. The sound of running water crashed over her highly sensitized senses. He hadn't pushed it. She let out a relieved breath.

She was relieved, wasn't she?

She peered behind her shoulder. He raised a glass to his lips and the well structured muscles along his back showed beneath the soft cotton shirt he wore. She swiveled her head back around and closed her eyes. Pirates, Nazis, *and* a super sexy time traveler. What more could happen?

The faucet shut down and silence filled the room. The back of her neck prickled again so she knew he was watching her.

"Hailey." The deep sound of his voice felt like a soft embrace. She jumped when she felt his hand against her cheek. She looked up to see his features tight with desire. Her heart thudded to a stop and she blinked her lashes rapidly trying to shake herself from the crazy trance effect he had on her.

The man had a thousand years of experience. It baffled the mind how much experience a man could accumulate in a thousand years. The thought helped to break the spell and she pulled back from his touch.

Derian dropped his hand and lifted his lips into a half smile. "I won't lie to you—I want you." He returned to his chair across the table. "But my first responsibility is to your safety and to teach you how to jump without getting yourself killed."

He reached across and grasped her hand. She stared as his thumb rubbed a gentle circle into her palm. "When you come to my bed it won't be because of what I can teach you. At least not regarding time travel."

What could she say to that? "Ah, thanks?"

He grinned and released her hand. The arrogance of the expression made her bristle. The man seemed to think he could have her in the sack at the snap of a finger. Once she learned how to travel through time she'd show him a thing or two! Probably. He stood and walked toward the door. She got a great view of his ass in the exquisitely fitted pants. She was toast.

The crunch of tires on gravel vanquished all thoughts she had about Derian's beautiful butt. Jumping up, she joined him just as he opened the door. "Who? Oh shit."

He pushed her back inside and slammed the door. Grabbing her by the elbow he propelled her toward the back bedroom.

"Do you think they saw us?" she asked.

"I don't know," he said as he grabbed his bag and pulled out a sleek black gun then checked the clip. "I'm going to assume they did."

Car doors slammed and the brusque German language carried through the house. A frighteningly familiar voice barked orders outside. Hailey looked out the small window as two German SS approached the back door.

The back of her neck started to tingle. "Derian." She grabbed his arm. "I think I can do it now."

He pulled her roughly into his arms and kissed her on the lips. Then let go of her just as abruptly. "That would be extremely helpful at this time. Think about your aunt in California."

"Do you think that will work?" she asked. He just stared at her expectantly. "Alright, but I hope you have a fall back plan if this doesn't work."

He reached a hand up to her cheek. "Don't worry, I can follow you."

She relaxed and focused on the tingle in her neck. The sensation radiated out and flowed through her entire body until all she saw was a blinding white light and then it all went dark.

**

Derian waited as Hailey shimmered out of sight, then pushed the bed against the door to give himself a few extra moments. His eyes closed and he focused in. The only person he had connected to in the past was Lucius. More than just a friend and Magister, he was Derian's *praeceptor*.

Now he had to search his system for the piece of Hailey that flowed through his veins and would lead him to her. It took a moment to identify hers beside the other. But where Lucius was heavy with intensity Hailey's was soft and beckoning.

He grasped at the thread and propelled through time. When he solidified he found himself in a small apartment living room. A bright green couch with white stripes screamed out against the periwinkle walls. He grimaced. It wouldn't have been his first choice in color scheme.

"I was experimenting. It didn't exactly come out how I expected it," a meek voice spoke. Hailey lay sprawled on the floor at his feet. One arm held her belly and the other flopped over her forehead. "How do you do it standing up? I always end up on my back and sick as shit."

"Practice." He reached down and pulled her to her feet. She wavered a moment and held tightly to his arm. He liked the feeling of having her turn to him. The desire to pull her in for a much less hurried kiss than before overwhelmed him but he had to secure their safety first. "Where are we?"

"My apartment."

"You thought about your apartment?"

"No, I thought about my Aunt Sue. She used to own this place." Hailey let go of him and took a few teetering steps toward a small hallway.

"Used to?"

"She died three years ago." She braced herself against the open hall doorway. "I'm going to take a shower and hopefully not puke. Make yourself at home."

Disappointment flared. He had hoped to ask her aunt for answers. He wandered to the window facing out toward the complex's common area. The sun shined bright across the aqua blue pool. The shrieks and screams of the splashing children created a cacophony of sound. It was in stark contrast to his recent adventures.

He turned to explore the rest of the room. Hailey's eclectic tastes and slightly off the wall sense of style stood evident in every corner. Chachkies and knickknacks covered every available flat space. A collection of CDs lined the shelves of her entertainment center. Bands like Offspring, Green Day, and The Beastie Boys evidenced a distinct predilection toward late 90s music.

When he reached her collection of photographs he paused. Hailey's good natured smile sparkled beside a number of unique characters. Most were of her and a short dark haired woman with soft green eyes and a carefree smile. Aunt Sue, he surmised. The most prominently placed frame was of Hailey and her aunt at the pool. Sue had the gaunt features and thinning hair of a cancer victim.

Empathy for the loss of a loved one tugged at his insides and he quickly stepped away from the sad reminder. The white noise of running water ceased and he listened as the whoosh of the shower curtain told him Hailey had finished her shower. The fatigue from days on alert set in and he wondered if he were to walk into the bathroom would he notice a delectable and naked Hailey or only have eyes for the shower.

The door clicked open and she emerged from the hall in a fuzzy bright pink bathrobe and hair wrapped high in a garish yellow towel. The woman did not shy away from color. Her smile was blissfully ecstatic and her voice significantly perkier than before, "Your turn. There's an extra towel in there for you. I'm sorry I don't have any clothes that will fit you, but I can run out to the store and pick something up if you would like."

She looked up and down at his clothes. "I don't think we want you walking outside looking like a Nazi."

"Probably not."

Her cheeks were scrubbed to a rosy shine. The scent of flowers and cleanliness hit his nostrils. The call to shower took over and he walked past her to answer his body's needs.

"If I'm not back before you get out feel free to take a nap in the guest bedroom. It's down the hall and to the right," she called as she disappeared down the hall. The click of a door closing was followed by the blast of pop radio.

The cold shower held his exhaustion at bay and he was thankful she had at least one towel in a reasonable color — navy blue. He was wary of putting any of his clothes back on, but settled on wearing just the trousers.

The guest bedroom lacked the personal Hailey style that the rest of the house did. Jewel tones and simple furniture made it feel warm and inviting. Did she know the uniqueness of her style enough to create a haven from it? Or was this evidence of another hand?

Derian wondered at the many things her home had told him about the woman but he drifted off to sleep before he could make any conclusions.

***

He woke to a sun setting and the apartment silent. He moved silently down the hall to check Hailey's room, hoping to find her safely sleeping. When a thorough search of the apartment turned up negative his insides twisted with worry. Had she jumped again?

He stood in the center of the living room and reached toward the thread in his blood that connected her to him. The sound of the front door lock sliding open halted his jump and Hailey sailed frantically into the room.

"I am so sorry! I really hope you didn't worry!" Laden with plastic bags and her purse tucked under her arm, she waddled toward the couch. "I totally forgot my car was at Rizzo's back when I did my first time travel thing, and then I remembered all my cards and stuff were there too. So I had to call a friend, go to the bank, tell the cops I was ok and then I was finally able to make it to the store!"

Dumping the bags on the floor, she slumped onto the couch. She continued, "Do you know how hard it is to explain disappearing into thin air?" She let out a huge sigh then looked at him. Her eyes went wide, "Oh, right, I have a shirt for you."

She slipped off the couch and onto the floor and started sorting through the bags. Amongst the food and toiletries she pulled out a bag of underwear, socks, three pairs of shorts and three plain black T-shirts. "I wasn't sure on your size, so I guessed and bought three different ones. I can return whatever doesn't fit."

"Thank you. You should sleep." He took the clothes she offered. She nodded, her eyes already drooping. He reached out a hand and caressed her cheek. "I need to see to a few things. I will be back as soon as I can."

She nodded again then pushed off the couch and stumbled out of the room. Sleep would catch her quickly. Taking a moment to secure the house, he focused on what needed to be done, not the worry that always sat waiting in the wings. He needed to check in at the *Domus*. Plans had to be made, updates given.

He snuck up to the door to her room and looked in. Limbs were thrown out like she'd fallen from the ceiling onto the bed. Squashing the urge to enter he turned and walked down the hall. She would be fine.

8

Hailey slept so hard the sheets pressed squiggly wrinkles deep into her cheek and forehead. The cruelly twisted faces of the pirate captain and SS commander had threatened to invade her dreams, but somehow Derian, with a constant presence at the edges of her consciousness forbade them from entering. Once they had been banished from her mind she'd fallen deep and hard into a slumber that was almost painful to leave.

It took the clanging of pots to pry her lids open from the iron grip of sleep. The sun shined brightly through her bedroom window and the smell of breakfast wafted under the door. A silly smile tugged at her lips. Not only sexy, but apparently Derian could cook. She hadn't expected him back so soon so she hopped out of bed and skipped to the door.

She followed her nose down the hall but stopped short before entering the living room. A petite woman with the longest, blondest hair she had ever seen stood over the stove quietly humming. A quick scan of the room turned up no other guests. Hailey tempered her nerves but reached for something that could serve as a weapon. Fingers closed around a grotesque little tiki doll she'd picked up years ago at a neighborhood rummage sale. She growled from the hallway door, "Who the hell are you and what the hell are you doing in my home?"

The woman swung around brandishing a spatula. "Oh my, you're up!"

She had a thin jaw line and high cheek bones combined with a small nose and full lips that would have been the envy of any aspiring model or actress. But her eyes, though wide and enticing were hooded with sadness.

"Who are you? And why are you in my kitchen?" Hailey took a step into the living room, her tiki doll held loose and ready in her hand.

"My name is Moina." The woman turned back to the stove and flipped a pancake. "I'm your mother."

"What??" Hailey squeaked.

Moina turned off the burner and let the pancakes finish cooking as the pan cooled. "Your mother." She pulled two plates from the cupboard. "I know it is a surprise, and I hope I didn't frighten you."

Hailey placed the tiki on the nearest bookcase and approached the woman serving out pancakes, bacon and eggs. Moina continued, "I had meant to come much sooner." She glanced with sorrow at the picture of Hailey and Sue. "But the situation wouldn't allow it."

Moina sat at the table and looked expectantly at Hailey. Twenty-nine years, the woman had been gone for twenty-nine years and now she sat across the table. Across Aunt Sue's table! There was a nearly irrepressible urge to go back to her room and slam the door.

"I have things I have to tell you—important things," her mother pleaded.

That decided it, Hailey needed to know what she'd inherited. Talking now didn't mean they had to have a relationship. She sat heavily in the chair kitty corner to Moina.

The woman gave a tentative smile and handed over the syrup. "What I have to tell you, you may not believe."

"Is it stranger than jumping through time?" Hailey pierced the small stack of pancakes.

Moina's mouth dropped open in disbelief, but quickly recovered. "You have jumped."

"Yep. A couple days ago."

"And you were able to get back here? That is phenomenal."

"Well, I had help."

Moina's whole demeanor changed. The air charged with tension and all Hailey's warning bells rang like sale announcements on Black Friday. Moina breathed, "Who?"

Hailey tipped her chin in defense. This woman had never *been* there for her and a home cooked meal and friendly face was hardly enough to build up trust. She had to bite her tongue not to point this very thing out in the most inappropriate of terms.

Moina reached a hand across the table and placed it over Hailey's. Her hands were soft and cold. A nervous shiver ran down Hailey's spine. "Hailey, you have to tell me." She tightened her fingers and her nails dug slightly into Hailey's skin. "You are in very serious danger."

Danger? This lady didn't know the half of it. But Hailey held her tongue and Moina released her hand. Her eyes narrowed and the caring mother illusion evaporated. "There are things in play you couldn't possibly understand," Moina said.

"Yeh? Try me."

Moina stood and started to pace. Imagine that, pacing was hereditary. "There are people that if they knew what you were," she paused to give Hailey a hard look, "would use you to do the most unspeakable things."

Hailey's brows shot up. "What I am? You mean a time traveler?"

Moina waved off Hailey's comment and began to pace again. "No. No, jumping time is the least of your talents, my dear."

My dear? Hailey rolled her eyes and crossed her arms over her chest. "What other talents do I have?"

The pacing stopped and Moina took a deep breath before she continued, "I have no idea."

Hailey threw up her arms and got up from the table. "Ok, this conversation is getting really old." In the back of her mind she hoped Derian would walk through the door—or just blink into existence at the breakfast table—just to see whether sparks would fly. "You have told me nothing. And to be honest, I have no reason to trust you or even believe you are my mother. So either get to the point or go."

Moina grimaced and said, "You have your father's temperament."

"Tell me what you want or get out of my place!"

The two women stood staring at each other, one seething the other cloaked with latency. Moina was the one to break the impasse. "I do not have the time to tell you everything. As it is, there is much even I do not know. You are not just a *viator*. You are the result of years of experimentations and study of our people's very natures. When you were born I felt I needed to hide you from the man who did this—your father."

"I'm an experiment?"

"You are the final product of experimentation. Through you he thought to master time, not just move through it. He is brilliant, but ruthless. And he will do anything to bring you back."

"Sounds like a great guy."

Moina looked down at her wrist and lifted a thin band of leather to look beneath. "I must leave. He will notice that I have gone. I just needed to see you, to see that you were safe." Her expression pleaded and her voice cracked a little under the force, "You must leave as well. It is not safe for you here."

"And where exactly am I supposed to go?"

"This person who helped you, did they seem—experienced?"

Experienced? Oh yes, but maybe not in the way Moina meant. Hailey tempered her reply, "He seemed kind of new to the whole teaching thing."

Moina frowned. "A new *praeceptor* will not be able to handle Nikanuur."

"Nikanuur?" Hailey asked. Was she serious? What kind of name was Nikanuur?

"Yes, he has been alive for thousands of years and is one of the most powerful *viators* that has ever existed. Your *praeceptor* will be no match for him." Moina's nervousness increased and Hailey began to think a personal freak out moment was on the horizon. "You must find safety. Go to your *praeceptor*. Have him take you to the Magister. He will, at the very least, make it more difficult for Nikanuur to get to you."

Moina strode over to Hailey and pulled her into her arms. "I am very sorry I could not come to you sooner. I had hoped to give you a good life with Sue." She glanced at the photo of Hailey's lost aunt, "She was a dear friend and a good woman. I have missed her dearly."

She pushed away from Hailey with suddenness. "I must go. I will do everything I can to protect you. I am so very sorry."

Moina closed her eyes and her body shimmered. Hailey called out to the translucent woman, "Wait! I can't just go to Derian! I'm not very good at it yet!"

The petite *viator* opened her eyes and smiled as though she spoke to child. "Of course you can, you just aren't trying hard enough." And then she faded from the room.

"Shit!"

Hailey ran from the room and down the hall. She dug into her closet and pulled out a plain grey t-shirt and a thin springtime jacket. Wherever she ended up could be chilly, who knew. Then she pulled on jeans and tied on a pair of running shoes. After her fiasco with the pirates and Nazis, she wasn't going to screw around with stylish treads.

Hailey stopped. She was running around and not really thinking. Should she do something about the apartment? Would she need money? Supplies? What if she wasn't able to pop in next to Derian? What then? She felt like a rabbit stuck between two hound dogs.

There wasn't a reason to believe everything Moina had said. And yet, what if she was correct and her dead beat Dad was on his way to use her in some nefarious scheme to — what had she said? Rule time?

That decided it. She had absolutely no desire to meet her father.

Hailey threw on her jacket and then took a moment to remove the last photo of her and Sue from its frame, folded it in two and placed it into her back jean pocket. The house and things in it weren't really all that important, but her memories of Aunt Sue were. What would the kind old woman think of her life now?

Two hours later she sat on the floor leaning against the couch with her head hanging between her knees. She was ready to throw in the towel and beat a hole in the wall. Focusing on the back of her neck, like Derian had taught her had come up with a big fat zero. She couldn't just imagine herself where she wanted to go like she had with the apartment because she had no idea where Derian was. Moina had said she hadn't been trying hard enough. It was painfully obvious the woman didn't know what she was talking about.

The fear grew less terrifying with the passage of time, but she felt a heavy dread building up and she had no idea what to do next. It would be so much easier if Derian would just pop in next to her. Hailey sighed. Where on earth was he? And who was this Magister that Moina—she just couldn't bring herself to call her mom—insisted she find?

She slumped onto the couch and groaned. She was royally screwed. Hailey smiled. Ha, if only being screwed were her only problem. Her thoughts ran toward the sexy dark haired Derian and the promise of passionate pleasure she knew he could deliver. If she wanted him to, of course. Oh who was she kidding? Of course she wanted to. And she'd jump right into bed with him if she could figure out how to get past this unfortunate daddy dilemma.

As she thought about Derian and his yumminess her body felt an awareness flow through her blood. A strange sensation created a pull toward something, like someone tugging at a small thread that ran through her veins. Her breath caught in her throat and then she felt the tingle at the back of her neck. Finally! Things were looking up.

***

When Hailey materialized she faced three very handsome and utterly flabbergasted men.

"Hailey!" Derian reached for her just as her knees buckled.

"Dude." She held on to him gratefully and waited for the nausea to pass. It was definitely getting better and the headache didn't make an appearance, so all in all she was pleased. "That was trippy."

Three men stared at her, words lost on gaping lips. Concern wrote a clear pattern across Derian's feature. Beside him the two other men recovered from their surprise enough to show vastly different incarnations of interest. One considered her with stoic seriousness the other with thinly disguised humor.

Hailey turned her attention to Derian. "At least I didn't end up on my back this time!"

The voice that replied was a heavy Scottish brogue, "Has that been a problem for ye?"

Hailey blushed and Derian sent a scathing glare toward the light haired man with twinkling blue eyes. Derian's voice rumbled like a train over a steel bridge when he spoke, "Hailey, this is Lucius and Roderic."

"So this is the lass that kept ye from us for so many days," Roderic responded, his pale eyes scanning her body in overtly male appreciation.

Derian stiffened beside her. He warned, "Roderic."

The Scot laughed, "Dinna worry my friend, she is infinitely more interesting to science — for now." He flashed an unapologetic grin at Hailey.

Derian emitted a rumbling growl. Unaccustomed to the tense testosterone that filled the atmosphere, it took a moment before she realized Roderic was testing territories. And Derian was making it very clear she wasn't available. She grinned up at his dark scowl. How fun to have a guy get all manly over her.

The dark haired man with olive skin and exotic Mediterranean features — Lucius by process of elimination — raised a hand to stay the two chest thumping *viators*. "Enough, Roderic." He turned his attention to Hailey. "How did you get here?"

"I'm not exactly sure. I needed to find Derian and just kept trying. This weird pulling thing happened, then my neck tingled, and here I am."

The three men exchanged a look.

"What?" Hailey asked, "Is this another time I did it faster than everybody else?"

Derian responded, "No. This time you did something no one can do."

Great. She raised her eyes to the ceiling and sighed. "What did I do?"

"This is the *castellum*. No one can land here," Derian answered her with a hooded expression. Hailey was getting the impression that she hadn't even begun to understand the level of weird she was going to experience today.

"What do you mean not possible?" she asked.

"Not possible, until today." Roderic leaned against table, humor conspicuously absent from his expression. Hailey preferred the twinkle. The abrupt shift made her anxious.

"There is a barrier established, an electronic field that disrupts a *viator's* ability to land within the established boundaries. Not even the oldest and most experienced can do what you just did."

All three men stood staring. Her heart thudded. If she looked down the over active organ had to be visible against her chest. Could she seriously take any more of this?

She turned to Derian and lowered her voice, "I need to talk to you."

"What's wrong?" he asked. She cast a glance at the other men. He replied to her implied comment, "I trust these men with my life. You can say anything in front of them."

That would remain to be seen. But fine, she'd play along. "I had a visitor when I woke up. My mom stopped by."

"Your mother?" Derian didn't hide his surprise. "I thought you didn't know your mother."

"I don't—didn't. She just showed up in my kitchen, pancake breakfast and all. She told me some things, not a lot, but enough to really freak me out."

Lucius listened intently and despite his relaxed posture, she was certain Roderic was too. She wondered who these men were that Derian trusted so well. She continued, "Anyway, long story short, she said I'm some kind of weird time traveler experiment and I am in big trouble with my dad."

"We're going to need more details than that," Derian replied.

"Well, what it sounded like to me is my father wants to rule the world and he did some stuff to me that would help him do that."

Lucius scowled and Derian looked like a storm had broken across the horizon and thundered toward them. She held up a finger. "Before you ask, I have no idea what he did or what I can do. She just told me I was in danger and I needed to have you take me to the Magister."

Lucius' eyebrows rose at that. "Did she tell you her name?"

"Moina," Hailey answered.

A flicker of recognition crossed Lucius' face. "And your father?" He was leaning forward and it was apparent to Hailey that her answer was of the utmost importance to the man.

"Nikanuur."

The air seemed to whoosh out of the room as all three men collectively hissed in their breath. Roderic was the first to recover. "Well, that explains quite a bit actually."

Lucius addressed Derian, "Take her to your home. Her safety is in your hands."

"Do you think Nikanuur is the one leading this conspiracy?" Roderic asked. And like that, she was lost. She couldn't wait to get Derian alone so she could beat the answers out of him. Ok. Maybe not beat him, but plead, beg and definitely weasel.

"It is possible, but—I don't know. He doesn't have the personality of a leader. I do, however, believe he would experiment on his own child." Lucius returned his attention to her. "Derian will protect you. But we must know what it is you can do. If we are to stop your father from his plans we need to know how he intends to use you."

Hailey nodded. She was pretty interested to know herself. Lucius then turned to the prowling Scot and asked, "What do you need from her?"

"A sample of blood would be enough." Roderic smiled at Hailey, but rather than the irreverence, this time it was filled with cautious warmth.

Derian took her arm. "I will take her down to the lab. Then we will leave."

They snaked through the halls, twisting and turning in a manner that was so random in direction it had to be intentional. After a few minutes Hailey knew she would never make it back to the large office they had just left. Derian, on the other hand, stalked the halls like he knew exactly where he was going. He led her at a breathless pace.

The last jump's effects were sneaking up on her and fatigue cried out from her muscles. She wanted them done, gone, and somewhere safe so she could comfortably freak out about everything she had learned in the last several days. A total screech-fest waited in her future and she preferred to do it alone, in a locked room where no one could make assumptions about her sanity.

"So, my mother seems to think that you aren't qualified to help me with this."

Derian kept up the pace but replied with a tinge of humor in his voice, "That would probably be true. If I were *praeceptor*."

All these stupid names. If she got through this alive she was definitely going to sit down and write a manual. "You're not?"

"No, I'm a *venator*." He pulled them to a stop and faced her. "I hunt rogue *viators*. I am very good. I won't let anything happen to you." He lifted a hand to tuck a stray tendril of hair behind her ear. Hailey's stomach did a topsy-turvy roll and her cheeks flushed.

And then they were off again. They passed through a series of security doors that Derian accessed with a flurry of codes and a press of his finger against a pad. Finger print access, very high tech. She tried not to freak out about being in a super secret agency with people she hardly knew. They had to be safer than a father willing to experiment on his own child.

He left her sitting in a small break room as he went to find a technician. When he returned, a short and dumpy woman followed. She had the look of one that had settled into a comfortable life with little to no excitement. Hailey wondered what that felt like. Even when she worked in the marketing department in a sea of cubes she'd never come to terms with life as usual. For the first time ever she envied those that had found a comfortable routine in their life.

As the woman prepared her arm for a blood draw Hailey focused on the handsome man at her side. Hopefully he wouldn't notice her face losing all color and her shallow breathing. She didn't want this man to see her weakness. She wanted him to see her as strong and capable. Someone that could take on the challenges that life threw at them. But she really, really hated needles.

"So, who is this Magister that Moina mentioned?" Hailey asked, simply to distract herself from the imminent prick.

Derian took her hand in his and gave her a reassuring squeeze. "You have already met him. Lucius is the Magister."

"Oh. So that makes him what?"

Derian thought for a moment before replying, "The Council of Seven established the *Domus* a long time ago. It was created because a number of *viators* would use their talents to manipulate history and gain power. It became a threat to our survival. Guidelines were developed and we began policing our own. Through the years we've added a group that helps new *viators* adjust, and a research division. The Magister is appointed by the Council of Seven to oversee the *Domus*."

"Wow, you guys are crazy organized," she said. The technician finished and left. Hailey rubbed absently at the puncture wound. Who would have thought a super secret organization of time travelers existed? She sighed heavily. "How is it that no one thought to write a manual?"

Derian didn't laugh, but she was convinced he really wanted to. He seemed like a man that needed to laugh more. A strong hand reached out and he helped her from her seat.

"Where are we going?" she asked.

A worried crease settled between his brows. "My home."

9

They walked out into the sunlight and the intense light pierced her eyeballs like searing hot kebabs. It felt like all the moisture in her body was suddenly sucked out. Did she stick her head into a hair dryer? "Where are we, Hell?"

Derian walked them toward a wide parking lot. "Arizona."

"Why are we in Arizona?" Hailey asked then got distracted when they approached a classic Land Rover. She whistled and said, "I always wanted to drive in one of these."

He held the door open for her. Impressed, she hid a smile. A guy who opens a door for a girl; now that was a unique characteristic. She never understood why anyone wouldn't like something as simple as a held door; it always made her feel fuzzy inside.

The good vibes faded quickly when the door shut and she found herself engulfed in a man-sized oven. Who in their right mind chose to live in a place like this?

"Ow." She burned her hand on the seatbelt buckle. Derian slid into the driver's seat and turned the key. A torrent of hot air flew from the air vents and slashed her face. "Dude!"

"It will cool down in a minute." He reached over and pointed the vents away from her.

"Ok, why are we in Arizona?" she asked, relieved that the air from the vents had at least cooled to lukewarm.

"Cheap land and most of the year the weather is really nice," he answered as Hailey grimaced. "And the locals leave us alone. They're used to strange government installations out here."

They drove for over an hour along desert highway, through a small town that had seen better days, and then up over a mountain pass. Derian stayed quiet and for that she was eternally thankful. As they wound through switchbacks and hill crests Hailey let the landscape sweep away her thoughts.

Mountain pines rose up like giant sentinels and only the small low lying cactus and succulents reminded the travelers that they were still in the Sonoran Desert. The sun slid behind the trees and the air shifted to the eerie phase between sepia-colored dusk and the grey black of oncoming night. Hailey rolled down her window and stuck a hand out into the rushing air. The temperature must have dropped thirty degrees since the afternoon. She was glad of the jacket she had stashed in the back seat.

Derian pulled the Land Rover onto a forest service road. Her hand gripped the door handle, her knuckles white as they bounced over and through the ruts and rivulets that plagued the unmaintained trail. Off-roading had never been on her list of weekend entertainments. The novelty of the situation fled when she looked down and saw they were feet away from a sheer drop-off of dead wood and brush.

"Do you have something against living in the city?" Hailey asked.

He sat relaxed in his seat but Derian's eyes never left the road. Everything about the man was cool and controlled. Hailey wished he could share just a little of that with her.

"I'm not here very often. It's just easier to deal with if I don't have neighbors," he said.

With his focus entirely on driving, Hailey let her gaze fall over his shadowed features. Dark brown hair looked inky black as night overtook the cab. The color seeped from her vision and the sharp angles and strength of his bone structure stood in stark contrast in the shadows. Not nearly as big and imposing a figure as Lucius, he was also not a small man. He wasn't tall or short, skinny or fat. He was just plain strong.

He took his eyes off the road for a moment to catch her staring. Heat rushed to her cheeks and she swung her gaze to the trees. At least this time her embarrassment lay hidden in the night. Blushing had become entirely too common-place.

The vehicle crawled over another crest and a flash of light peeked through the trees. When they drew near she could make out a two story house illuminated by a bright outdoor security light. They pulled forward onto a solid concrete driveway and into a two car garage. The door slid quietly shut behind them. "Wow, you wouldn't expect a place like this out here."

Derian slid out of the car and held the door for her just as she was hopping out. He led her into the house and flicked the switch as they entered a narrow hall. Exhaustion creased his brow. She imagined she didn't look much better.

They entered the main rooms and she paused to gape. Solid wood floors were polished without removing the rustic look. There wasn't much furniture but what was there was solid and matched the woodsmen adventurer theme he seemed to be going for.

The ceilings were high and the living room had one wall entirely made of glass. The morning view must be incredible. As it was she could see the inky blackness of the sky peppered with millions of stars. A light from an adjacent room switched on and the view lost its brilliance.

She entered the kitchen to find Derian pulling cans from a cupboard. The room was a classy mix of light woods and stainless steel. Pots and pans hung from a wrought iron apparatus over a long center island. It was something right out of Martha Stewarts's Living.

Her gaze still on the various modern amenities, she wandered over to his side. Just as she reached him he turned and they bumped into each other, sending a happy jolt of electricity through her. Never had a man had this kind of an effect on her. Perhaps it was the strangeness of the situation or the sense of danger. Or maybe it was simply because he was the hottest man to enter her life outside the T.V. screen. She was shallow, she could admit it.

He apologized and went back to the cupboards to pull out several cream colored ceramic bowls. "I don't keep fresh food here unless I plan to stay for a while. So today we will have to deal with canned food."

He popped a bowl of soup into the microwave, then lounged against the counter. Despite tired eyes he still watched her with a hot intensity. Hailey hopped onto a barstool across the island from him and asked, "So...what's the plan?"

"We stay here and I protect you."

"That's it?"

"That's it."

How boring. Waiting for something to happen was definitely not her style. The last time she'd been stuck in a house with nothing to do was when she had mono in college. By the time she'd been able to see the light of day she was a frenetic lunatic starved for action. "How about we practice time traveling?"

"No."

"Why?"

He perked an eyebrow. She was being difficult. She knew that. But if he kept her cooped up in this place he would learn how very difficult she could get.

"You can't control your jumps. I would have no idea where we were landing or what we would face," Derian said.

"Yeh, but wouldn't it be harder for the bad guys to find me if we were on the move?" Hailey did her best to keep the whine out of her voice. But seriously, you don't just leave a city girl in the middle of nowhere with nothing to do. Could she possibly cope without a fast food joint down the road or a theater showing the latest movies? He didn't respond. Hailey sighed. "Well, you have to give me something to do, I'll go nuts."

A slow wolfish smile covered his lips. "I can think of something for us to do."

"Ok, sure. But we can't do that all day."

His smile widened and he pushed off the counter. He strode toward her and her heart started the thumpty thump song that had been playing so frequently. The microwave dinged. Miracles from heaven! She jumped off the stool and ran to the microwave. "Dude, I'm starving."

She heard the soft rumble of his chuckle as she singed her fingers on the ceramic bowl.

***

Hailey kept up a nervous chatter throughout dinner. She'd started with the weather, moved onto his choice of dinnerware, and finally settled into an interrogation over everything and anything *viator*. It was amusing. She wanted him, he had no doubt of that. And she knew it too.

After the soup and two beers she finally lost the nervousness and relaxed. But when she started asking about his family, it was time to change the subject. "You are certain your mother told you nothing of what your father did to you?"

Caught off guard by the change in topic she processed his question. The thoughts rolled across her face. There was very little she could hide behind her almond shaped hazel eyes. "No. She didn't exactly hang around."

He nearly swallowed his tongue when she placed her hands on the back of her stool and stretched her back, jutting her breasts up into the air. Did she have no idea what that did to a man? He coughed to clear his throat then said, "It would be easier if we knew."

Hailey waved her hand at him and yawned. "Yeh, I know. If you have any ideas on how to figure that out let me know." She slipped off the stool and started toward the door. "Do you have an extra bed, or am I couching it?"

Her round backside swayed as she walked from the room. He had to blink several times before he was able to get up and follow her from the room. It was going to be a long couple of days with her in this house. It was already shrinking in around him.

Derian settled her into the guest room then wandered out onto the second story deck that extended off the master bedroom. The night was crisp with the scent of pine. A stealthy movement in the brush below drew his attention. His hand fell to his side where the cool Glock sat at his hip.

The tension lifted as the slinking shadow of a mountain lion emerged. With a slight nod in salute he watched as his fellow hunter stalked the night.

"They are amazing creatures."

Derian swung around and pointed his gun at the man sitting in the dark enshrouded deck chair. When he realized who had snuck up on him he lowered the weapon and scowled. "You are going to get yourself shot."

"Well, I dinna want to interrupt you and the sexy *novus*. Dinna know if you had tucked her into your bed yet," Roderic said.

Derian bristled. The man was a rogue, just not the kind he hunted. He said as he leaned back against the deck rail, "She's off limits to you."

"Aye, you've made your claim clear, *venator*." The last word oozed derision. They had been friends for hundreds of years, yet a piece of the man had always been held back. Something had happened between Roderic and a *venator* and perhaps someday the man would confide in his friend.

"You have learned something?" Derian asked.

"I have, we found the mother in our databases." Fire flashed between Roderic's hands as he lit a cigarette. "Her first jump was in the Norse lands."

"She's old."

"Verra." Roderic paused and took a drag. The smoke curled through the shadows. "She kept to herself from thebeginning. Never had any relationships that we know of and never worked for the *Domus*. Then, twenty years ago she was reported dead."

"But she's not dead. Who reported it?"

"Now that is the interesting thing." The Scot grinned like a schoolgirl with a new secret and continued, "She went off the grid around that time and a *venator* was sent to apprehend her. It was he who reported her death."

"And where is he now?"

"Dead. One of those murdered by that damn poison," Roderic said.

The hair along Derian's arms rose as he felt the call of the hunt. There was no doubt now that the murders were somehow connected to Hailey. But he was torn between following the scent of conspiracy and staying behind to protect the young *novus*.

Roderic stood and flicked the cigarette off the balcony. Derian watched as it plummeted to the ground, wincing at the possibility of it starting a fire. If they weren't desperately in need of his friend's brilliant mind, he would enjoy throwing him over after it.

"I came to warn you, not recruit ye for the hunt. The *novus* is our best weapon against whatever we're facing," Roderic said as he faded from view.

Derian seethed. Roderic would feel compelled to use Hailey as a tool to protect the *Domus*. Derian was unwilling to let it come to that.

The night deepened with his thoughts and his body settled into Original Time. A *viator* always felt most comfortable in Original Time, the body knowing somehowthat this was the natural way to exist. It was the soul that pulled the *viator* out of time to explore the possibilities.

He never spent much time contemplating his existence despite his thousand years spent on Earth. The *Domus* had its share of philosophers debating the meaning and purpose behind traveling through time. It also had a large contingency of scientists determined to dissect the mechanisms that made what they did possible. And just as found in the human society at large, these two groups rarely saw eye to eye. Derian had just found it easier to stay away from the debate and simply learn to exist.

Now he was faced with a puzzle; one that did not fit into the constructs developed by either group. Was it possible that Nikanuur had altered Hailey's DNA? Enhanced the piece that was uniquely *viator*? Even Roderic's army of scientists hadn't yet discovered what governed a *viator's* talents. He had made significant inroads in the last two centuries as the science of Original Time opened avenues previously unavailable. But, even so...

Derian had already witnessed Hailey's advanced development as a *viator*. Even Lucius, with his age and experience, could not break past the barriers that guarded the *castellum*, yet she had followed him there. Were there others that Nikanuur had enhanced as well? Was the inner sanctum of the *Domus* threatened more severely than assumed?

He rubbed his eyes with the palms of his hands, grinding the tension away and breaking his deep contemplation. Action was the language he understood. The years had mellowed him and taught him patience, but the rash boy on the battlefield of Hastings still beat a thunderous rhythm against his heart. Hailey exhibited similar aversions to waiting for the battle to come to them, but they would both have to fight against their natures.

He returned to his room. Closing the blinds to the inky black night he pulled off his clothes and pulled back the bed sheets. The morning would do much to soothe the desire to hunt.

***

Three days. Three of the most agonizingly boring days had gone by and Hailey was about ready to take an axe to the door and run screaming into the woods. If it hadn't been for the satellite television she would have already done so. Now she couldn't find the remote.

She glared at the huge flat screen. Without the remote it was a useless piece of metal and glass. She vaguely recalled that there had been a time when a person could manually change the channels on a television. Those times were done and gone and she wondered what would happen if all the remotes of the world just disappeared. Would society survive?

Derian was off somewhere doing who knew what. He had made himself scarce over the last couple of days, though he was never too far. The morning before she had stubbed her toe, creating the perfect opportunity for her to practice profanity. He had run to her side, his face an image of steely resolve and his hand hovering inches from his Glock. The protection was there, but the company was not.

This had Hailey confused, annoyed, and most of all bored. He had made it clear he enjoyed her company. Well, maybe not enjoyed, but it seemed he would be willing to pass some time in recreational activities of the adult persuasion. But since that first night in the kitchen he hadn't made another move in her direction, innocent or otherwise.

She looked down at the voluminous pajama pants and t-shirt she had on and grimaced. After two days in the same clothes she had left California in, she had rummaged through his dresser to find something else to wear and it wasn't exactly the most attractive she'd ever worn. A trip to a mall was in order. Her miniscule cash stash was about to get even smaller.

The pale gold watch on her wrist told her a trip to town would have to wait until morning. The black television screen stared back at her. The night would drag agonizingly on if she weren't able to find that damn remote. Where had she seen it last?

Looking back into her memory she visualized the last time she had the remote in hand. It had been that afternoon, before she had wandered off for another shower. She hadn't really needed the shower, but it wasted time, and time was apparently something she could afford to waste.

A buzz rolled up from the back of her neck. This wasn't quite like the feeling she got right before a jump through time. Instead it was soft and lacked the sense of impending danger. It traveled along her shoulders and down her arm until a mild heat warmed the palm of her hand. The air shimmered and an object formed out of nothing onto her hand.

She stared at the remote. "Dude."

10

"What's wrong?" Derian asked from directly behind her shoulder.

Hailey put out her free hand to prevent a fall from the couch. Focused so intently on the remote she hadn't heard Derian walk in. "Nothing. What makes you think something is wrong?"

He walked around the couch and squared his shoulders. His eyes narrowed and she wondered if he could read her mind. He said, "You squeaked."

"I didn't." She never squeaked. Mice squeaked. Bikes left in the rain squeaked. Silly girls squeaked. She did not squeak.

"You did." He folded his arms. "You're a terrible liar. What happened?"

Resigned, Hailey handed him the remote. "Did you happen to forget to tell me that *viators* can make things teleport?"

His face darkened and Hailey's nervousness rocketed to a new high. He answered, "No, I did not. We can't."

Just great, another freakazoid thing to deal with. She was bound to hit a break sooner or later, right? She sighed, then pointed toward the remote. "Well, that just appeared in my hand when I thought too hard about it."

Derian looked down at the remote, then back at her. Disbelief flashed for a second before he replaced it with the customary steely resolve. "Do you think you could do it again?"

She stood up, threw up her arms and started to pace. "Ah hell, I don't know." With all the pacing she'd done over the last week she could eat a party's worth of cupcakes and not worry about calories. "I don't know how any of this is happening."

A strong hand wrapped around her wrist to stop her mid-stride. Derian pulled her into his arms. He was warm and strong. She laid her cheek against his chest and allowed his gentle breathing to calm her nerves. She had known him less than a week and yet he was the closest to home she had felt since Aunt Sue passed.

She pulled away and brushed her fingers through her dirty-blond hair. Pillows fell to the floor as she flopped onto the couch. "Alright, let's try to figure this out. Right before it teleported into my hand I was trying to remember where I had seen it last."

He settled onto the loveseat kitty corner to the couch. "Do you want to try it again?"

"I guess." She sat quietly for a moment. What could she try? Something small for sure. Maybe something from the other room? The perfect item popped into her mind. Focusing her thoughts on the last time she saw it, she waited. The buzz at the back of her neck was subtle and she barely noticed the warmth in her hand before she held the slim silver cell phone she'd left in California.

She looked up at Derian. His face was still a mask of steel, but a flicker of something suggested he was far from unsurprised.

"Whoa! Far out!" A strange voice echoed in the room.

Derian's head snapped up. The intensity that stiffened his body relaxed and Hailey let herself breathe. She twisted around as a woman with chocolate brown hair dressed in the height of 1970's style strutted into the room. She had to be in her mid-forties, yet she sported the shortest skirt Hailey had ever seen. She'd grown up with Hollywood wannabes and beach bum babes where short skirts were the norm. This one beat them all in crossing the line to obscene.

Derian stood and the woman slinked up to him in a come-hither way that sent a wave of cattiness through Hailey. The perfectly tanned complexion and erotically inspired attire was designed to perk a man's interest. If Derian was that kind of man, Hailey would walk right out that minute.

Despite the woman's giant platform boots, her head only reached the bottom of Derian's chin. He asked, "What are you doing here?"

Hailey stood and moved a little closer to the two, but restrained herself from inserting her body between Derian and the little tramp.

"I felt a disturbance in the Force! I just had to come!" The woman giggled in the obnoxious high-pitch that made Hailey think of pink princesses and bubble gum. Had the woman walked through a helium cloud?

"Reena," Derian warned.

Her slinky hand snuck out and rested on Derian's forearm. "Oh Sugar, they call me Poppi now." She turned to Hailey and winked. "It's 'cause I love me some Pop."

That had to be the lamest excuse for a nickname she had ever heard. But she was more concerned with the woman's hand gripping Derian. Would it be bad if she ripped the slender arm out of its socket?

Something must have shown because Poppi dropped her hand and flounced toward the loveseat and fell into the cushions. Hailey winced as she was given an unnecessary show of skin before Poppi pulled her legs into a ladylike pose.

"Reena," Derian emphasized the use of the woman's first name and she stuck her tongue out at him. "What are you doing here?"

"I told you! I felt something in the Force!"

Derian growled in exasperation and Poppi started wagging her finger at him. "Don't you deny the Force! It's for real, man. Anyway, I knew something was up and I was right." She looked pointedly at Hailey. "You must be Nikanuur's baby."

"How do you know that?" Derian was coiled tight and the room thickened with tension. Hailey held her breath. He was in a very dangerous mood and Poppi appeared completely oblivious.

"Come on now Baby, he's been looking for his girl for years." She pointed at his wrist and said, "But, you're still working for the Man so you wouldn't know that."

Hailey cut her eyes toward the thin leather band around Derian's wrist. "What is that?"

He lifted the band and beneath was a small metal patch with three green lights. "It's how I communicate with the *Domus*."

"My mother had one," Hailey said.

He frowned and lost the hard unfazed look, clearly frustrated by the turn of events. All of his attention was now trained directly on Hailey. "Why would your mother have one of these?"

"I have no idea."

"Freaky deaky, Man," Poppi said and stood up before flouncing toward the door. "You got food? I'm starving!"

After a moment Hailey could hear cabinets slamming and the very clear sounds of rummaging. She leaned toward Derian and asked, "Who is she?"

"She's..." He raised his eyes to the ceiling. "I couldn't even begin to explain."

"Well, how did she find us and how does she know about me?"

Derian sat beside Hailey and laid his head against the top of the couch. "She's old."

Hailey scrunched her forehead, "She can't be more than 45."

"She first jumped with she was five."

"Holy crap, five? How the hell?"

Derian glanced toward the kitchen. "She's developed some interesting survival skills." He looked back at Hailey and clasped her hand in both of his. Rather than a jolt of energy she felt the warmth spread from his hands up through her arms. Boy, she was getting it bad for this man. "This is a problem, Hailey."

She looked up into his eyes, confused. "What? This? I mean, we haven't done anything yet."

He was about to say something but stopped, then cocked his head. Hailey realized he hadn't been speaking about the feelings elicited by his touch. She blushed and looked away.

His fingers touched the side of her face and he pulled her toward him. His lips brushed hers before she thought it was even a possibility. Puffs of air tickled her lips as he whispered, "You are distracting me."

"Dude, I..." His lips found hers again. They were warm and insistent, but clearly testing her response. Now who was distracting? Her belly fluttered and she felt the hairs at the back of her neck rise. She pulled back from the kiss as confusion overwhelmed her. One moment she felt inexorably pulled toward this man and in the next she wanted to run.

There was uncertainty in his expression. Did he have the same conflicting feelings as she? "Derian, I...ah hell." They could sit in limbo forever doing the pre-romance two-step or she could go ahead and make a decision. What was the worst thing that could happen? She leaned in and planted a solid kiss against his lips.

A deep rumble filled his chest and vibrated against hers. He wrapped his arms around her back and took over the kiss. Hailey held on for dear life. The sensation at the back of her neck was far from the fight or flight tingling. Instead, it was flushed with a heat that spread through her body.

She slid a hand and grasped behind his neck, holding him to her and securing herself solidly in his embrace.

"Whoa Man! You're robbing the cradle!" Poppi called from across the room.

Hailey flew out of the embrace feeling like a teenager caught necking in the park. Poppi stood in the door a can of tuna in one hand a fork poised halfway to her mouth in the other. "Nikki's not going to like you kissing on his baby girl."

"Nikanuur is a rogue." Derian confronted the garishly dressed woman.

"So? He's still this little girl's daddy," Poppi replied.

Hailey had enough. Who did this woman think she was? "Hey. I don't care who Nikanuur is. He has nothing to say about me."

Poppi dismissed her with a wave of a hand. "Whatever, he's coming anyway."

Derian advanced on the woman who finally showed the sense enough to be nervous. "Reena, if you led him to her…"

"I didn't." Poppi ducked out of the way. She ran, but with the huge platforms it was more of a shuffle, to the backside of the couch. "Listen. Nikanuur has been getting pretty powerful. He's got a hand in more stuff than anyone knows."

He stopped pursuing Poppi, but stood with his hands clenched at his side. "Then why are you here?"

She gave a snarky grin that sent shivers down Hailey's spine. "I like to be where the action is. And this is where the action is going to be."

"This isn't a game, Reena," He said and she replied with a derisive snort. Derian swung around and grabbed Hailey to pull her from the room.

"Do you really think you can keep her safe from him?" she called. When he kept them walking through the door Poppi hustled after them. "You can't take her to the *Domus*!"

Derian whirled around and Hailey scooted out of the way. Poppi gripped the back of a chair, her tendons popped up through her hand and her jaw tensed. Warning bells clanged.

"Where do you think her mother got the com band?"Poppi breathed.

"What are you saying?"Derian asked.

"Something's going down Man, and it stinks in the *Domus*."

"You have never cared for politics before." The tone Derian took with Poppi was a little more familiar than Hailey liked. Did the two have a past? She couldn't imagine the outrageous woman being Derian's type. But did she really know? Here she was considering a relationship — ok, so just a physical one — and she didn't know anything about him.

"Derian, this isn't politics," The petite woman relaxed the heavy nineteen seventies slang. Her eyes sharpened and a trace of keen intelligence flashed.

Derian stared at Poppi, distrust evident. Hailey felt it too, but she wasn't quite sure why. Gut feeling she assumed. Poppi wasn't forthcoming with information, which led to a rather uncomfortably quiet moment. Hailey sighed in frustration. She was getting really tired of cagey time travelers.

"I am so done with you two," Hailey said with exasperation. She walked out the door and up to her room. There was too much to think about and she couldn't do that with Derian hovering and Poppi making a nuisance of herself. If there was a time she wanted to disappear into history, this was it.

***

Derian watched as Hailey stormed from the room. He could understand her frustration. He had very few answers from the start for her. Now, he was faced with more questions and even fewer answers. Reena, now Poppi, had been the occasional nuisance since he started as a *venator*, but he had been warned well in advance of her chaotic nature.

After thousands of years traveling for survival, the woman had gotten bored. Latching on to one *viator* or another, she would stumble through the years causing at the very least trouble, in many cases catastrophes. Nearly three hundred years ago Reena had run into Derian and had been a thorn in his side since.

And yet again, the woman was true to form. When he should be focused on protecting Hailey, he was dealing with her and her highly questionable motives. Derian said, "I am sure you are not surprised that I question your intentions."

Poppi stuck her bottom lip out in an overtly contrived pout. "After all the time we've spent together baby?"

"My patience is not limitless," he answered.

Poppi lost the conniving tilt to her head and narrowed her eyes at the frustrated *viator*. Her angles were rarely complicated, though at this junction he was unsure what her investment was with Hailey and the rogue. Poppi never took sides as her best interests always came first and never aligned with others. She finally replied, "Your sweet tart is the catalyst for a war. The big fish at the *Domus* have no clue what is coming at them."

"Nikanuur is leading this war?"

She shook her head and said, "No, as far as I can tell he's just a minion. He screwed up big time when he lost track of Hailey."

"Who are you working, for?" he asked.

The dark haired woman twirled a strand of hair around a finger. "You know I never work for anyone, sugar. Keep that baby girl safe." Poppi leaned in and planted a quick kiss on his cheek then started to fade away.

"Wait! Who's involved with this at the *Domus*?" he asked.

She shrugged and then was gone. Derian kicked at the foot of the couch. The damn woman had left him with nothing but more questions.

He left the room to find his exasperated *novus*. So much for getting to know Hailey a little more intimately. It unnerved him that someone was involved at the *Domus*. Lucius would need to know, but he would have to get Hailey and himself into the *castellum* without alerting the entire *Domus*.

Derian entered Hailey's room and found it empty. The tell-tale sound of car door slamming shut sent him running to the window. An unfamiliar SUV threw dust into the air as it sped away from the house. Dread settled in his stomach as he ran from the room. Someone had gotten past him while he'd been distracted by Poppi and somehow gotten Hailey out of the house.

He didn't know if Poppi had been a party to the kidnapping, nonetheless he would strangle her the next time she showed up. He grabbed his Glock and keys and ran to the garage where he was met by four flat tires. He cursed and ran back into the house.

Stalking to the rarely used office on the first floor to make a call he processed options. There were few and those he did have he did not like.

11

Derian looked out across the green and white landscape surrounded by the Ochachi-Daira caldera. The chill wind struck the back of his neck. It kept his mind sharp and the senses alert. These volcanic peaks on the island of Hokkaido had been a place of sanctuary for all his years traveling through time.

The small shack behind him had survived well. Unable to return to a time and place he had been to previously, he always worried that time in his absence would take its toll. One day he might return and find it uninhabitable. But Derian had timed this arrival well. By his calculations, the shack had last felt his touch only three days ago. For him, it had been nearly 300 hundred years since his feet tread on this frosty ground. He smiled, explaining this little quirk of *viator* physical reality to Hailey would be a challenge.

He immediately sobered. His only solace in Hailey's capture was that she was invaluable to whoever had her. She would be safe — in theory. He would need to get to her soon, but jumping into the situation without backup or knowledge of what he faced could be disastrous.

The crunch of gravel alerted Derian to Lucius' arrival. Both men stood silently, allowing their souls to settle with the landscape. The caldera had been the destination of Derian's first jump. Lucius had found the young Anglo-Saxon injured from battle. Confused from a time jump he had never been prepared to experience, he had been ready to lash out at anything in his vicinity. Lucius took him in hand and taught him about being a *viator* and even more about being a man.

"She went off the grid," Lucius said. The stolid Magister stood strong against the lashing wind; his tense shoulders the only hint that unease bracketed his thoughts. "You are the only link we have to her now."

Derian cursed and then said, "If they know I have bonded with her, they will be waiting for me. I will be going in blind." He had never actually gone into a situation not knowing at the very least where he would find himself. It was unlikely that her kidnappers had gotten her to jump to another time, so they would be restricted to physical travel in Original Time. But this still did not provide Derian with much work to with.

"Has Roderic come up with anything?" Derian asked.

"Nothing that would help us here." Lucius turned a considering eye on his *venator*. "Why did you request a communications white out?"

"Moina has a com band."

"You are certain?"

"Enough not to risk it." Derian puffed warm air into his hands. The cold had seeped into his fingers, stiffening the joints and numbing the skin. It had been a long time since he had felt the cold. It was a welcome sensation that reminded him of his past and focused his thoughts on his future.

"There seems to be much that has gone on without my observation," Lucius said. The man prided himself on his ability to foresee possible challenges. The current turn of events was obviously not sitting well with him. "You are going to follow her."

"Yes," Derian replied. Hailey may remain unharmed, but he wouldn't leave her in the hands of this threat.

Lucius stood unmoving his thoughts unreadable. "It would be a challenge." An understatement, but the comment fit his stoic nature.

"We can't afford to leave her with them," Derian countered. It wouldn't have mattered if they could. Even though the man was his friend, he did not want Lucius questioning his true motives. And at the moment, he wasn't quite sure of them himself.

"No, you are correct. It is imperative that we retrieve her," Lucius said. Another moment passed in silence. Then he continued, "I will go with you."

"That is not a risk you should take."

"You will need assistance. You are the only one that can follow Hailey. I am the only one that can follow you," Lucius answered.

Derian could not argue that, although he wished he could. Having someone to watch his back on this mission would be invaluable. But the loss of the Magister would be disastrous for their kind. Derian would have to take pains to prevent that from happening.

"We need supplies," Derian said, turning his gaze back to his friend. "Without being seen."

A twinkle lit in Lucius' eyes. The man was no doubt looking forward to a little action. "I think we can manage that."

***

The world outside was moving — again. Hailey rubbed at her eyes as she waited for her stomach to settle. The nausea felt more like motion sickness than the after effects of time travel. She groaned and rolled onto her back. The wood floor vibrated beneath her and she picked up the distinctive sound of steel wheels on tracks. It sounded suspiciously like a train. What was she doing on a train?

A haze filled the car and thin streams of light sliced through the dark from between the joints in the door. Dust particles hung in the air in an ethereal dance. She held her breath, listening for others that shared her moving cabin. Nothing stirred above the clanging metal and she relaxed.

As she sat up, she held her stomach to quell its roiling reaction. She scanned the room and nothing moved. Whoever had taken her had left her alone. She thought back to her last moments of consciousness. She had just reached her room after walking away from Derian and Poppi in a snit. Her reaction to the bantering *viators* had been childish, but she hadn't been able to spend another second in the room with them, wondering what kind of relationship he'd had with that silly woman.

They'd been waiting for her behind the door. When she'd crossed the threshold they'd grabbed her, jabbed a needle in her neck and out she went. And now she was alone, freaked out and confused.

From what she could see, the room was empty save for a plastic bucket and a cooler. Hailey crawled over to find the bucket filled a quarter the way with kitty litter and the cooler full of bottled water and various snacks. Apparently, they expected her to be in here a while. She sniffed at the kitty litter toilet. They had to be out of their minds if they thought she would use that.

Bracing her arms on the floor she pushed herself up to examine the rest of the car. A small mattress with a hastily thrown comforter sat in one corner. The rest of the car was empty. The giant steel door didn't budge, as expected, but it's never good to just assume. "Never assume anything dear, when you do, it just kicks you in the butt," Hailey smiled as she quoted her Aunt Sue. But then frowned, remembering that the kind old woman hadn't really been her aunt after all.

Slumping down against a wall she banged her head in frustration. So what if she hadn't been related to Sue. The woman had been more family then any of her newly realized relations. They hadn't been particularly endearing since they had made their presence known. Just like bad relatives, only coming out when you got something they wanted.

Well, Nikanuur wasn't getting whatever it was he wanted. It was time to get the hell out of there. She shut her eyes and focused on Derian's home in the Arizona mountains. Hopefully she could get back before he noticed she was gone. It was nice having him protect her and all, but truthfully, she wanted to prove to him she could take care of herself. Who wants a teacher-student relationship with the guy you want to sleep with? That sure as hell wasn't her kink.

Nothing happened. She tried for several more minutes before crying out in frustration. She could do this, she'd done it before. It wasn't that hard, was it?

Hailey took a deep breath and then changed her focus to the piece of Derian that flowed through her veins. It felt like she was floating in a fog but she eventually caught a thread and tried to follow it. Her neck tingled and her heart thumped in anticipation.

"Arghhhh!!" A white pain shot from her neck strait toward her forehead. She lost focus on the connecting thread to Derian and the pain ceased. "What the hell?"

Her fingers touched the back of her neck and she frowned. A hard metal square was planted into her skin. Hailey pinched her fingers around it and pulled. The same white pain pierced her head again. "Shit!"

The bastards had implanted her with something! She slammed her fist on the wood floor. Whatever it was, it obviously prevented her from leaving. Tears burned behind her eyes. So much for showing Derian she could save herself. She banged her head against the wall again. It was totally not fair.

It could have been hours before she moved again. Her sense of passing time was skewed. Quiet thinking hadn't led to any epiphanies and now it looked like she would have to breakdown and use the damn kitty litter. Could things get any worse?

Three bottles of water, five cheese sticks and one annoying experience with a bucket toilet later she was cursing herself for asking the obvious. If you can ask if things can get worse, then they undoubtedly can. Proof of this stood across the floor from her in the form of three very mean—and scruffy—looking men. Each held a nasty-looking weapon and an equally nasty expression.

Hailey eyed the nefarious weapons with unease. They looked like cattle prods, though perhaps a little less humane. What exactly had they expected to find in here?

They mumbled heatedly before the one with the longest prod started forward with a snarl. He poked at her and she skittered to her feet. "Dude! Seriously?"

He stepped back and then glanced at his partners in crime. The other two scanned the room, arms ready, waiting for something. Realization struck. They were expecting her rescuer.

"I'm all by myself boys," Hailey said. They didn't pay any attention to her. She rolled her eyes. "Seriously, it's just us. If he were here he'd have shot you by now."

This got a reaction at least. A cell phone flipped open and a curt reply was barked into the phone. The language sounded like nothing she'd ever heard. Arabic maybe? Greek?

The air beside the three henchmen shimmered as a figure materialized. Despite the darkness Hailey could see the imposing shoulders of a man. She had a sneaking suspicion she wouldn't be happy when she learned his name.

He stepped from the shadows into the only portion of the car with enough light to see. He looked like Prince on steroids. Or was he still formerly known as Prince? She could never keep it straight. Hailey sighed. Let the fun and games begin.

"Daughter," he said, his voice rumbling deep and silky. It sent shivers of unease up her spine. Could she seriously be related to this rat?

"You must be Nikki." Hailey held out a hand. "I've heard so much about you."

Taken aback, he paused and she pressed her advantage. "So, I hear you want to rule the world — or something like that."

She turned her back on him and wracked her brain for a plan. Simple moxy wasn't likely to get her out of this one. "That's totally cool, but really," she paused and waved her hand over the car's contents, "did you have to go to all this trouble?"

"Sit down," Nikanuur ordered.

She felt like a child in a lion's den. But he needed her. That meant she was safe. Didn't it? When in doubt, redirect blame. She pointed at the three men standing to the side. "They just told me to get up. Did you want to make up your mind?" She whirled away, turning her back on him again. Think. She had to think.

"Sit down," he barked. Ok, he seemed to really mean it. But the boxed in feeling made her reckless. How dare he treat her like this?

"No," she said.

"What??"

That sounded a lot like a roar. Ah well, in for a penny. She propped her hands on her hips. "No. I'm not going to sit down. You're going to tell me what you want from me and we are going to negotiate. But you are not going to order me around."

His mouth flew open in preparation of a shout, but he closed it before a sound came out. Hailey held her breath. She was valuable, right?

He smiled, and she wasn't sure if that was a good thing or not. "You, daughter, are nothing like your mother."

"Yeh? How's that?"

"You seem to have a well developed back bone." His lips curled as he spoke and if she had known nothing about him, she would have disliked him anyway.

"Hmm. She kept me away from you didn't she?"

His expression darkened with his evidently volatile temper. He said, "Yes, that was significantly out of character for her."

Hailey crossed her arms over her chest. "Perhaps you don't know much about her character."

"And do you?"

"Nope." Hailey stepped back until she felt the wall against her spine. The solidity of the metal added strength to her stance. "So, what do you want?"

"Information."

"Call a librarian. I have nothing."

Irritation flared in Nikanuur's expression and Hailey knew she was pushing buttons. When he flicked his hand and one of the ogres advanced with the prod aimed for her middle she decided perhaps it was time to put aside the snarky comments. "Fine."

A hand stayed the advance and an eyebrow rose in triumph. So, the man anticipated her reaction to a physical threat, she was a wimp, what could she say. "What do you want to know?"

His smile was crafty and Hailey hated it. If she hadn't been sure the three goons were expecting it, she would have prayed to heaven that Derian would choose this time to come in guns blazing.

"You have learned to jump time."

It was a statement, so she just stood quietly. She wasn't going to make it easy. He continued, "And have you learned to control it?"

"Not really." She could tell he didn't like that. What had he expected?

"Have you noticed any other new abilities?"

"Do you mean like shooting fire out of my hands?" He looked so excited about the prospect she couldn't help herself from waiting an extra moment before continuing. "Yeh, no. Can't do that."

His response was so swift she didn't see it coming. His hand swiped across her cheek, snapping it sideways. Sparks flew through her eyes. Oh how she wished she really did have the fire super power now. The bastard deserved a serious torching.

"You will learn to respect me."

"Not likely," she spat out.

He slapped her again. Tears streamed from her eyes and down her face and numbness crept over her cheekbone on a course toward her eye. "Dude, you seriously need people skills."

A third strike and she fell to the floor. Somewhere she vaguely remembered being a wimp about pain. Perhaps stupidity just trumped it.

Nikanuur stood back, waiting, watching. Snarky comments weren't working for her, so she opted for silence. He resumed questioning, but she stopped listening after awhile, retreating inside herself, wishing he would just go away and let her pull herself back together. Eventually he did, taking his three thugs with him. It wouldn't be the last she saw of her good old daddy, that she knew, but perhaps between now and then she could come up with a better strategy than taunting the snake.

She woke with her heart pounding. There was nothing worse than falling asleep without realizing it. After fighting through the haze of disorientation she found herself nose to nose with Poppi.

"Dude!"

The back wall was far too close and Hailey clonked her head as she scrambled away from the woman and her giant eyes and frizzy hair. Poppi just laughed then stood and took a few steps back. "Rise and shine baby doll."

"You're a little nuts, you know that?"Hailey said.

Poppi narrowed her eyes and her mien transformed from slightly dazed ditz to something far more complex and complicated. "Sanity is not always what you have been taught it is. More often the crazy are the most sane."

"So, what are you doing here?"

The giant smile returned and her eyes sparkled with mischief. "Well, baby doll, it seems you are in need of rescuing. I just happen to be in a rescuing type of mood."

"Why would you want to help me?" Hailey stood and the blood rushed to her legs letting her know that they too had fallen into a deep sleep. "Argh, dude. I hate that."

Poppi giggled as Hailey stomped her legs and cursed in a frantic attempt to bring circulation through the offended appendages. Poppi said, "For some reason I like you. Plus, Derian seems a bit attached."

Hailey's temper flared. "What exactly is your thing with Derian?" It wasn't jealously. She was just a little protective. He was her *praeceptor* after all.

"Don't get your panties in a bunch. He's like a kid brother," Poppi said then wandered over to the cooler and popped open a soda. When she noticed the bucket of kitty litter her nose wrinkled. "Gross! So, are you ready to go?"

"I would love to go. But, I can't jump and the doors are locked." Hailey lifted her hair and showed Poppi the implant.

"Well that sucks. I guess you'll be going out the door." She faded from view before Hailey could respond. An hour passed and she was once again sitting against the wall waiting. So much for an escape plan.

Hailey was contemplating the makeshift potty again when a loud bang sounded against the door to the train car. Hailey was up and running before she thought to worry about whatever waited on the other side. A second bang was followed by the screech of metal against metal as the door slid open. A pair of bolt cutters flew into the car and distracted her from the body flying in behind it. Hailey landed in a pile of limbs and grunts.

"Shit baby doll, what were you doing in front of the door?"Poppi asked.

When Hailey extricated herself from the nutty *viator* she brushed off her pants and pulled herself together. The woman obviously thought she was in Mission Impossible or something. Not only did she have to worry about being killed by her dad, but now by a well-intentioned crazy lady.

"This was not exactly the rescue I expected," Hailey said.

"No? Well, it's what we've got. Come on, out you go." Poppi grabbed her elbow and started pulling her toward the door.

"What? Out the door? It's moving!"

Poppi didn't stop and Hailey tried to dig in her heels. Only movie stuntmen and fugitives jumped from moving trains. She was neither. Ok, maybe a fugitive in the broadest sense of the term, but really, there were other options. There were always other options!

They stopped at the edge and Hailey could see the landscape flying by. Vegetation was sparse and the ground was relatively flat and free of obstacles, but not any more reassuring.

"It's not that bad. People do this all the time," Poppi said.

"No they don't. People get killed doing this all the time."

"Now, when was the last time you heard of someone getting killed doing this?"Poppi stuck her head out into the air careening past the train.

Hailey didn't respond. Poppi was a font of optimism, there would be no arguing there. She looked to the side to see the thin metal rods that made up a ladder leading up to the car roof.

"You have to get off this somehow. Jumping is your best deal," Poppi said.

Hailey filled herself with resolve. She could do it. She had to do it. But she was damned if she was going to do it alone. "You go first."

"Oh, I'm not jumping."

"Excuse me?"

"Just roll when you hit the ground," Poppi said then struck out with both hands.

Hailey felt the air rush past as she flew off the car. Her last thought before she focused on the imminent collision with the desert was a new determination to kill Poppi.

12

A million different scenarios passed through Derian's mind as he prepared to jump after Hailey. Landing beside a freight train with Hailey hurtling through the air toward him was not one he had anticipated. Bones crunched when she hit him and he knew pain would be his companion for a number of days to follow. They both spiraled backward hitting the ground in what could only be described as a bounce, except, the experience was significantly more violent.

They settled in a heap of limbs and pain. Lots of pain. Centuries of experience told him his body would mend. Nothing serious or permanent had happened in the crash. But his certainty did not extend to Hailey. She was uncharacteristically quiet. He untangled himself and looked down to see her face blossoming with bruises and blood trickling from a shallow slice at her temple. "Hailey! *Léof*, please wake up."

"Shit. I was sure she'd land better than that."

Derian swung around to where Poppi stood beside them. "What the hell are you doing here?" She flinched at his tone, but he didn't care. With a snarl he turned back to the woman that had somehow found a chink in his armor. The terror he felt at that moment was unlike any he had faced. No army or rogue was as daunting as losing her before he knew why her loss would haunt him.

A gentle throb responded to his questing fingers and he breathed a sigh of relief. A pulse, soft, but true. Her head injury worried him. The blood still trickled out, though thankfully not a gush. Head wounds bled like hell, but the real danger lay in the likely concussion. His hands roamed over her body searching for further injury. He was nervous to move her, but there were few options out in the middle of the desert.

He looked up, searching the mountains for a familiar shape, anything to tell him where they had landed.

"I had to get her out. I had too." Poppi kneeled beside Hailey and dabbed at the wound at her temple with a soft cotton cloth. Derian bit back the harsh comment he had prepared for the meddlesome *viator* when he saw the tears streaming down her cheek.

"Reena?"

No words came from her mouth, but a quiet hiccup wracked her body. The woman never cried. In fact, she had never shown any emotion. She was simple, obnoxious, and uncaring. The moment was strange, but fleeting, as they both gasped at Hailey's soft groan. "Oh baby doll! Wake up girl! You got too much to do to just lay here out in the desert."

Hailey groaned again but didn't open her eyes. The bright yellow and greenish tint of a bruise covering the side of her face came to view when she turned her head. Derian's sucked in a breath as his heart clenched.

"Those were there before she jumped," Poppi said.

"Who?"

"Nikanuur I'm sure. He's a mean son of a bitch." The vehemence was out of character again. Derian looked closely at the tiny woman. She had changed out of her usual outrageous attire, clothed simply in jeans and a t-shirt. It was an extremely fitted shirt, but a t-shirt nonetheless.

"What is your interest here?" He asked Reena. It didn't make sense. Another piece, like Hailey's mother, that didn't seem to fit in the puzzle.

Poppi ran her hand over Hailey's hair, a strange wistful smile on her lips. "I'm on your side. You have to just trust me on that."

"I don't have a reason to," he growled. Hailey groaned again, taking his attention away from the conversation. The sun rose high and pressed its scorched fingers into the land. The heat would become unbearable and they would need water. Until she was conscious they couldn't jump. Where was Lucius? He was supposed to land soon after him.

"Help me move her," he said. Bracing her head with his forearm he reached under her shoulders as Poppi slid her hands under the knees. They shuffled awkwardly toward a copse of cottonwood trees. The desert pavement was flat and relatively free of vegetation, but it was littered with rocks and pebbles with a heavy patina. Each precarious step challenged their grip on Hailey's limp body.

When they made it into the shade Derian was relieved to find several puddles left from a desert monsoon. The cottonwood always told the weary traveler where water could be found, in most cases it flowed far underground. They were fortunate to find some on the surface, despite its muddy quality.

A slight breeze moved through the branches. That and the shade would be enough to keep them safe from the sun's rays. With that worry removed, he focused on the other. Hailey was still unconscious and the longer she stayed so the more severe he suspected the injury. His hand slid from behind her neck, scraping against something hard and metal where her spine met her neck. "What the hell?"

A small silver square of metal clung to her neck. The skin around it rose in an angry swell. When he tugged gently Poppi hissed, "Don't!"

"What is it?" Derian asked and laid Hailey's head down, wishing he had something to serve as a cushion, but glad it was the soft sand of the desert wash and not the hot desert pavement. "What is this thing? And how is it you know so much about what is going on?"

"It's a leash. And it hurts like hell when you try to pull it off." She absently rubbed the back of her neck. Derian took three steps and grabbed her arm, pulling it away so he could look under the ancient's hair. A series of puncture marks in the shape of a square sat at the nape of her neck.

"You had one. Why?" he asked.

Poppi pulled her bottom lip with her teeth. Irritation flared. He was tired of her skirting, holding back. If he didn't get information from her soon he was bound to shake it out of her.

Haunted eyes peaked out beneath long dark lashes. "Nikanuur grabbed me a while ago. Kept me locked up for almost five years. Bastard thought he could compare my brain to others and discover what makes us tick. He almost killed me. He'll do the same to your sweet heart, but I think his plans for her are a lot worse."

Hailey moved and they both jumped back to attend her. "Come on now, baby doll. You got Derian all worried; it's time to wake up."

Hailey's eyes fluttered open then quickly squeezed shut. Derian realized the sun was shining directly onto her face. He shifted, then lifted her head onto his lap. "Hailey?"

"Tell me I didn't get pushed off a moving train," she said her voice weak.

Derian's head snapped up to glare at Poppi. A soft pink blush spread suspiciously across her cheeks. He looked back down and Hailey was staring into his face, her expression unguarded and filled with trust. The moment passed quickly when she noticed Poppi standing just behind him. Her voice sounded significantly stronger, "You! You psycho bitch! You pushed me off the train!"

"Well, you weren't going to jump and it was the only way off." Poppi said, the soft hearted expression gone. That piece of Poppi locked itself securely behind a shallow façade.

"I was going to jump! You almost killed me!" Hailey struggled to get up, but Derian pulled her into his lap before she could spring at the ancient *viator*. Poppi more than likely deserved whatever Hailey had in mind, but he was still nervous about her head injury.

"Girl, you aren't dead and it would have been worse if you stayed on that train." The fact that she knew more than she was telling crashed to the forefront again.

"What exactly do you know about what would have happened, Poppi?"Derian asked.

"Oh, its Poppi now, is it? Finally decide to call me by my real name now that you want something?" she replied with agitation.

Why had the catty woman attached herself to his *novus*? The stiff set to Hailey's shoulders leaning against his chest suggested her thoughts ran much the same way. Then she let out a long breath with a shudder and the tension seemed to melt away from them both.

"I appreciate you helping me," Hailey softened her voice. Poppi shifted uncomfortably at the thank you. "Just don't push me off any more moving vehicles okay?"

Poppi nodded, then walked away, mumbling something about finding a little girls room. Hailey asked, "She's putting on an act, isn't she?"

"Yes. But I don't know why," he said. The sun reached its highest point and the breeze that had tickled the leaves earlier grew still. Derian felt the need to get out of the unfamiliar desert. A jump with a head injury could be dangerous. But they had to get out, and preferably to a hospital where a doctor could take a look at her head. Unfortunately, they would have to come up with an explanation for the damn implant in her neck.

"You keep coming to my rescue. I like it, but I wish you didn't have to," she said. Derian wrapped his arms around her and pulled her tight against his chest. As she relaxed he rested his chin on her head. With Poppi gone his entire body and mind focused just on her. Desire flowed through him despite the heat and untenable situation. Leg muscles twitched as she absently ran her fingers over his heavy canvas pants. With her backside pressed up against his lap the position was liable to get uncomfortable fast.

"We need to get going. I'm not sure how far we are from a town and I don't think we should risk a jump through time until we know you don't have a concussion."

Hailey nodded. "Yeh, well, I wouldn't be able to either way." Her hand rose to touch the back of her neck. "This thing won't let me."

So that was what Poppi meant when she called it a leash. He pulled back her hair and took a closer look. It was smooth and silver, almost like a computer component. It was pressed so deep he couldn't find how it was attached.

"You need rare earth magnets. That's the only thing that will get that off." Poppi stood a few feet away, her return eerily silent. Hailey tensed, suspicion and anxiety poured into the atmosphere.

"She was captured by Nikanuur as well," Derian told Hailey before the two women could start bickering again. He turned a considering eye to Poppi. "How exactly did you get away Poppi?"

"I had help."

"Who?" Derian asked.

"Moina."

Hailey let out a frustrated grunt, then pulled herself to her feet. "I am really getting tired of not know what is going on. Why do you keep showing up? And how do you know my mother?"

Poppi held her hands up in submission. "Chill baby doll. I'm on your side."

"Yeh, well, I find that hard to believe. I think the only side you are ever on is your own." Hailey stalked up to Poppi and glared down at the woman. Both women squared their shoulders in confrontation and Derian wasn't sure if he should try to diffuse the situation or let the pieces fall after the match.

"You got bigger problems than me. I'm here to help, and you and your beefcake Saxon over there are just going to have to deal with it."

"Beefcake what?" As Hailey fisted her fingers Poppi began to fade from view. "Where are you going now?"

143

"I'm going to get you a magnet."

Hailey threw her hands in the air. "I don't want your help!" she yelled. Poppi just stuck her tongue out and then was gone. "Argh! That woman is so irritating!"

Hailey turned toward him and he was struck once again by the ugly bruise that covered her left cheek. He reached a hand up, but stopped before he touched it. Confusion crossed her features, and she raised her hand to her face. She let out a hiss as her fingers pressed into the tender skin. "How bad does it look?"

"It's not pretty."

"You know, before this all started happening, I had never even been in a fight." She gave a tremulous smile. "Kind of wishing I had taken some martial art classes or something. If we live through this I should have plenty of time though right?"

The very real danger this astounding woman faced was stark and frightening. Could he always be there to protect her? The evidence suggested otherwise. It hit deep. "Have you ever shot a gun before?"

"No."

Derian pulled his Glock from the holster at his waist. With a hand on her elbow he walked them out from beneath the cottonwoods and onto the desert pavement. He showed her the way it loaded, how the safety worked and explained how to fire. She wrapped her fingers around the cold metal and stood nervous and unsure. He spoke quietly, "You have to relax, don't stiffen up, you'll break something that way."

Running a hand down her arm he soothed her tension. Her breathing was shallow so he stood behind her and rested his hands on her waist. Leaning in to her ear he calmly gave her instruction. He could feel her body respond to his touch; his own breath became shallow for reasons other than nerves. An ache built in his belly. He wanted to pull her close and strip her down so his hands could continue to explore, to know her body, to help him find a release for the building desire. "Always aim for center mass then squeeze the trigger."

The recoil pushed her into his chest and she started to laugh. "That is totally crazy!"

She pulled out of his arms and turned, her face still wrinkled in levity. The gun was held out for him to take, but all thought and action fled when she looked into his eyes. She was so very beautiful. Dust had settled a soft coat against her skin that amplified her carefree and adaptable nature. The woman didn't just roll with the punches; she danced with them and threw some of her own.

"You know, I would be totally cool with you kissing me right now."

"Hailey," he breathed.

"What? Back at your place you seemed more than interested."

Interested? He was far more than interested. But, there was a very good chance he couldn't stop with a kiss. "I was. But you weren't" There were other things they should be focusing on. Important things. But heaven help him, he couldn't remember what they were.

"I am now." She stepped closer. The laughter was gone and in its place a naked appeal. The temptation swept through him, drawing him closer. He lifted a hand and cupped her jaw-line; her soft skin was like silk against his rough calluses. Strength and softness soared through her character in a dance for supremacy. To capture it for a moment promised blinding ecstasy.

"This isn't because I keep coming to your rescue, I don't want—"

Hailey reached up and put her free hand against the back of his neck and pulled him toward her. "Shut up and just kiss me, will you?"

There was no arguing with that. Her lips tasted of salt and sunlight and she held nothing back. She pressed into him, showing him the passion she had to share. The tip of her tongue ran along his bottom lip in a tentative tease then met his where they were lost in a dance of heat and intensity. She groaned and he pulled her tight against his body.

There was ecstasy to be found in the arms of this woman. Halfway wouldn't cut it, Hailey was an all or nothing kind of woman. What surprised him was his willingness to give her everything at that moment. He gripped the back of her neck and pulled her deeper into the kiss. How could a woman he knew for so short a time tempt him so completely?

The heavy thud of rotors echoed above them. Startled, she pulled back from the kiss. Reluctant to let the moment pass too quickly he held her as he gazed up. Shading his eyes against the bright rays of the late afternoon sun, he spied a Black Hawk helicopter beating the air into submission as it coasted across the sky. Considering the landscape and the military presence they had to be near the small city of Yuma, Arizona. The question was, did the helicopter come from Yuma or was it on its way back to the army instillation at Yuma Proving Grounds? He needed to get oriented.

If he could get them to Yuma, Hailey's injuries could be looked at and he could call into the *Domus*. The fact that

Lucius had yet to turn up was a concern. His friend knew the danger that Derian could have faced when he jumped to find Hailey. Nothing but the direst of circumstances would have kept him from following.

He pulled back the protective covering on the small communication band at his wrist. The bands were simple, limited to three contact lights connected to the main computer at the *Domus*. A red light meant the connection was active but no communication necessary; green was a command to return. Yellow meant the connection was lost. Looking back at Derian were three deceptive red lights. He didn't believe for a minute that all was well.

Only a few people had access to send communications to agents in the field, Lucius as the Magister, Roderic as the head of the research division, and the seven members of the Council. Would they call him in if there was trouble? There was no doubt that someone connected to Moina had infiltrated the *Domus*. Did Nikanuur have a contact as well? Were they the same? The depth of the conspiracy was an unknown and frustrating as hell.

Scanning the distance he spotted a road just beyond the tracks—convenient, but empty. Hopefully the road served more than the occasional rancher or the wait would last a while. He grabbed her by the elbow and said, "It's time to go."

13

It was hot. Not the kind of hot you remark on in small talk. No, this was the fry your brain kind of hot. Twenty minutes passed and they still stood on the side of the road waiting for someone to be kind enough to pick them up. There had apparently been a time when stopping for stranded people on the side of the road was considered a patriotic duty. Now, with all the trouble with illegal immigrants, drug smugglers, and psycho killers people were just wary of bedraggled travelers standing stupidly with their thumbs out.

Finally a highway patrol sedan pulled off and Hailey sighed in relief. Derian, on the other hand, did not look happy. She asked, "What's wrong?"

"Not quite sure how to explain why we are out here." He looked pointedly at her and continued, "Or why you look like you met the business end of a lead pipe."

Hailey reached for her cheek. That could be a problem. "Well, considering your acting skills back with the Nazi's, I trust you to figure it out."

He responded with a wry smile. "Thanks."

The officer stepped out of the blue and white Crown Victoria and approached. Hailey plastered on her biggest and most relieved smile.

"Officer," Derian said, holding his hands out in front, fingers splayed. Hailey looked down at the black glint of his gun sticking out of his shoulder holster. They presented a very interesting picture. She looked up at the officer who had stopped a good ten feet from them. Perhaps interesting wasn't quite the word for it. How could they possibly explain being out on the side of the road looking like they'd been in a five car pileup with no car and no pileup? Screw it. She was in this deep. She might as well add lying to the law as a new skill. "Oh...My...God! We are *so* glad to see you! You would not believe the day we have been having!"

Derian stiffened but she was all in so he was going to have to come along for the ride. Hailey started toward the officer.

"Ma'am please stay where you are." She froze. So he wasn't inclined to believe it was all a just a crazy accident. Why couldn't they have the gullible cop so often found in comedy sitcoms? Life would be so much easier that way.

"I know we look bad, but believe me, it isn't what it seems," she said.

Derian hissed at her. He had been brilliant when dealing with the SS officers. But at the moment he wasn't exactly forthcoming with alternatives. Hailey hissed back at him, "What exactly do you suggest we do?"

"Let the officer take the lead," he answered. Hailey rolled her eyes. So, the officer could what? Throw Derian in jail for beating her up? The story about a crazy time travelling scientist slapping her around and then a daredevil jump from a racing train lacked some serious believability. Jail would be their first stop on the way to the nut house.

"I'm not loving that option," she said.

The officer approached again. He stopped close enough so they didn't have to shout at each other to be heard. "What happened here?"

Derian laced his fingers through Hailey's. "We were hiking and had an accident."

"Hiking?" Skepticism dripped from the officer's eyebrows. Hailey didn't blame him, only criminals and nutcases hung out in heat like this. Since they weren't criminals that only left one option.

"Yes sir," Derian said.

"Where's your vehicle?" the officer asked.

Movement flashed at the corner of Hailey's eye. Across the two-lane highway the three goons from the train materialized. Each held the same nefarious pole weapons.

Hailey elbowed Derian in the ribs. "Dude."

The only indication that Derian noticed the new development was a stiff spine and a small tick in his jaw line. He continued speaking to the officer, "We pulled off onto a dirt road a couple miles back."

"Um, Derian," Hailey said under her breath. The three men made their way across the road like crabs over hot sand.

"Officer, we have not been entirely honest." Derian nodded toward the three goons. "We have been running from these three men. They are armed and dangerous. I recommend getting to cover."

Derian hauled Hailey behind him and pulled out his Glock. The highway shoulder went along a steep embankment where her feet perched precariously on the edge. The landscape didn't provide much for cover. Hopefully, the officer would decide to be on their side; otherwise, they were severely under-armed.

"Hi baby doll." At the sound of Poppi's voice at her side Hailey's feet slipped and she tumbled down the embankment. When she skidded to a halt she heard shouts and bodies meeting in violent confrontation.

"Damn it Poppi!" Derian's curses carried down to where she'd landed. "Get down and take care of Hailey!"

The dark haired nuisance popped her head over the side then flew down the embankment. Poppi's descent was significantly more graceful, just another thing to hold against the woman. Her giant grin spread like a Cheshire cat as she offered a slender hand to help Hailey up. "Looks like I got back just in time."

"Depends on who you ask," Hailey said.

Poppi just laughed and pulled a round black slab of metal from her pocket. "Time to get that leash off you."

Hailey looked askance as Poppi reached toward her. Gunshots popped from above. Terror slammed through her heart. Shrugging away from Poppi's grip Hailey ran back up the embankment, determined to be at Derian's side. Just as she reached the top, he swung over and crashed into her. They rolled down the rocky slope, landing in heap at the bottom. Hailey sucked in a painful breath. "Dude, we really have to stop doing that."

Derian pressed a quick kiss to her lips, his eyes sparkling with excitement. "Time to go, *léof.*"

They ran across the desert. Poppi followed close behind. Through the huffs of exertion, Hailey asked what had happened with Nikanuur's goons.

"The officer's backup showed. They have the three pinned down," Derian answered, his voice didn't even register the fact that he was running at full speed. Hailey glared at him, after twenty minutes her legs burned and threatened to mutiny.

When she stumbled over a small rise in the desert pavement Derian slowed the pace. Hailey was grateful, but at the same time grew increasingly more nervous the farther they ran from the road. Another fifteen minutes passed and she had to call it quits. If they didn't find shade and water she would fry to a crisp.

Derian led them toward a small cactus covered hill. In the distance the plants looked like soft fuzz but as they drew closer the devious spines sparkled in the sun. Little buds covered the ground making for a treacherous trail. They stepped diligently around each yellow spiked landmine until they reached an overhang with the sweet promise of shade.

"Stay here. I am going to find water," Derian said.

Hailey nodded then leaned her head against the hard rock wall. Her throat was so dry she doubted her voice could produce much more than a croak. Poppi sat beside her and closed her eyes. Something had finally proved effective in shutting the woman up. Hailey was grateful for small blessings.

Nearly an hour passed before the sound of boots across gravel heralded his return. A small piece of her mind warned that she should be more wary of who approached. Exhaustion argued that if it were anyone beside Derian she would just pass out and make it easier on everyone involved. Luck was with her. The handsome *viator* turned the corner into their small haven, a grocery bag in each hand.

"What, did you find a grocery store out here or something?" Hailey straightened up and reached for the bags.

"No. I had to jump time. I brought ice cream," he said a slight smile on his face as he watched her rustle through the bag. She pulled out a box of chocolate covered ice cream bars. There was a good reason she loved this man. Hailey coughed just as the first bite slid down her throat. When had she started thinking she loved him? It must be the hot sun and crazy circumstances.

Poppi reached over and plucked the box from her hand. "Too slow baby doll." Wrappers were ripped open and a gallon of water filled their bellies before anyone spoke.

"This whole jumping through time can be pretty convenient. Who would have thought I could get ice cream in the middle of the desert?" Hailey said.

Poppi sniggered, "Girl, you don't know the half of it."

Derian growled, "She doesn't need to learn from you."

"Oh please. Stop being such a fuddy duddy. There is nothing wrong with my methods." Poppi pulled out the black metal magnet. "How about we get that thing off your neck now, baby doll?"

An excellent thought. Hailey pulled her hair away from her neck and leaned forward. "There's one thing I don't get Poppi, Derian had to do the blood thing with me in order to follow me in time. But you seem to be able to find me without it."

Silence filled the overhang. Hailey looked up to see Derian staring hard at Poppi. The other woman's face was deceptively blank. They were at another impasse. A piece of her wanted to trust Poppi. Everything the nutty woman had done seemed to be in Hailey's best interest. But the lack of forthcoming honesty troubled her, and from every indication, Derian had his own reasons to distrust Poppi as well. The frustrated feeling that she had jumped into the middle of a story with half the information overwhelmed her. "Dude. I've got enough shit to deal with. How about you just tell us the truth?"

Poppi sighed and said, "You won't believe it, even if I tell you baby doll." She nodded toward Derian. "And he definitely won't."

Derian stood with his arms crossed. Poppi probably had it right. Though, if Poppi spent years hounding her, she would probably be just as hostile. "Try me."

"I'm your great-grandmother."

"You're shitting me."

Poppi laughed and pulled out another ice cream bar. It practically oozed from the package, but Poppi found a way to eat it nonetheless. "No. Girl. I'm serious. You and I are related. And that is why I can find you in time. Your mother can too. And your father." She licked the melted cream from her fingers.

"Dude."

Derian started to pace, his head barely missed scraping the ceiling of the overhang. There had been so many revelations in the last several days Hailey could hardly say she was surprised by this recent turn in events. In the span of a week she had gone from no family to too many. "Any other family members I should expect to come popping into my life?"

Poppi's eyes turned dangerously dark. They showed a depth that in the past Hailey would have sworn wasn't there. Why the woman hid behind a ditzy exterior was a mystery, but she was learning never to underestimate the woman's capabilities or motives. "All that is left is your mother and I."

"And Nikanuur," Hailey added.

"Yes, and that rat bastard."

"Weird that I have light features like my mother and not dark like you and Nikanuur. Aren't dark features dominant or something?"

Poppi just shrugged and lifted the bottle of water to her lips. Derian stood over her and asked, "What do you know about his plans?"

Poppi looked up, unimpressed by his attempt at intimidation. "Nikanuur? He's a simple man. He wants to increase his abilities. He has watched as the ancients develop strength and new talents. He wants those for himself." She laughed and shook her head. "Without waiting. Hasn't the *Domus* noticed the number of ancients that have disappeared lately?"

Derian pursed his lips. Hailey didn't know much about the *Domus* or what it did, but it seemed this was something they should have known.

"Why haven't you come forward? Why didn't you tell the Magister?" Derian asked.

Poppi snorted, "You're a good man, but there is so much dirty going on in the *Domus*, you can't know who to trust." She looked pointedly at Derian. "Even the Magister can't be trusted."

His nose flared in response. Hailey was fairly certain Derian had a close relationship with the Magister. Even the few moments she spent in their presence suggested Derian would trust the man with his life. She jumped in, "Alrighty then. So, it sounds like we are all on the same side then. We all want to stop Nikanuur from whatever it is he is doing. What's the next step?"

Both *viators* stared at Hailey. She gave them a blinding smile. "Does he have a secret lair or something?"

Poppi nodded. "He does. It's in Babylon."

"Serious? Hasn't that place disappeared?"

"His lab is in the past, baby doll."

Hailey's lips formed in an 'oh'. It would take time for her to fully appreciate her new reality. Time wasn't a constant, not any more. She would need to learn quick if she wanted to survive whatever lay ahead. Once again, she wished for that manual. Her life felt like the blinking time on a new VCR and she had no idea how to fix it.

"Well, then we should go burn it down," Hailey said.

"It's not that easy. We don't know when or where it is exactly. Babylon existed for thousands of years and who knows where he decided to set up shop." Poppi smiled indulgently at her. It ruffled her feathers a little, but then again, they were both getting used to being family. Hailey would give her a little leeway — for now.

"Yeh, but he's my dad. So I can follow him, just like you can follow me."

Derian stared incredulously at her. The idea had merit and she knew it. The logistics were a bit blurry, but it seemed to be the only option they had. That or running around trying to hide from the maniac. If she had the choice, she would rather confront the bastard.

"I don't like it," Derian finally broke his silence as he scowled at her.

"Why?"

"It's too dangerous." Stubbornness filled his stance but her heart did a little skip. His concern for her made her feel all gooey inside. It wouldn't do him a lick of good, but it was sweet. The sooner they got her family issues straightened out the sooner she could show him how much she liked his protectiveness.

"Whatever," she said and pointed at her swollen face. "It's not any more dangerous than what we already have to deal with. He won't expect it."

"No." He crossed his arms across his chest.

"Come on." Hailey stood up.

"No."

It wasn't so cute now. "Well, then. Poppi and I can do it without you. Can't we Poppi?" Her great-grandmother smiled with mischief and nodded.

"Hailey," he growled out a warning.

"I don't know if you have noticed, with all your jumping through time and all. But men can't tell women what to do anymore," Hailey argued. Derian grabbed her elbow and pulled her out of the overhang.

"Hey!" Hailey tugged her arm, trying to extricate herself from his grip. She did not like being manhandled.

He stopped when they were far enough from the overhang that Poppi couldn't hear them. He hissed, "You are in over your head."

"So what? I've been in over my head since this thing started. I am the only one that can get us to Nikanuur and you know it!"

Derian threw his hands in the air and turned his back on her. "You're what he wants. Do you just want to serve yourself on a silver platter?"

Hailey reached out her hand and touched his shoulder. The tension radiated through him and Hailey knew he was worried for her safety. But she couldn't think of anything else, and she was tired of hiding. "Derian. We have to try. Please."

He turned and wrapped his arms around her, laying his chin on the crown of her head. The thump of his heart rattled her core and she knew that she truly had fallen in love with him. If she were in his shoes would she let him take such a risk? "We should at least consider it. Maybe talk to the Magister?"

He pushed away, but kept his hands on her shoulders, his face full of concern and frustration. "I don't know what is going on at the *Domus*. Lucius was supposed to be here with us. He didn't follow."

"I don't understand."

"Something stopped him from following me, and very little could have made him do that. The *Domus* may not be safe. Until we know for sure, you are going nowhere near it," Derian said and rubbed a worried hand into his shoulder.

"What do you suggest we do then? Sit around in the desert?" Hailey asked.

Derian frowned down at her. There were few options that appealed to either of them. The sun sank toward the horizon. Hitching a ride was an opportunity lost, but it was an aspect that reminded her of how fragile their safety was.

"You know, they can show up anytime. If Nikanuur can track me, then what is stopping them from showing up now? Is there any place we can go to be safe?"

"Safe-zones are rare. The *castellum* is one, but with the *Domus* potentially compromised we have to stay away.

There is another that I know of, but, I haven't been there for decades and haven't heard if it is still secure," Derian said.

"Well, do we really have any other options? You don't want to storm the lab right now, and we can't stay here."

Derian shook his head. "We need to get you to a hospital first."

"I feel fine."

"Humor me."

Hailey rolled her eyes. He was being domineering. It helped a little that it was due to concern for her, but not much. There was a lot the man had to learn about the modern woman. Letting her make her own decisions was going to be lesson number one. But she would wage that battle later.

"If we are going to have the doctor look at my head, I want this thing off my neck," Hailey said and started back toward the overhand. When they returned dusk had settled and the light grew dim.

Poppi sat against the wall, her head hung in exhaustion. Hailey wondered how long her great-grandmother had been battling against Nikanuur. Hailey reached down and shook the woman's shoulder, "Poppi. Do you have that magnet? I'm ready to get this thing off."

If her exhaustion hadn't been obvious before it would have then, as Poppi pushed heavily off the ground and silently brought the magnet out. When this was done, Hailey would make sure Poppi found a safe place to get some sleep. It wasn't that she liked the woman, but she might come in handy, and they needed her alert.

Poppi yawned and she felt a twinge of guilt. Alright, so the woman was growing on her. Hailey pulled the hair away from her neck. "So, does this hurt?"

Poppi shook away another yawn. "You may want to be sitting for this."

The ancient *viator* placed her hands on Hailey's shoulder, pushed her to the ground then placed the magnet against her neck. Excruciating pain shot through Hailey's head and blackness filled her vision. Then her stomach rolled. Not again! She wasn't ready for a jump.

When Hailey came too she was face down on a hot concrete sidewalk. She rolled to her side and watched as an old beat up Cadillac drove past. Shouts rang through the air and the sound of broken glass propelled her to her feet. The street was packed with running bodies, undulating like amorphous human gelatin. Were those parachute pants?

14

"That was not supposed to happen," Poppi stared dumbfounded at the spot where Hailey had just occupied and unexpectedly left.

"Where is she? What did you do?" If Derian had it in him to strangle Poppi, it would have happened right then. As soon as the magnet hit Hailey's neck she'd blanched, screamed and faded away. There was nothing he could do but watch as she jumped time.

"I didn't do anything." Poppi shook and tears filled her eyes. He really could not deal with a weepy female. Things had gone farther beyond his control than he had any intention of letting it.

"You need to hold it together." Her sniffles amplified. Derian shouted, "Poppi, knock it off!" She started to hiccup. He reached out and grabbed her upper arm. "For crying out loud woman! That is not going to help us."

"I...know...I just...I just can't stop screwing up," she cried.

Derian raised his eyes to heaven. He prayed for the patience not to strangle her just so he could move on. "Poppi, did you know that was going to happen?" She shook her head. "Did that happen when you used it to remove yours?" She shook her head emphatically. "Then it isn't your fault. Now, stop crying. We have to catch up to her and there isn't much time. With our luck she's in the middle of the American Civil War."

Derian checked his Glock for ammunition. As long as he didn't find himself in the middle of a firefight, they should be fine. But if they followed Hailey's pattern to this point, they could be facing a barrage of scud missiles. He looked to the woman beside him and asked, "Are you coming?"

She sniffled, but she straightened her back and a determination was present he had never seen on the woman before. He said, "I can almost believe you really are related to her."

Poppi bared her teeth and flipped him the bird. He grinned then focused on following Hailey. They materialized on a dark street, the air heavy with smoke and screams. "Where the..."

Poppi stepped in front of him and peered down the street. "Riots," she whispered. Grabbing his hand she tugged him toward the nearest brick wall. They followed the wall until they reached the corner then crouched as they watched a crowd tear apart a local grocery store. "Twenty bucks says were in L.A."

"What year?" Derian asked.

"Based on the clothes? I'd say the Rodney King trial just ended. 1990's."

That was impossible. Hailey had been in Los Angeles in the 1990's. A *viator* couldn't physically travel to the same location at the same time. The barrier usually went at least a thousand miles around the previous self. "It's not possible. She can't be here."

"Do you really think so?" she said as she pointed a long well manicured finger toward a huddled figure crouched beside a trashcan.

Derian stood and ran, conscious to not draw attention. It didn't take much. Most of the souls with the courage to be on the streets were focused on taking advantage of the chaos by looting and destroying everything in their path. When he reached Hailey's side he pulled her into his arms. "Why can't you land in a boring location?"

Hailey's eyes were glazed and her face twisted in a grimace. "I tried. But it really hurts. The headache won't stop pounding."

Poppi reached them just as Derian brushed her hair from her eyes. "We need to get her to a hospital. She has a concussion and it's getting worse."

Poppi nodded then ran off. He hoped the little woman knew where to go because at the moment, all he could do was shield Hailey's body from the mob intent on violence.

"Derian?" Hailey whispered hoarsely into his ear. "Aren't you tired of coming to my rescue?"

Wrapping his arms around her, Derian cradled her against his shoulder. "I don't think that is possible."

She sighed. "Well, I am. I would like to come to your rescue at least once."

Sirens wailed in the distance and the crowd dispersed in a crazed mass exodus, leaving a trail of destruction in their wake. It always amazed him what excuses people would use to do things they otherwise found morally reprehensible. This was not the first he'd seen and would probably not be the last. Hailey whimpered and his thoughts were drawn back to the fragile woman in his arms. She proved her resiliency time and again, but no one was indestructible.

The sirens grew louder and then Poppi was once again at their side. "Here they are baby doll. We'll get you to someone to make the pain go away."

The paramedics had Hailey loaded and ready to transport when one approached him and Poppi. "Are you family?"

"I'm her grand... I'm her mother." Poppi grabbed onto the paramedic's sleeve. "Can I ride with her?"

The man nodded and she ran off toward the ambulance, calling back as she went, "Meet us there Derian!"

An officer approached before he could follow and proceeded to grill him for details of the accident. Luckily, Derian didn't have to worry about the authorities suspecting him of domestic abuse. The rioters provided a convenient excuse for her injuries. A believable story came relatively easy. After the cop left he walked toward a back alley where he could make a jump.

The hospital bustled with activity. Victims from the riots filled the beds and the staff had their hands full with simply trying to control the insanity. Anger and fear raged strong in the city that night. It would only last a few days, but an entire nation would be glued to the television set waiting to see what would happen next. Derian wondered at Hailey's ability to find the most inconvenient locations to land.

At least this time they were able to get her medical attention. Though the full impact of the concussion on her ability to jump time hadn't yet been determined, it seemed to be as effective a leash as Nikanuur's implant. There were a number of safe-zones scattered across the globe and through time that could provide sanctuary to them until she could heal, but Derian did not have the knowledge or resources to find the nearest one.

People packed into the waiting room like New York businessmen on the subway. He found a corner and wedged himself between a large man with a holey shirt covered in sweat stains and a woman holding a squirming toddler on her hip.

Poppi found him after only a few minutes. "They have her hooked up to an IV. The doctor is pretty sure it is a concussion. They want to keep her overnight but then will want her on bed rest."

"I need to get in there with her."

Poppi shook her head. "They are only letting in family."

"Tell them I'm her husband."

"Derian. She's fine. I will stay by her side."

"And if someone tries to take her? What then? Are you going to fight them for her Poppi?" He kept his voice low, not wanting others to witness his irritation.

She poked her finger into his sternum. "I have as much, if not more riding on this Derian. She is my great-granddaughter. No one will take her from me. I have a lot more in my bag of tricks than you think."

"Poppi." The need to be by Hailey's side was nearly undeniable. The ancient *viator* was trying to put a wedge between the two of them and he wasn't about to let it happen.

"Go find a safe-zone for us," she said, flashing one of her toothy grins. "Trust me. I didn't just hang around you 'cause I thought you were cute. Someday maybe you'll figure it out, but right now, you have to trust me. Hailey will be fine until morning. Then we are going to have to book it." The years suddenly filled her face. The youth and exuberance that made up her façade grew fractured by wisdom and weariness.

"It would be easier if you just told me what was going on," Derian said.

"Maybe." She turned and slid through the crowd back down the hall that led to the wards. Frustration bit into his iron control. Fists tightened as he held back the temptation to throw it all to hell and go to Hailey. Nothing suggested that Poppi intended her great-granddaughter harm. But taking care of her was his responsibility. At least, it should be. Shouldn't it? He was her *praeceptor*, her mentor. And he hadn't been particularly good at it as it was.

A figure caught his attention at the door. Roderic glared into the room, impatience radiating from his stance. Perhaps some of the answers Derian needed would be forthcoming.

When they met outside the emergency room doors Roderic said, "Ye are a hard man to track down."

"We've had some trouble."

"I can see that. Is your lady *novus* well?"

"Considering what she has been through. What is going on?" Derian asked.

The Scot nodded toward an out of the way corner of the sidewalk. "I'm no closer to finding the rogue. Nikanuur is our only connection and the trail is cold on his activities. According to everything I have found he is working on his own. But it just isn't possible."

"Where is Lucius?"

Roderic frowned and glared into the building beside them. "Gone. After ye jumped no one has seen him."

"Do you think someone has taken him?" Derian asked.

"Tis possible. But it would have to be someone from high in the *Domus*." He looked at Derian. They both knew the only *viators* with clearance levels that could have made it

166

into the room with Lucius were the two of them. Or someone in the Council.

"Any word from the Council?"

Roderic snorted, "They wish to see the two of us. There are murmurs of them appointing an interim Magister until we know what happened to Lucius."

"I don't trust it. Someone from the Council has to be involved."

"Aye, but we canna deny them." Roderic looked up in the air and sighed. "They want ye to bring your *novus*."

Anger flashed. Taking Hailey to the Council was akin to walking into a snake pit. And if one of them were indeed connected to Nikanuur and a master rogue she would be far too vulnerable. "Not going to happen."

Roderic laughed, "You have it bad for the chit."

Perhaps his old friend was correct. The physical attraction and severe protective instinct served a heady mix. The last kiss had been enough to derail his focus. A focus that had to be absolute. With his own *praeceptor* missing it was clear he would need to go on the hunt. He could not do that and protect Hailey. That was a problem. "I need a safe-zone, one that is off the books."

"Aye, I thought ye might. There is one near here. But ye aren't going to like it."

"Why won't I like it?"

"Tis run by Thomas Roy."

Derian groaned. He and the old hippy had a history. "I don't have another option do I?"

Roderic laughed and walked away. The benefit to the situation was Thomas had no love for the Council. He had no love for *venators* and more specifically, Derian. But there was little doubt that Thomas would be game for helping

Hailey. The man was a sucker for the oppressed. They were in for an interesting visit.

***

The traffic sucked. Hailey made a promise to herself that once she got through this mess she would never sit in traffic ever again. After only a week or so of jumping time she had already been spoiled by the convenience. It was also quite apparent that the three other occupants in the vehicle were unaccustomed to traveling in this manner.

When she'd been rolled out of the hospital that morning they found Roderic grinning beside a cherry red 1967 Mustang. Poppi squealed and proceeded to argue with the Scot over who would get the chance to drive. Derian had grabbed the keys and ordered everyone into the car. Hailey could have told them that a stick shift wasn't the best choice for sitting through the Los Angeles rush hour, but why pour salt on an already gaping wound?

Roderic and Poppi crow barred themselves into the back seat. They had just made it through L.A. proper when the bickering started up. "Christ Reena, what is that god awful stench?"

"It's Eternity. Popular stuff. And the name is Poppi."

"Since when?" Roderic grumbled.

"Since forever."

Hailey laughed. "You've met my great-grandmother before I take it."

Roderic's jaw dropped. "Not possible."

"It is too toots. Can't you tell she's inherited my brilliant wit?" Poppi said.

He grimaced in response. Hailey took pity on him and asked Derian if they could stop for something to eat. They pulled off the freeway that currently doubled as a parking lot and stopped at a Denny's.

"I hope they have Grand Slams! Did they have Grand Slams in the 90's or was that something that went away after the 70s? I do love Grand Slams!"Poppi practically bounced in the back seat.

"I'm pretty sure they're still around. I think you're safe." Hailey waited as Roderic peeled himself out of the two-door Mustang. "Where did you get the car?"

"It was waiting for me when I got here," Roderic replied

Hailey shook her head. She couldn't even imagine the logistics involved in keeping vehicles available in every time and place. "Do you keep it in a garage or something?"

Derian took her hand and led her through the restaurant doors. "He found it on a corner. It's not his."

"What??" Her shriek carried through the small diner packed with people taking a few moments for sustenance before the daily grind. Lowering her voice she whispered irritably at Derian, "He stole it? We've been driving in a stolen vehicle? Are you nuts?"

A heavy hand landed on her shoulder. "Borrowed. Only borrowed." Roderic's smile was full of mischief and vinegar. The man obviously had questionable morals. Was it possible that Roderic was the traitor at the *Domus*? She looked at Derian. He seemed to count Roderic as a friend. Could he be blind to the possibility?

Derian pulled her close. "It is a survival tactic, *léof*. We often don't have a choice but to steal what we need." He kissed her temple and continued, "But, we try not to if we can help it."

A dumpy waitress with frizzy hair and too much eye makeup led them to a booth. Hailey slid to the side and grabbed gratefully for a menu.

"Oh they do have Grand Slams!" Poppi bounced in her seat.

"Well, how about money? Do you have to steal that too?" Hailey asked.

Roderic rolled his eyes. Derian replied before the Scot could say just what it was he was thinking. "No. I have accounts that cover most eras. It helps to know where to invest and how."

"That seems unfair," Hailey said.

Derian shrugged. "It is an advantage, but without it, we wouldn't have many ways to make money. We have to survive."

She thought about that a while. There were so many things that still didn't make sense about the whole lifestyle. It would have been nice to have learned how to do this without running for her life. But there was no point crying over what wasn't. With any luck the pancakes to come would provide the much needed answers to their dilemmas.

Number one for her was figuring out how not to jump randomly from one time to the next. Derian told her it took practice. She really didn't have the time for all that. Who knew when she would need her talent to be in working order? They couldn't run from her father forever, and she was more and more certain that she was the key to stopping him, despite Derian's desire to keep her locked up out of harm's way.

They kept mentioning a safe-zone, which she assumed was a place she could be safe from her father. But, there wasn't much that inspired her confidence in the whole situation. She would play along long enough to make sure her head wouldn't explode. A day of rest should be more than enough, right? But they sure as hell weren't going to keep her out of the loop. She may be new to the whole *viator* time travel thing, but it was her family. It was her problem and she was the answer. At least, well, part of the answer.

Traffic was significantly lighter after breakfast. Despite sleeping heavily through the night before Hailey nodded off to the soft roar of the engine. When she woke Manzanita lined the road and they were in the middle of a switchback turn. In the back seat Poppi dozed against Roderic's rock hard chest, his own head thrown back in a heavy snore.

"Are we in the mountains?" Hailey asked.

"Big Bear," Derian responded from the driver seat, his eyes intent on the road.

"Really? I don't live too far from here." Hailey peered out the side window at the pines rising in the distance. "Aunt Sue loved coming here. She said it made her feel free. If she didn't feel free every once in a while, she couldn't stand living so close to so many people."

"Did you live here in 1992?"

"California? Yeh. We never went far from home. Big Bear was the closest to traveling we ever did. Though, we went to Sequoia once. That was awesome. I think I would like to go there again. Maybe after this is all over." She turned toward Derian. The point between his brows wrinkled and the edge of his mouth tipped just enough to imply a frown. "Why?"

"When a *viator* has been somewhere before. They can't go back to that point," he said, slanting a glance at her before returning it to the hairpin turn.

"That whole can't inhabit the same space as you self thing? A paradox."

His brows furrowed. "I suppose, though Roderic might know more about why than I do. All I know is that you physically can't do it. There is a thousand mile circumference around your previous self that you just can't cross."

"Even if you jump outside the thousand miles and walk in?" Hailey asked.

"No. You would trigger an immediate jump."

"Hunh. But, I am only a hundred miles away, if that."

"Exactly," Derian said.

Great, another one of those weird quirks courtesy of her father. Hailey rested against the headrest. Just what had the man done to her? Was it some kind of weird DNA manipulation? Gene splicing? Did it really matter? She was a freak. If being a time traveler wasn't enough, she was a freakish time traveler.

The rest of the drive Hailey sat quietly. Derian provided some comfort sitting beside her, but as the landscape flew by, memories of Aunt Sue enveloped her mind. Heart sick and vulnerable she tried to think what Sue would say. *Keep your chin up and walk like the world is yours for the taking.* Sue was a true believer in faking it until it came true. Why did she feel like that wasn't going to help?

Derian turned onto a dirt lane that meandered down into a picturesque hidden valley. In the distance Hailey spotted a compound of buildings dotting the valley floor. Bodies rustled in the back seat. Roderic's rumbling voice filled the tight space, "Ah, so we're here. Just in time, my bones canna take being crushed by this woman anymore."

Hailey couldn't help but laugh. Poppi was half Roderic's size. If anyone was doing the crushing, it wasn't her. The drive ended at a chain-link fence that ran around the compound. A small turbine creaked and birds chirped with the breeze. No one came to greet them, so Derian unhitched the gate and the four of them walked up the gravel driveway toward the largest of the white clapboard buildings.

"There isn't much security. I would have expected more from Roy," Roderic's hushed comment did little for her confidence. Who was this dude they kept bringing up? Neither of the men seemed particularly fond of him, which made her wonder why they would trust him in a situation like this.

The stairs leading to the front door were old and questionable. Screens hung half off the windows and the door looked unsecured. The whole place reminded her of every zombie movie ever made. She was about to recommend that they go back to the car and come up with a new plan when Derian knocked on the door and shouted, "Come on you old hippie! Stop playing games!"

The door flew open and three shot gun bells pointed out at them. Around each side of the house four more people appeared with guns. Hailey grabbed at Poppi's hands and the two women slammed themselves between Derian and Roderic. When they got through this, she and Derian were going to talk about how much information he gave her beforehand.

A handsome face with a full beard and hair that shone like sunlight off a glassy lake poked out one of the windows. "Give me one good reason I shouldn't blow a hole in your face *venator*?"

15

Derian was gone. With not much more than a kiss on the cheek and a promise to return, he and Roderic walked out of the compound to 'speak to the Council'. Whatever that meant. So now she was stuck with Poppi and a bunch of, if not hostile than trigger-happy, wary strangers. Several minutes of fast talk by Roderic and Derian had at least gotten the guns lowered. Most of it seemed to be about past history between the three men, but the last piece, the piece that seemed to be the deciding factor was an elaborated version of her story. And the people of the compound ate it up like birthday lasagna. By the end she felt like tying herself to a tree and waiting for a dragon to fry her just to get it over with. Playing the maiden in distress just wasn't her thing. But there she was, nonetheless.

Hailey sat in a bustling kitchen. Fresh flowers stood in vases on every available flat space, heartwarming smells emanated from the small oven, and laughter rang through the house. Poppi and two other women sat across from her discussing the traumatic loss of style by the American people since the mid 1970s. It was all too surreal.

A plate of cinnamon rolls slid in front of her. A chair was drug out and a portly woman sat beside Hailey, two forks in hand. "Here you are honey, nothing better for a head injury than Momma's famous cinnamon rolls."

"Are they really famous?"

"In this house they are." The woman's laughter was infectious. Her smiling eyes and hearty attitude made Hailey feel immediately more comfortable. If only there weren't shotguns lying all over the place. "Dig in, honey."

Hailey took a fork and tasted. The sweet icing melted across her tongue like the smoothest cream. The bread was soft and doughy with a slight crunch of cinnamon and sugar. "They should be famous."

The woman's laughter rang out, making the old 1950s furniture ring from the vibration. Hailey looked at the large woman, a thought percolating in her mind. "May I ask you a question?"

"Of course dear, whatever you need to know, Momma Joe will tell you." Hailey smiled. Momma Joe. If that didn't sound like the name of a backwoods breakfast joint, nothing did.

"What is this place? Are you all *viators* too?"

Momma Joe's mirth grew serious, "Well now, yes we are. Though most of us don't practice like we used to."

"You don't practice?"

"We're what you might call, retired." She slanted a glance at the door. "Some by choice."

Hailey nodded in understanding. From what she'd gathered, Derian's job as a *venator* required him to force a number of the inhabitants into early retirements. Momma Joe continued, "Now, Thomas Roy, he's more or less running this place. He likes to call it Shangri-La. Though, to some of us older folk it is a rather silly name, but you would have to go to the real Shangri-La to understand why."

"Shangri-La is real? I thought it was a myth."

"Oh, no, honey. It is very real. Just not a place to take the faint of heart."

Hailey tried to keep her bottom lip from falling into the gooey pastry. What next, Atlantis and aliens? There was so much she had to learn, it was exciting just thinking about the adventures she could have. Strange enough, in her mind's eye Derian stood by her through it all. It was something to think about. Definitely, but she would have to wait until after she stopped being annoyed with him for leaving her here while he ran off to be heroic.

"So why are you retired Momma Joe?" Hailey realized the question might be a little personal so she amended it, "I mean, if you don't mind talking about it."

Her heady laughter burst out again. The only head that turned at the outburst was Poppi's. Apparently everyone was used to Momma Joe's raucous exclamations. "No, I don't! You are a polite peach though. I just got tired, that's all. When you've been travelling as long as I have, you get tired."

She didn't mark Momma Joe as someone that had been around that long. Though her only experience with the really old *viators* included Nikanuur, Moina, and Poppi. Her parents hadn't stuck around much for her to get a feel for their age and Poppi—well, she just didn't fit any preconceived ideas, period. "You can't be that old, Southern accents have only been around for a little while."

Momma Joe grinned. "Well now, love," her accent shifted dramatically to British, "with age you can try on accents much like you try on clothes." She nodded toward

Poppi. "Your great-grandmother has done the same. She chose a style she liked. As did I."

She laughed again, then placed a hand on Hailey's arm. "Now, let's find you a room for you to rest. You are going to need all the energy you can find for what is coming."

"Wait, what is coming? Do you know what's coming?"Hailey asked the retreating woman.

Momma Joe's called back as she walked from the kitchen, "Why the war darling. There is going to be a war."

***

Silence filled the *Domus*. Unease rippled through the air like waves against concrete barriers. Derian and Roderic moved through the halls, each person they encountered hurried past with their head down and nerves shot to hell. A Magister had never gone missing before; add to that the breakdown in security and very real threat from unknown renegades and there was enough to terrorize a people that had grown accustom to the expected and mundane. Derian wished he had answers for them. He doubted the Council would provide anything but more questions.

A cadaverous woman with skin practically translucent approached them, a clipboard assertively braced on her arm. "Gentlemen. You are the last to arrive. The Council waits in the Hearing Chamber."

"Everyone?" Roderic asked, his lips tipped at a sardonic angle.

"Everyone."

They stopped at an elaborately carved double door. She stepped to the side to let the men pass before her.

"The old man is never on time for anything. Either we are very late, or something is very wrong," Roderic said. His grandfather, Rusa, had been on the Council since anyone could remember. Few of the oldest *viators* were still active within the *Domus*. As an ancient Minoan, Rusa, sat as the senior Council member and undisputed head. He was not, however, known for his adherence to the more modern concept of punctuality.

"I'll let you do the talking," Derian said.

"Aye, you can try."

Seven heads turned as Derian and Roderic waited to be acknowledged. A heavy wood table filled the room, leaving just enough room to walk around. Dim light muted against the hardwood paneled walls and cast the faces into shadow. A heavy set man with broad shoulders and a cantankerous demeanor stood and pointed to the two empty seats left at the table. "Sit."

Derian felt his friend bite back an acerbic comment. He had the opportunity to observe Roderic and his grandfather interact only once. It ended with Gaelic insults and a broken door. Roderic would hold his tongue among the members of the Council as long as he felt it necessary. Derian hoped it would last until they walked out the door.

"Where is the *novus?*" Rusa asked. Roderic looked pointedly at Derian. So much for Roderic taking the lead.

"Safe," Derian answered. The silence was deafening. No one denied an order of the Council.

"Derian, you are understandably protective," a regal woman with thick black hair that grayed at the temple responded. He had never met her before; but she, like all on the Council had an air of authority and false omniscience. "But, we mean her no harm. You should have brought her."

"She's injured. She couldn't make the trip." A hushed mumble filled the room in response to Derian's declaration.

If an enemy indeed sat on the Council, then he had given them an invaluable piece of information. But, if the doctor's prognosis had been correct, by the time they could utilize it, she would be back to full strength and ready with a few surprises of her own.

He watched each Council member closely, each facial tick, flick of the eyes, hooded expression noted. How deep did the conspiracy go? Lucius and Roderic assumed they faced a devious and highly placed enemy, but one with limited numbers. Derian didn't like assumptions. Just because a rogue had never created a large network in the past, did not mean it couldn't happen.

A second woman, this one small in stature and riddled in pock marks spoke, "What do you know of this renegade? Why has he targeted the young *novus*?"

Derian tempered his reactions. Apparently, Lucius held back quite a bit of detail from the Council. How he wished his mentor were there. What knowledge had the old centurion disappeared with?

"She's his daughter," Roderic replied with bored brevity.

Another mumble rolled through the room. One voice spoke louder than the rest, "What does this woman have to do with the dead *venators*? There is no proof that the two are connected! There's no proof there is a conspiracy!"

"Lucius has disappeared. That is no accident!" another lashed out. Derian and Roderic sat back and folded their arms. The reason for Roderic's grandfather being there before them became apparent. The Council had clearly been arguing before their arrival.

"I say we are dealing with one renegade. That is what we should focus on! Not some *novus* that hasn't gotten her legs yet!"

"Enough!" Rusa roared. The room erupted into more shouting. Control wasn't just slipping away; it had bought a ticket and left for better weather. Twenty minutes of arguing later the room degenerated into several strings of ancient expletives and the room emptied.

A little stunned at the veracity of the disagreement, Derian could not determine a source of the discontent. It seemed everyone in the Council had something to be upset about and it wasn't coming from a single episode.

Roderic grinned at his grandfather. "Not exactly holding the reins tight on the group are ye?"

The ordinarily bombastic man's shoulders were slumped, but his glare was as heated as ever. "This would not have happened had you and your Magister come to us sooner."

"Oh, I dinna believe that the problems ye have here have anything to do with what we have had a hand in, grandfather," he let the last word slide out silkily. "So who is the snake in your tree? Who is making this happen?"

Rusa folded his arms against his chest. "I do not know what you are talking about."

"I dinna believe that for a minute, but ye can keep your cards hidden. It will come out eventually. Now, are we going to talk about the conspiracy or is this where we stop?"

The old man closed his eyes and leaned back in the chair, the weight of four thousand years settled heavy on his shoulders. "What have you learned of the dead *venators*?"

Roderic set aside the combativeness and everything became about the issue at hand. "The poison was a fast acting neurotoxin. Fast enough to impact our systems."

There were few drugs that impacted a *viator's* system. With the cellular aging processes slowed as theirs were, most pathogens didn't have the ability to secure a foothold on the system to cause any damage. Those that did were extremely fast acting, the kind that could kill a human on contact. But none had ever been found to be fatal to a *viator*. The speed at which the new poison would have to work was terrifying. Such a drug could not only be a danger to *viator*, but could wipe out entire populations of humans.

The knowledge of this showed like clear crystal in Roderic and his grandfather. An enemy with this weapon could wield a power unlike anything humanity or *viator* had ever seen. Nothing would be the same.

"We must stop this from being used any further," Rusa said.

But how? There was only one piece they knew for sure, and that was Nikanuur played a part in the dangerous game. Derian agreed with Lucius. Nikanuur may have the brilliance required to develop the poison, but he was not the man pulling the strings. Was his obsession with his daughter a personal project or one also tied to the conspiracy?

He watched the old man and Roderic as they sparred. There was very little information available and even fewer options. Derian knew he had an option. But it meant putting Hailey in harm's way. Rusa slammed his fist on the table and shouted, "There is no proof of a conspiracy!"

"Yer a fool old man!" Roderic answered. The conversation quickly became unconstructive.

Derian jumped in to stop it from drowning in anger, "Someone is pulling Nikanuur's strings. He has muscle and assistance. Nikanuur has never commanded the respect of others. Either he is paying the men helping him, or someone has told them to. I doubt very much Nikanuur could pay enough for someone to work with him, he doesn't have the charisma or vision." Lucius had told him as much before he disappeared. Now, with what he had seen of the men coming after Hailey, there had to be someone coordinating the force.

Roderic replied, "Nikanuur is the man behind the poison. I am positive of it. His interest in his daughter does not bode well. If her capabilities are possible to recreate, it could be even more dangerous for us. Especially if it is taken advantage of by a strong leader."

Rusa sat down heavily in his seat. His hand ran over hair kept high and tight. "What exactly are the girl's capabilities?"

"Enhancements. She can do things faster than any *novus* ever has," Roderic answered.

"That is not much to be excited over," Rusa said.

"Considering his extreme interest, it is likely more will manifest," Roderic answered.

"She needs to be brought in. You need to discover what she can do," Rusa said.

Roderic turned to Derian. This was where the two friends disagreed. Roderic wanted to pick her apart. Derian wouldn't let her near Roderic's lab, not with the security breach. And something about her being poked about and tested rubbed him wrong.

"Not going to happen," Derian said.

Rusa puffed out his chest, but Derian refused to be intimidated. "Derian! You will…" The man was building up a roar.

"Nikanuur has a lab in Babylon," Derian offered and it halted Rusa's rant and brought Roderic's full attention to Derian. He hadn't had a chance to tell the Scot the newest revelation.

"And how do you know this?" Roderic asked.

"Poppi."

Roderic cursed and said, "What has that woman gotten her hands in this time?"

Lost, Rusa swung his head between the two men, a frustrated flush building up across his face. "Damn it, who is this Poppi? What does she have to with this?"

"It's Reena, grandfather. She is Poppi."

"That woman! Why is that woman..."

"She's Hailey's great-grandmother," Derian said.

Rusa's mouth flapped shut. It reminded Derian that he had left Hailey and Poppi with Tom Roy's band of renegades. It wasn't the choice he had hoped for. A decent man with decent intentions, Tom lacked the sense to do anything with it. Having fried his brain on drugs prior to his first jump in the mid 1960s, what intellect he might have had, was woefully missing. But she was surrounded by *viators*, many with years of experience. And she was protected by the no jump zone. It would take a huge effort for the conspiracy to go after Hailey at the compound.

"Do we know the location of the lab?" Rusa was back to business. His bombastic nature often hid his high intelligence. The same intelligence had been passed on to his grandson.

"We don't, but Poppi might," Derian said. And Hailey certainly could take them there. The connection between a child and their parents was similar to the blood tracking used between a *novus* and their *praeceptor*. Following the familial connection was, however, a skill that usually manifested as a *novus* developed. It was a skill Hailey more than likely already had, if all the patterns continued.

"We can't depend on that woman." Rusa stood and started to pace the room. "Where is Lucius?? There isn't a man out there that can mobilize the *venators* like he can."

"The last place he was seen was in the *castellum*." Roderic frowned at his grandfather. "Either Lucius left on his own or there is someone with access to the *castellum* and devious intent."

"There is nothing that proves that this comes from the *Domus*. Rogues have always come from outside the organization. There are safeguards, checks...," Rusa said.

"Stubborn old man! Everything points to a contact inside! Are you so attached to your pride that you won't see what is right in front of your nose?" Roderic countered. Neither man would budge until indisputable proof came forward. The Council vetted everyone that had access to the *castellum*. If someone got in, it was their under-sight. Roderic set up the system that established the *castellum* as a safe-zone. He was understandably unwilling to believe that anyone could land in the *castellum*.

Except, someone could. Derian groaned. The answer to finding what happened to Lucius became crystal clear. But it was even more dangerous than Hailey's idea to track down Nikanuur's lab. He couldn't follow her into the *castellum*. Could he ask her to put herself to such risk? He offered slowly, "I may have a solution."

16

Momma Joe hadn't been particularly forthcoming about the impending War. In Hailey's opinion she was far too jovial about the whole thing, suggesting she had a few bolts missing nuts. At the moment those nuts seemed to be running around like hopped up squirrels. They were definitely too enthusiastic about what was going on.

"We count five on the north side of the ridge, Tom!"

"Three more on the South!"

Thomas Roy strode into the room, his shirt off and hair cascading over his shoulders as if he had just walked off a bad romance novel cover. He swung his head then cocked the shotgun with one hand, as only someone with far too much time in front of a television would do. He had a flair for the dramatic, but failed to elicit any sense of confidence in her. Now would be a great time for Derian to walk back into her life.

A constant stream of children and *viator* flooded into the house. There had to be close to a hundred people packed behind its walls. Nightmares of badly executed FBI and ATF raids sent shudders down her spine. Poppi snuck up to her side and placed a hand on her shoulder.

"So, they call this a safe-zone why?" Hailey asked.

"It's impossible to land here. Or jump," Poppi answered, her eyes sparkling with anticipation. If there was any doubt that her great-grandmother wasn't nuts, it was laid to rest. She belonged with these people.

Hailey peered out the window at the huddle of thugs standing just beyond the fence to the compound. "Too bad they know how to walk."

Momma Joe hustled past, her laughter shared with several other women hauling ammo boxes. There was enough firepower in that house to supply the D.C. Fourth of July Celebration for decades. Hailey breathed, "They are way too prepared for this."

Poppi reached out and snatched a shotgun from a young man running past. "There's no such thing as too prepared, baby doll." She grabbed Hailey's hand and dragged her up to the second floor. "Next lesson: Always take higher ground."

They entered a large bedroom that faced the front of the house. Several others were already hunkered down. Poppi started yelling instructions as everyone jumped up to move furniture in front of the windows, leaving just enough space to shoot through. Why did she feel like she was in a bad 1980s shoot-em-up movie?

The shouts amplified on the first floor and Hailey hurried to the window. More of Nikanuur's goons had arrived. It looked like they were facing close to thirty and each had a mix of alien looking weapons to choose from. Apparently messing with his offspring's DNA wasn't all he had been up to in that lab of his. She scanned the area for his dark curly hair and autocratic stance. With both her great-grandmother and father with dark features it was a mystery that she turned out looking like she did. Maybe it is all a mistake. Maybe.

Nikanuur did not show. He was probably too busy torturing small children and animals, she thought, then sighed. Her head had stopped pounding, and she had gotten in several hours of rest before the recent crisis. It boded well for her jumping capabilities. It was very likely she was an exception to the no jumping rule, considering her impossible jump into the *castellum*.

Hailey looked over at her great-grandmother giving instructions to several younger *viators*. Unfortunately, these people wouldn't be able to jump if they had to.

And yet, they were practically giddy with anticipation. Hailey shook her head. She hoped she never got so bored that she looked forward to a shootout. A hush fell over the house as everyone chose a spot to settle and it became a game of wait and see. Hailey kept an eye out on the growing number of goons. They were like roaches, crawling out of cracks in the earth to congregate until the light was turned on and they all went skittering back into their respective holes. With all this trouble, she should feel honored.

Hailey watched through a small crack between a propped up sofa and the edge of the window. The goons weren't really doing anything. It was worse than watching a football game during a referee review. A voice whispered from across the room, "What are they doing?"

Poppi popped up behind Hailey's shoulder to check out the situation. "I think one just picked his nose."

"What are they waiting for?" another piped up. It was a good question. They kept milling around like husbands at a garden tea party. If they were preparing to take the compound by storm they were doing it all wrong.

"Hold on. Who's that?" Everyone ran to the left side of the room to get a look. Hailey wedged herself between two scruffy teens. Something had definitely gotten the attention of the goons because they were all making pains to look busy. A dark figure walked up to the main gate entrance. Five mean and far too competent looking men flanked his sides. As he drew closer they were finally able to get a good look.

"Whoa! Now that is one sexy man!"Poppi practically drooled out the window. Several of the women huddling around them murmured in agreement.

"He's one of the bad guys!" Hailey replied.

"That doesn't stop him from being hot! The things I could do with a man like that!" Poppy leaned in further for a better look.

Hailey threw up her arms and headed back to her own spot. His approach brought him in view to all the windows. He did cut a dashing figure. But, the way the men around him deferred, Hailey suspected he wouldn't try to win any hero medals.

He looked up, straight into her window. Hailey shot away, her heart thumping against her ribs. Her palm pressed against her chest. It had to be a coincidence. He couldn't possible know she was at that window. She slunk back to peer through the glass. The mystery man spoke with a small group of goons, each nodding to whatever orders they were being given then they turned and hurried away.

Hailey called out, "Everyone get ready. It's going to start soon."

Poppi came up behind her. "How do you know that?"

An explosion rocked the side of the house. "Just a hunch."

The house erupted in chaos. The air rang with explosions, gun shots, and shouts in various unfamiliar languages. Hailey hoped they had at least gotten the children somewhere relatively safe. She looked out the hall just as a six year old ran past with an armful of ammunition. For the love of God!

She streaked toward the door. There was no way in hell she would let children fight this battle. Running down the stairs, she had to jump over several women hurriedly unpacking boxes of grenades and other devices of devastation. Someone was going to blow off an arm and it wasn't going to be on Nikanuur's side.

She found Tom Roy in the living room, pacing the length as several awe struck members of his retinue waited for orders. From what she could tell, he had little knowledge of strategy or battle in general. "Tom."

He lifted a finger for her to wait. Did the man just put her off? That was it. She'd had enough. "Tom Roy. If you don't come talk to me I am going to open the front door and let them in!" She wouldn't. That was just ridiculous, but she got the needed reaction. He ran to her side. A second major explosion hit the house and splintered siding flew through the hall behind them. Screams replaced the shouts as the compound felt the first major injuries.

Tom looked a little green and when she shouted at him he was slow to respond. Grabbing his arm she hauled him away from the wreckage and into an interior room where the youngest of the children were being watched by nervous mothers. At least someone had the sense to be worried.

"This isn't going to work!" she yelled into his ear to be heard over the noise of attack. He nodded. Hailey rolled her eyes. He hadn't tried to hold on to his leadership position for long. "They want me, so that's what we are going to give them."

He nodded again. If there had been a bus in the vicinity, she would probably have been thrown under it. "Just get your people ready to go out the back. Those assholes aren't going to be happy after what I do, so you will want to get everyone out of the valley fast. I might be able to give you five minutes. Tops."

Without a comment he turned and started shouting. She could feel the love. It was staggering. Sarcasm wasn't going to solve the issue, so she turned and ran back up the stairs to find Poppi. The nutty woman was hunkered down where she'd left her, gleefully pumping lead out the window. Hailey called out, "Poppi!"

She didn't respond. Hailey stomped over and grabbed the woman by the shoulder, pulling her away from the fight. "You have to go, and get everyone out of here. I am going out the front."

"What? You can't do that!" Poppi shouted as another barrage of gunfire hit the front side of the house.

"Don't worry. I'm just giving you time to get away."

Poppi grabbed onto her shirt. "I'm going with you."

"No, You can't. Trust me on this. Catch up with me when you get to a place where you can jump."

Poppi looked at her incredulously. "If they take you, Derian will kill me."

Hailey smiled. "Don't worry about it." And then she ran out of the room before Poppi had a chance to respond. The front room was empty. Hailey found Tom with about twenty of his followers squished in the back kitchen. Others were filing in from other parts of the house. She got their attention with a sharp two-finger whistle. "Ok, listen up, I am going out the front door. Give it about thirty seconds, then start running like hell."

As she turned to leave, a strong hand grabbed her elbow. Momma Joe grinned down at her. "Keep your head on your shoulders, honey. We'll catch up later."

"Oh, I don't know if you all need to…"

Momma Joe just patted her on the shoulder and disappeared into the crowd of waiting bodies. All Hailey could do was shake her head. Heaven help them if this group showed up again.

Hailey strode to the front door. Her hands shook and her knees threatened to make a mess of things and give out. But she didn't give it a thought, her body and fear would have to wait. There just wasn't time.

When she peered out the door, a shadow flashed across her vision from the porch. The goons were trying a frontal assault. Lucky them, she was going to come out and save them a lot of trouble. At least for a few minutes. Hailey took a deep breath. It was a big risk, one she wasn't one hundred percent sure of, but it was better than trusting the idiots in the compound not to shoot her accidentally. Derian would be pissed he missed this fiasco. Not as pissed as he would be when he found out what she was about to do. But, he was the one that left her here, so really, she didn't have any sympathy.

Another flash of movement, and Hailey peered out the window. An earlier shot had left a gaping hole in the bottom half of the glass. A man dressed in black slinked up to the door, a small canister held in his hand. Smoke bomb. As he lifted his hand to throw the canister into the hole in the window, she opened the door.

"Hi."

Surprise threw off his aim and the canister bounced off the wall and back into the yard. Hailey walked past the man and down the stairs. A gruff voice called a cease fire as the men stood with mouths agape. The mysterious dark man that they had spied from the second floor moved toward her. His features were excruciatingly clear. His nose was long but not so much to detract from the strength of his jaw-line. His eyes were a deep coffee crowned by heavy brows. Beauty held him captive like carved marble. Everything about him asked you to trust him. Except for the cruel twist to his lips.

Hailey stopped just before the gate. Heart thumping, she flexed her hands, but kept her head up and shoulders strong. She promised Tom Roy five minutes, but damned if she knew how to stall for that long. The back of her neck tingled. If she weren't positive they needed her alive... well she was mostly positive. "So what's the plan? You just blow the house up then look for my body in the wreckage?"

His smile spread slowly across his face and she shivered. "It seems you were far too intelligent to let that happen." Oh, his voice was silky smooth. The man wore bad boy like a pair of custom made Italian shoes.

"Right." Hailey scanned the mass of nasty looking men, each stood uncomfortable and still, shifting the weapons from hand to hand as though it were the first time they'd touched the things.

"This seems a little like overkill. Did you really need this many guys to pick me up?" Hailey asked. His reactions were slight, minor, the kind that made you know he was ready for anything. The kind that didn't tell you anything except that he was waiting.

He also wasn't much for conversation. She wracked her brain for something else to say. "Um, so, would it be better if I went back inside and let you guys throw some more firepower around? Make you feel like the walk was worth it?"

He reached down and lifted the latch to the gate. Hailey took a step back. She was babbling a little. Just trying to waste time. She needed a few more minutes, but by the looks of things, he was done talking. She pushed up on her toes and shifted from one foot to the other. "We could always talk about you surrendering, you know, because I really don't think I will be going with you after all."

He stepped into the yard.

"Dude, seriously. You don't know what you are getting yourself into. I am a loaded weapon. Didn't my dad tell you anything?" Now she was making things up. Just another minute. He stalked after her, and she spun around. Tom Roy had better have run like hell, because she was out of time.

Dirt kicked up in front of her as a barrage of bullets riddled the space in front of her. It worked, she stopped. When she turned the dark haired demon man was standing five feet away. He barked at the men behind him— apparently the gun shots were not his idea. Nonetheless, they were at an impasse again. Now was the time to find out if her gamble had paid out.

Hailey focused on the back of her neck where the tingling had begun. As the sensation filtered down through her shoulders, she smiled. The man swung around just in time for her to lift her hand and give him the finger. "See ya."

***

Derian found Hailey stretched out on the soft sand of a beach, her hand thrown over her eyes to block the sun. He said, "You are supposed to be in California."

"I had a sudden desire for a vacation." The ocean spread out before them, calm and clear. A slight breeze rustled through the trees that lined the small cove. The lapping of waves and harsh calls of tropical birds were the only sounds that surrounded them.

He sat beside her on the sand. Taking her hand from her eyes she smiled up at him. It took his breath away. When he had arrived back at the compound and found everyone gone and evidence of battle, terror had filled his gut. Guilt and fury followed him on the harrowing drive out of the valley.

The relief staggered him when he found her thread within his veins. With gun drawn he landed on the beach and promptly fell to his knees when he saw her lying quietly and alone.

"Did you have a nice meeting?" she asked, peering into the distant horizon.

"Christ, *léof*."

She sat up and smiled again. Her hand grabbed his and she leaned against his side. "No worries. I'm fine. Though I think you guys should rethink calling that place a safe-zone. It really wasn't all that safe."

Pulling her into his lap he wrapped her in a crushing embrace. She breathed, "Dude, if I have to be in mortal danger to get a hug, what do I need to do to get a kiss?"

Derian groaned, and nuzzled her neck. The temptation to taste her there on the beach was overwhelming. But the threat they faced continued to beat against his desires. Hailey moaned and leaned her head to the side, exposing her throat. All good intentions nearly slid away with the tide. They had a little time. He needed a little time. He groaned again, and pulled away. "They can track you here."

Her sigh was torture on his discipline. "I guess we don't want to be caught with our pants down." She crawled out of his lap and sand flew as she brushed her pants. "So, what's the plan? You got another idea for a hiding place?"

The pressure from running sat behind her eyes and in her shoulders. Her fighting instinct was strong; it certainly explained why she had jumped so late in life. Most *viators* jumped the first time in their early to mid-twenties. Fear was a very important catalyst for the first jump. Fear was definitely not one of her dominant emotional states.

"We need your help. It is a risk, but it is the only way to find out what happened to Lucius," he said.

"Oh yeh?" The smile she flashed him sent dread through his knees. She was far too eager to say yes. "And I'm the only one that can do whatever it is you need, right?"

"Yes."

"Sweet." She clasped her hands together in delight. When this was over he was going to lock her away. She was almost as crazy as her great-grandmother. He smiled at the thought. A hunch told him Hailey wouldn't like hearing she was like Poppi in any way.

"So, what do I get to do?" she asked.

"We need you to land in the *castellum* and find out what happened to Lucius."

"Can you at least be in the *Domus*?"

"I was there at the time."

"Oh." Hailey looked down at her toes. She dug a small crater in the sand. The urge to pace was probably overwhelming her at the moment. He wanted her to say no, to tell him to find another way. But if he knew her as he thought he did...

"Can I take a gun?" she said. Derian raised his eyes to the sky. Loving this woman was going to kill him.

17

"Have ye never shot a gun afore?" Roderic raised a skeptical brow. Derian knew better.

"Of course I have." Hailey grinned up at the tall Scot. "Once."

"God save us," Roderic moaned.

Derian had to agree. When they arrived at the laboratory they walked in on a mussed up and pacing Roderic. The pressure must be reaching a pinnacle if Roderic's nerves were ruffled. When he had laid the plan before Rusa and Roderic the ancient Minoan had jumped on it as brilliant. He assumed there was little risk for something that was just a simple reconnaissance. Either that or he didn't care.

Roderic at least recognized the risk, but had agreed that there were few options. Everyone they could trust with the job had been in the *Domus* that day. Everyone except Hailey.

She tugged at her pants. "I must be losing weight, these don't fit like they used to. Who would have thought?" She perked an eyebrow when she turned to them. "Dude, you both need to chill. I am going to be fine. I'm just running in to see what happened. If it doesn't seem right, I'll just hop out right away."

Derian reached over and tucked her shirt into her waistband then pulled her pants up for her. With a laugh she kissed him on the cheek and said, "I better go, before you both figure out how to stop me."

Hailey stepped back and wiggled her finger in farewell. Derian didn't look away until the very last hint of her figure disappeared. Roderic already sat at his desk pulling up the tracking system. The communicator Roderic had given her transmitted a strong signal and both men breathed a sigh of relief. All they could do was watch and wait.

The system zoomed in and the blinking green dot that represented Hailey moved toward Lucius. According to the records, she had fifteen minutes before Lucius' own signal would blip out of existence. Within five she was beside the signal given off by the Magister. Derian breathed in a nervous sigh. Hope that the mission would prove successful flickered, until a second and third beacon appeared beside hers. "What the hell is that?"

Roderic's fingers flew across the keyboard, furiously trying to track down the unique identifiers of each signal. All four lights now blinked in unison in the very center of the *castellum*. "They came out of nowhere. If they came in through the main *Domus*, we would have seen them coming."

"They landed there?" Pages flashed and data scurried across the screen. The database didn't recognize the new signals.

"Someone must have disabled the safe-zone," Roderic said, evidence of worry strong in his hushed tone. Derian watched in horror as Lucius' signal disappeared. Another harrowing moment and Hailey's disappeared followed by another. The third waited, then moved through the *castellum* toward the *Domus*.

"Who could have disabled the safe-zone?"Derian asked.

Roderic turned to look at a large black box sitting ominously in the corner of the laboratory. His expression was dark and dangerous. "I was here." He looked toward an adjacent room. "It must have happened when I went in to the quarantine room to work with the poison."

"Who was here with you?" Derian asked.

Roderic stood and started toward the door, his shoulder stiff with barely restrained fury. "Millard."

The data analyst's office was empty. Nearly all the files were gone and the computer tower was condemningly missing. "Well, that explains why Moina had the com band. They've been able to track everyone in the database." Roderic looked at Derian. "It's how they tracked the *venator* and murdered them. If they get the system up and running elsewhere, no one will be safe from them."

Derian's fists clenched. Understandably, Roderic concerned himself over the implications the issue had on the *Domus*. But Derian couldn't care less about it. Hailey had disappeared and he'd been the one to send her right into Nikanuur's waiting arms. He stormed out of the office toward the *Domus*. He didn't have much time; he had to get out of the safe-zone and to Hailey. They would no doubt be waiting for him, but his wrath saw no other options.

"Derian, don't be an imbecile!"Roderic shouted down the hall.

He ignored his friend. When he burst out of the *castellum* doors a dozen heads flew up. He closed his eyes and desperately sought the thread to Hailey. But it was gone. Somehow they had cut his ties.

"Damn it!"

***

Hailey watched in horror as Lucius faded from view, a slow spread of red soaking the fabric across his chest. "You shot him!"

The dark stranger from the compound dug his fingers into her elbow as he hauled her to her feet. Her own gun lay across the room, mocking her inability to do anything effective to prevent the tragedy. Shock gave way to a frenzied fear. If they were willing to kill the head of the *Domus*, what were they willing to do to her?

She had to get out of there and fast. Just as she started relax so she could jump, his silky voice slammed her back to reality, "If you care anything for your great-grandmother, you will not be running."

"What?!"

"You will come with me, or your great-grandmother will die as easily as Lucius," the dark haired man said. A movement caught her eye as a small weasel of a man reached down to retrieve her gun.

"You're lying to me," she said. The only response was an evil smile."You bastard."

The little man approached with a syringe in one hand as her captor roughly exposed the skin of her arm. His fingers dug deep into the muscle above her elbow.

"What are you doing??"Hailey cried. She struggled, but before much could be done the needle slid into her vein. The pain of the prick was slight, but the liquid seared through her veins and her head pounded. "What the hell is that?"

She was let go and the little man scurried out of her reach. The other loomed over her and reached to tuck a tendril of hair behind her ear. Hailey flinched. The creepy vibe nauseated her. "We wouldn't want anyone interrupting us, now would we?"

"Derian."

"Ah. Is that who has you on a leash? I wondered. Not entirely a bad choice. But moot now." He stepped away and leaned leisurely against Lucius' heavy wood desk.

"Who are you?" she breathed through clenched teeth, her hands fisted in frustration.

"Carlo."

"Just Carlo?" He just smiled, again. "Do you work for my father, *Carlo*?" Her fear retreated as her ire rose. She took a deep breath, her nails biting into her palms. Reacting to irritation always seemed to get her in trouble. She should think of kittens. Or moonbeams. Anything that kept her from strangling the asshole in front of her.

"I do not work for your father," he said. Why was she blessed with men that gave short answers? With all the teeth pulling she had to do, she should have been a dentist.

"Does he work for you?"

"Not as such, no." He stood and looked toward the weasel. The man held the gun like a hot potato. Carlo grabbed it from him. "Thank you Millard. Go reset the safe-zone. I recommend that you take a vacation."

"But...but, I was supposed to —" Carlo bared his teeth and Millard's body shook and he looked away. Carlo turned back to Hailey.

"Now, *cara mia*, let's go visit your great-grandmother, shall we?" He tucked the gun into his slacks and smoothed the fabric with long, elegant fingers.

"I don't know how," she answered.

"You will figure it out. Her life depends on it."

She had a nearly irrepressible desire to stick out her tongue and make farting noises in his general direction. With a glance at the ceiling she hoped for inspiration. When nothing came to her she closed her eyes and gave it a shot. Things were definitely not going her way. Was it too much to ask for luck to be on her side for once?

He was right, of course. The jump was relatively easy. Hailey landed beside her great-grandmother. Unfortunately that meant she was on the wrong side of prison glass. Poppi was alive, but she'd looked better. Her shirt hung like shreds and she'd lost a heel to one of her pumps. Puffy eyes with dark shadows told of sleepless nights.

"What happened to you?" Hailey asked.

"I'm not going to lie, baby doll. It's been a rough day." Poppi glared at Carlo standing on the other side of the glass wall. He spoke adamantly with three men in plain black t-shirts and heavy cargo pants. It was the universal security uniform. The old *viator* pounded her firsts on the glass and shouted in a language completely foreign to Hailey.

A door in the room beyond the glass opened and a fourth man in black entered, his hand wrapped solidly around Moina's wrist. Poppi went nuts. Ranting and screaming, her eyes filled with tears as she did everything in her power to break her foot against the wall.

Hailey put a hand on her shoulder. "Come on Poppi don't break down on me now."

She turned wretched eyes toward her great-granddaughter. "I couldn't do a damn thing about it. If I knew, god, Hailey if I knew what she was doing."

Confusion blanketed her mind, but she didn't have time to think about it before a small window slid open on the door to their cell. Carlo sneered through the grate that stood between them. "Your mother wants to say something to you."

Moina stumbled up to the door, her eyes red-rimmed and puffy. "I'm so sorry, Hailey. I'm so very sorry."

"What? What are you sorry for you?" Hailey stuck her face close to the grate and her mother flinched like she'd been struck. "What did you do??"

"She's the one that told them you existed," Poppi voice grew quiet and cold.

"She what?" Hailey said, her voice raising an octave.

"I love him, I had to tell him. I didn't know what he wanted to do, not really. I'm so sorry." Moina wrapped her fingers around the grate. Hailey considered biting them off.

"You're crying? Why are *you* crying?" Hailey hit the door with her fist. Poppi laughed. "You're the reason my life has been a constant hell for two weeks!"

Moina stumbled away from the door, her body shook in wracking sobs. Hailey's shouts followed, "The best thing you ever did was leave me with Aunt Sue!" The traitorous woman turned and ran toward the door. "Go to hell!"

Moina's wail flowed back from the hall she'd disappeared down. The grate slammed shut and Hailey gave Carlo the finger. He just smiled.

"Argh! I cannot possibly be related to that woman!" Everything Moina told her in her living room had been a lie. The woman lied over pancakes for crying out loud! Who lied over pancakes? Poppi grinned at her. Hailey snarled, "What?"

"You are something else, baby doll."

"Why are you on my side Poppi? You don't work with the *Domus*. You don't seem loyal to anyone. Why are you here?"

The grin disappeared and Poppi said, "You're family."

Hailey pointed to the door. "So's that woman."

Poppi sighed heavily and turned toward the only seat in the room. She settled her frame on a wood stool of questionable stability. The room was stark, like one would expect for a prison cell. Three walls made of solid packed mud completed the room. Straw hung down where some of the mud had started to crumble. A tiny square window opened to the air high above.

"Family is a rare thing, baby doll. You and Moina are all I have left." The distance between her and her great-grandmother opened into a gulf as Poppi retreated into memory. "I loved your grandmother with all I had. I was a good mother then, responsible, smart." She looked to Hailey openly challenging the young woman to doubt her. Hailey slid to the floor, her back leaning against the glass wall.

"Death is just as rare as family for *viator*. But it took your grandmother. She had an accident with a water wheel in the Norse land. I wasn't there. I didn't learn about it for nearly two hundred years. All that was left was a shell of a man that was your grandfather, and a girl. Moina. She learned to jump long before I met her and became who she was long before I could have any say."

"That's not your fault."

Poppi snorted and shook her head. "No. It's not. But she was family."

"What happened?"

"Nothing. Not a damn thing. Until she showed up ten years ago telling me she wanted a relationship," Poppi said, her nose wrinkling as if the air was filled with a stench. "That's how I got here the first time."

It didn't surprise her. Moina had been Nikanuur's easy pawn from the beginning. She probably wasn't a terrible person—just weak. Terribly weak. And it destroyed the people around her. "But you said she was the one that helped you escape."

"A temporary episode of guilt. As you can see, it didn't last."

They sat in silence for a while. Each left to their thoughts. Hailey's kept drifting toward Derian. No matter how much she loved him, she couldn't see herself becoming what her mother had. But then, Derian wouldn't ever expect it. Could she learn to forgive a woman for loving a man like her father? Probably not.

"You know, I kind of like you this way," Hailey said.

"What way? Not ditzy?"

Hailey laughed. Yeh, not ditzy was exactly the thing. "Did you ever think of going back and trying to stop my grandmother from dying?"

Poppi's eyes grew sad. "No. Not your grandmother. By that time I knew it wouldn't work."

Wouldn't work? It seemed so simple. How could it not work? Poppi continued, "I tried it once you know. Tried to go back and change something terrible."

Hailey remained still and just listened. Poppi sounded fragile, her memories flowed into the room and they were miserable company. Was it any wonder the woman chose to live a simple life away from the stress and drama of the *viator* community? "Donas, your great-grandfather, he was my whole life, my reason for living. I could have spent ten thousand years happily in his arms. But instead I only got three hundred."

How strange it was to see three hundred as too short a time. But then, if she had been around for two thousand she would more than likely see it as such. Hailey asked the question that sat tentatively on her tongue, "What happened?"

A fond smile played on her lips. "He was a *venator*. Like your Derian. One of the first. He was incredible." She winked at Hailey. "And sexy. Super sexy." Poppi leaned back and balanced the chair on the two back legs. A distraction, perhaps, from the pain of the past. "He was caught up in a battle with a master rogue."

"A master rogue?"

"Yes, A renegade, a *viator* that either threatens mankind or our ability to survive. The *Domus* has only really dealt with the relatively harmless rogues. Those that just want to be left alone or to carve or a little world of their own. But sometimes someone comes along that wants more. They get ideas of world domination and stupid shit like that. This isn't the first time we've faced problems like this, baby doll."

"And Donas?"

"He was killed." She slammed the chair back onto its four legs. "I tried to go back and stop it. And I did."

She paused, a hitch in her breath. "He died three days later in the final firefight."

"But that doesn't mean it isn't possible." Hailey refused to believe that nothing could be done. What was the point of being able to time travel is you couldn't stop bad things from happening?

"We change things in history. Just because we are on a different timeline doesn't mean it wasn't meant to be. But those things that are meant to be? They will happen no matter what you do."

"Dude. That sucks."

Poppi nodded. "Totally."

So how do you know what was supposed to happen and what wasn't? It was all too complicated. The outer room door opened and Carlo entered with Nikanuur. Her father looked more than pleased to see her sitting behind the glass.

Hailey stood and moved beside Poppi. Both women were tired and wary, nothing good could happen when Nikanuur looked like a kid in a candy shop. The door scraped against the hard earth floor and both men joined the women in the cell.

"Reena, you look terrible," Nikanuur said.

"Poppi, you stupid little man, my name is Poppi," her great-grandmother growled. Hailey made a mental note never to change her name.

Nikanuur ignored Poppi and walked up to Hailey. His body odor assailed her senses. Apparently bathing was not on the list of things to do when one was bent on world domination. "It seems we will finally be able to get to know each other, daughter."

There were so many things she wanted to say to the man, but she settled on giving him an evil eye. How she wished her words could make his ears bleed. That was a sight she'd pay good money to see. Unfortunately, that superpower had yet to show up in her bag of tricks. She would have to stick with her usual. "You're an ass."

Carlo grabbed her arm and propelled her toward the door. Poppi jumped up and started to screech. Hailey nearly lost it when Nikanuur lashed out and snapped her great-grandmother's head to the side with a brutal slap.

"Don't hurt her!" Hailey shouted. Carlo didn't pause and Hailey couldn't dig in her heels enough to prevent Nikanuur from striking again. "Let me go you bastard!"

It didn't matter. He hauled her through the room and Hailey could only hope Nikanuur would get tired of slapping Poppi around before something permanent happened. Her head reeled. There wasn't anything she could do. There were no white knights coming to her rescue. Derian wouldn't be able to find her and they had put the damn implant back in her neck the moment she materialized beside her great-grandmother. But even if she could jump, she couldn't leave Poppi.

If she had options it would be nice if they'd advertise themselves in bright blinking fluorescence, because right now she was in real trouble.

18

Carlo hauled her through a narrow hall with walls made of packed earth and straw. Every hundred feet, a small light bulb spit out a weak sepia-toned light that did little to illuminate the rut-filled walkway. They came upon several rooms with glass walls facing the hall just like Poppi's cell.

Except, these inhabitants were in significantly worse shape. In one, a woman sat curled in a ball with her hands pressed into her temples, a high keening sound rattling the walls. Across the way another room contained a man. Hailey flinched when he launched himself at the wall, his head slamming against the glass and sending a spray of blood droplets against the smooth surface.

"Dude. What are you doing to these people?"

Carlo didn't spare the prisoners a glance. "Some do not handle the tests as well as others."

"You're sick."

He stopped abruptly and pushed her into the wall. His hips pressed into hers and he reached up to cup his hand against her jaw. He was full of challenge and frightening promise. Hailey shivered but masked it by tensing her body.

"Are you frightened, *cara mia*?" He trailed a finger to her chin then traced her lips. "I could help you forget your fear."

"You're not my type," she spat out. He leaned closer his eyes boring into hers. When they shifted their focus to her lips her stomach turned. "Seriously, dude. I'd rather take a hot poker."

"I will speak to Nikanuur and have him add that to your experience," he drawled.

"Nice. I don't know how I got so damn lucky."

He turned and started to pull her down the hall again. Bile threatened to scald her throat. Could she really handle what was coming? She fantasized about Derian crashing in, guns blazing, just like he had on the pirate ship. Unfortunately, she was just setting herself up for disappointment. No one was coming to save her this time.

They flew up a set of stairs crowned by a heavy wood door. When Carlo pulled it open the hinges groaned. As he pushed her across the threshold brilliant sunlight blinded her senses. Blinking was an effort in uselessness as she tried to accustom herself to the brightness. Carlo didn't give her a moment, his fingers digging like nails into her upper arm.

"Dude. You can let go," Hailey said.

He didn't. When she could finally see where they were going she dug in her heals in an attempt to bring them to a halt. Since Carlo had no intention of stopping she was sent sprawling to her knees. He looked down with irritation and yanked her back to her feet. With the momentum she wrested her arm from his grip and took a step back. "I'm not going anywhere. You can chill."

He reached for her arm and she slapped it away. "Where are we?" she demanded.

They stood on a long porch several floors above the ground. Beyond the decorative wood rail, a small mud city emerged from a harsh desert. Beyond snaked a river of deep blue providing a strong contrast to the stark landscape. The city itself bustled with activity. People filled the streets and squares as the soft hum of humanity filled the air.

"Babylon," he answered.

Poppi had been right and hope flared in Hailey's heart. Derian may not be able to follow her, but he did know that the lab was in Babylon. That meant there was a small chance in hell that he'd show up. "Sounds like a rockin' place."

"They have been a generous host," Carlo said.

"I bet—what do you do? Bring them apple pie from the future?" She snuck a glance around the side of the building, hoping for a clue on how to escape. Sheer walls and no cover didn't make such an attempt plausible. Not here at least.

His fingers wrapped around her wrist like buzzard talons on carrion and they were on their way again. "We are late," he grumbled.

"I'm sorry. Am I keeping you from something important?"

He stopped, the irritation flew off like heat waves off hot summer asphalt. "You will learn to curb your tongue," he growled, his voice low and filled with menace. "You are not nearly as indispensable as you think."

Hailey bit her tongue. Being a smart ass was her only defense. Take that away and she was pretty certain she'd be a shuddering mass of hysteria. But perhaps it was better to let it slide. Just this once. Carlo was moving up on the scary meter and she was not eager to see him peak.

***

They were back in the Council chamber, but this time the lights blared and there was a marked absence of Council members. Roderic stood at the head of the table piercing the seated *viators* with heated glares. "What do you mean more have died? Why wasn't this brought to my attention before?" Roderic barked.

A stony faced man responded, "Since when are you the Magister?"

Roderic's face flushed and Derian felt it would be advantageous to prevent the tide of finger pointing. "This is not productive. Lucius is missing. Roderic is second in command. Period."

The grumbling retreated into the background. The woman beside Derian spoke up. Her daffodil blond hair and soft pink lips did much to lull the casual observer into believing her a simple beauty. But the young soviet was anything but simple. When Lidiya spoke everyone made the effort to hear. A relatively new *viator* she rose quickly within the *Domus*; her aptitude for database and information management went far beyond the norm. "Three documented dead *venator* in last week. This is five we have lost for certain, but three more unaccounted for."

"Are there any patterns to their disappearance?" Roderic asked.

Lidiya tapped her pen against the table in a staccato minuet. "We are running all circumstances through algorithms right now. Nothing is standing out except each was on personal leave."

"We need to call all *venator* in from personal leave now." Several heads bobbed in agreement with Roderic's order, despite the obvious lack of trust in his leadership.

Roderic was excellent as the head of the lab, but had always been a polarizing force. Lucius was the man that kept all parties working together. It was a terrible time for the man to disappear.

"What else do we know? Has anyone tracked down Nikanuur's laboratory? There has to be some indication of activity somewhere," Roderic asked and when no one answered he looked at the research team. "Find it!"

Lidiya spoke again, "There is also increase in number of *viator* falling out of system."

Roderic crossed his arms. "Why hasn't this been noticed before?"

Lidiya had worked with Roderic long enough that his gruffness and unsympathetic expectations rolled over her unnoticed. Her work was always above par and she never apologized. "The disappearances are small, running just above average, but there is increase, and there is pattern."

Derian was pretty sure he knew what was happening to the missing *viator*. It was unlikely that Poppi was the only *viator* taken captive. The question was, were they still alive to be rescued? Lidiya continued, "They appear to be targeting *viator*s one thousand or older."

The room sank into a deep quiet as everyone let the implications of her comment settle in. Few in the room had actually made it to one thousand. Derian scanned the occupants. He was the oldest by several hundred years at the very least. Reaching the thousand year milestone always inspired awe. Many of the more challenging skills and abilities only started to manifest after that age. If Nikanuur was truly trying to find ways to enhance a *viator's* abilities it made sense for him to target the oldest and most skilled.

The skills were innocuous enough on their own. Efficient jumping, shorter periods between jumps, and an ability to bring larger materials through weren't frightening on their own. But could they increase the effectiveness of a mobilized army? And what if they discovered that Hailey could teleport materials independently through time and space?

"What are our options? Where are the outliers? I need actionable items, not more questions!" Roderic's impatience shouted from his stance. Faces scrunched throughout the room as everyone tried to think of ways to proceed. Derian was frustrated more than most. He had lost contact with both Lucius and Hailey. Somehow Nikanuur had developed a way to block the connection between a *praeceptor* and their *novus*.

"I am going after Millard," Derian said, his quiet comment in stark contrast to the brusqueness of Roderic. A few heads nodded, while most remained non-committed. It had been a shock for the members of the *Domus* that one of their own had assisted the enemy. It had been equally shocking that it be an unassuming man like Millard. Suspicion skyrocketed as everyone realized anyone could be a traitor.

Assignments were given. The majority of viators were sent to gather additional information but a small specialized unit of would mobilize to investigate the five *venator* deaths. The room emptied and Derian faced a frustrated Scot and stoic Lidiya.

"Millard has fallen off the grid. How do you expect to find the man?" Roderic asked.

Derian looked to Lidiya. "Can you get me a print out to his most frequent jump spots?"

She nodded and stood to leave. "I will have it for you in my office."

"Do you really believe the man will know how to find your *novus*?" Roderic asked.

"He is the only connection I have to Hailey right now." Derian had thought to track down Poppi, the woman had a talent for finding her great-granddaughter. He'd already checked to see if there were any tracking data on the woman, but had come up empty. When Poppi didn't want to be found you'd be more likely to run into a ghost before you found her.

"I appreciate the offer to find the man, but I canna help but question your priorities," Roderic said, propping his arms on the table as he leaned toward Derian.

"What is that supposed to mean?"

"It means, I think ye will put the girl before the *Domus*."

Derian didn't respond to the comment. Roderic was correct. He would put Hailey's well being before the *Domus*.

Roderic sighed and sat heavily in his grandfather's chair. Rusa had left the basic operation decisions to his grandson. Roderic was capable, but the responsibility visibly weighed down his shoulders.

"We have no other leads on Lucius, do we?" Derian asked.

"No. I wish we did. Ye are correct in going after Millard; he is our only link to your *novus* and the Magister. He will have to lead us to one of them." Roderic didn't ask the question that blared between them. Would Derian be able to choose between Lucius and Hailey if he had to? Derian hoped on everything that was holy that the question remained untested.

Derian stopped by his office on the way to see Lidiya. He hadn't been to his desk since he'd met Hailey. It was rare for him to ever be there, the field was his office, but that hadn't stopped Lucius from insisting he have a location for his supplies in between assignments. In addition, they insisted he have a place for the accumulation of paperwork, memos, and directives that he never bothered to read.

The pile had definitely grown. He reached into a drawer and pulled out his Colt 1911. The grip fit his hand like a glove. It had been a gift from a friend who had found trouble during the First World War; trouble that Derian extricated him from. The gun was a man stopper, and when he first went for Hailey, he hadn't expected to need that kind of firepower. Now with the stakes high Derian wanted as much advantage on his side as possible.

An extra pair of clothes sat folded in his locker. Pulling them out, he closed the door to change. A shower would have been nice, but too much time had already passed. He would have to go just a little bit longer missing the finer things in life.

Lidiya sat at her desk buried behind three massive flat screen monitors. He knocked on the doorjamb and her hand went up and waved him over. "There are three locations that look promising. His locus of origin is the most visited, but I doubt he would hide there. He's worked in this department too long to hide anywhere obvious." She glanced up and slanted a devious grin at him. "But, he was never very smart. I can still find him."

Derian looked at her screen. "Vegas?"

"Millard has weakness for gambling," she replied.

This was not surprising. Millard seemed to have a general weakness of personality. A gambling addiction only fit.

"But what time?"

"He's partial to 1960's. He's hit most of time available, but there are small gaps in 1961 and 1969. You're choice."

Derian sighed. It would have to be the swinging sixties. He always stuck out in the relaxed atmospheres of the less conservative eras. They always pegged him for law enforcement and it only made his job more difficult. There was little he could do; he just wasn't a smooth kind of guy.

"That looks as good as we will get. Can you call Marianne and let her know I need a suit for 1960s America?" Derian asked. Marianne would get a kick out of this one. She always loved putting operatives in something beyond the usual black pants and t-shirts that most *venator* preferred. Unfortunately for the *venator*, world fashion didn't favor the combination as often as they liked.

***

Carlo took Hailey down a second set of stairs and through another narrow hall. They came to the end of the hall and it opened into a large room filled with bright fluorescent light.

"So, the Babylonians seem to have a pretty good grasp on electricity," she said, not bothering to mask her curiosity.

Carlo waved toward a closed door. "Generators. The locals have no idea what they do, but it helps keep the mystique."

A short, dumpy man approached, his feet moving faster than his fat body could keep up with. He squinted at her, his eyes scrunched together like raisins even behind the bottle lenses he had for glasses. He made her think of moles with his tiny nose that wiggled a little as he spoke. "I am so excited to meet you. You have no idea! You will help so much! It has taken years to get to this point. But with you, we could jump decades!"

Hailey wanted to slap him. But he'd probably bounce back like one of those wobbly clown toys that freaked her out as a child. He leaned in closer and his stale breath puffed out as he spoke, "You're blond. Is that natural?"

"Excuse me?"

"Are you a natural blond?"

"Of course I am," Hailey bit back.

He sniffed, then turned around mumbling as he went. "Shouldn't be blond. No. No recessive genes. There shouldn't be recessive genes."

Hailey looked up at Carlo. "Are you serious? You're planning to take over the world with people like him?"

Carlo pursed his lips, then pushed her toward a seat that looked far too much like a dentist chair. The mole-man pulled out a syringe.

"Oh hell no! That man is not coming anywhere near me with a needle!" Hailey said, her voice cracking with anxiety. He probably couldn't find a vein if it had flashing lights and puffed to the size of a watermelon. She grabbed a hold of Carlo's hair and yanked him down to eye level. He was too shocked to react. "You do it! He's going to dig a hole to China in my arm. He's blind as a bat!"

The mole-man blushed then started to mutter again. Carlo pried her fingers from his hair then strapped her down on the chair. Hailey's heart pounded so fast she thought it might bounce out and across the room. "Did I mention I hate needles? I really hate needles. And not like most people hate needles, I mean I really, really hate needles."

The needle came toward her arm. "Don't we want to wait for my dad? I'm sure he wants to see this. He's been waiting for this forever right? How pissed would he be if he missed this?"

Wrinkled eyes blinked at her like little strobe lights. "This is just anesthesia."

Anesthesia? What were they planning to do to her that required anesthesia? This was not looking good. Not good at all. "What do big bad dudes planning to take over the world need with anesthesia? Don't you just torture and run?"

Mole-man looked confused. Carlo was just annoyed and said, "Just do it."

"What? Is he your boss? Do you always do what this asshole tells you to do? 'Cause I think he might be a little crazy. I would check it out first. You don't want to find out later you've been doing stuff for a crazy man. It doesn't look good on resumes. Trust me. I know." So she sounded a little nutty. The minute they started pumping things into her body she knew it was all over. Then her only way out would be in a body bag.

Carlo grabbed the needle and pushed it into her arm. Hailey hissed at him, "Oh, dude. You are so going to regret this. I am going to get out of here, and when I do, you better run like hell."

The effects were nearly instantaneous. Whatever they had been working on, it was pretty heavy stuff. Her body melted into the chair. Carlo leaned down and cupped the back of her head, he pulled her toward him and whispered in her ear, "If you survive the next couple weeks you will be desperate to thank me."

She slurred, but she hoped he got the gist of her meaning, "Rot in hell, jerk off."

19

Derian stepped out of the way as women paraded past, showing off to their very best the influence of Jackie Kennedy. Several men strutted by in casual suits with wide ties. He stood uncomfortably outside the Sands Hotel where the sign boasted Dean Martin as the performer, and Maybe Frank and Maybe Sammy. He had never been up on popular culture, especially during the turbulent mid 20th American century, but he'd have to be dead not to know about the Rat Pack. So would Millard, and if the man favored 1960s Vegas, he was more than likely a fan of Frank, Dino, Sammy, Joey and Peter.

He entered the wide front doors of the casino. The room filled to the brim with warm bodies, he did his best to blend in with the crowd. He scanned the faces milling around him and hoped he hadn't chosen the wrong year. He wanted his hands on Millard before the night ended.

A young woman with legs that had to end just below her chin slowed as she passed and gave him an appreciative smile. Roderic would have had a field day with the feminine offerings in this crowd. There was a time when Derian would have found the diversion entertaining as well, but as it was, he had his heart and mind set on a very specific blond. Her legs might not be as long, but she did more to get his blood boiling than any of the candy walking the room. If Millard proved unhelpful, he would find it hard not to strangle the man.

"Sir, may I get you a drink?" A skinny woman with bright saucer eyes and tits far too exposed for any decade's sense of decency stood beside him holding a tray of cigarettes and empty glasses.

"No. Thank you, I am fine," he answered. She responded with a vague smile then slid through the crowd. She stopped at a high top table where three men with shoulders too big for their choice in jackets scowled out at the crowd. All three glared at him in unconcealed suspicion. Gambling in Vegas was legal, but not everything that went on in the city was. Derian's unfortunate look of authority would not be missed by members of organized crime. He needed to find a good excuse to be there, and just standing against a wall watching the crowd wasn't going to cut it.

He moved toward one of the high stakes tables. Gambling was not one of his hobbies, but he could pass off his skill enough to never be noticed. He motioned for a hand, but kept the room in his peripheral. He wouldn't chance losing Millard over a damn game of cards.

The night grew late and Derian still hadn't seen Millard. He may have the right time but been wrong about the attraction of the Sands. He started to question his choice and filter through the alternatives when a small commotion drew his attention to the far corner of the casino. The show had finished and the stars were making their way into the lounge as usual. The chance to see the Rat Pack in their element drew crowds like none other.

Men puffed out their chests and straightened their ties, the ladies ran to the restroom to check their makeup. The staff just smiled and watched the money come in.

He decided to wait to see if his prey would appear. Another hand did little to stem his impatience. Half of his mind watched for Millard, the other half imagined the terrible things that could be happening to Hailey, leaving nothing for the game of Black Jack. It was this very reason he nearly missed the small palm sneak in and nab a few of his unguarded chips.

His hand snagged the wrist of a young woman dressed to the nines and quite obviously shocked to have been caught. Gambling may not be what he wanted to be doing at the time, but no one stole from him. "Give them back."

Her lower lip trembled and a much practiced pout erupted. He leaned toward her ear. "I am willing to forget this happened and not tell the house, if you give them back."

The Dealer noticed and waved over one of the floor bosses. Derian nodded toward the oncoming authority. "Your choice."

She trembled, but opened her hands and dropped the chips into his. As soon as he let her wrist go she skittered down the packed lanes toward the door. Getting caught stealing in Vegas was at best career ending; she was obviously aware of the risk.

Security moved to intercept. He might not report the incident, but there was little he could do about what the Casino saw. His attention returned to the cards in his hand and then back to scan the room for Millard. His stomach hit the floor when he spied his quarry being shown to the emergency exit by the same three men that had watched Derian early in the evening.

He closed his hand and left the table. It should not have come as a shock that Millard had found his own trouble in Vegas. He grunted in irritation. The door they exited was now barred by another large man in an immaculate suit accessorized with giant beefy arms. Derian hightailed it out the front door and around the building in time to see the men drive away in a Chevy Impala.

Several yellow cabs idled at the entrance and he jumped in the one at the front of the line. Slamming the door he said, "I need you to follow the car that just left."

The driver turned to argue. "Listen Mack, I'm not playing any cops and robbers today. You can get right back out of here."

"Derian pulled his Colt and pointed it at the driver's head. "I'm not a cop, so I'm not worried about shooting you. Drive."

The driver narrowed his eyes and chewed on a thin toothpick with flagrant disregard for the cold metal pressed to his temple. Derian waited for a response and finally the man turned and pulled into traffic. They drove past milling crowds and late night revelers. At night the Strip transformed into a different animal, its bright lights, gaudy inhabitants and atmosphere of excess turned it into an alien wonderland. The Impala, unaware that it had a tail, made no effort to rush through the streets.

The beat up cab followed them off the Strip and into Las Vegas proper where desert and industry replaced the glitz and glamour. The driver eased the breaks when the Impala turned into a street block lined with warehouses. He pulled to the side at the corner and stopped, gripping the wheel like an iron lock. "This is as far as I'm going Mack. I know what goes on down there and I don't want nothing to do with it."

Derian pulled out his chips and dropped them into the passenger seat. The amount would more than compensate for the man's irritation. He stepped out into the black night and started down the street. He needed to get to Millard before the man jumped or his captors killed him.

The soft scuff of his steps echoed against the block and aluminum siding that made up the numerous warehouses. He walked nearly a quarter mile before he glimpsed the Impala tucked beside one of the smaller buildings. A slight yellow glow filtered beneath a thin steel door.

He considered his options. Three men accompanied Millard out of the Casino. Assuming no one had been waiting for them in the warehouse, then he was at best outnumbered three to one. He could scour the building for another entrance but he didn't like the amount of time that would waste. He strode up to the door and pounded against the steel.

The giant ox of a man that answered his knock stood dumbfounded by the unexpected visitor at the door. "You have something that belongs to me," Derian said.

"What?"

Derian shouldered himself past the thug and entered the bright light of the front office. The other two men from the Casino rose and started toward him. Putting a hand up, he stalled their attack. "I'm only here to talk to Millard. You can keep him and do whatever you want with him, but we need to talk before that happens."

"Why should we do that?" The two larger goons watched the shorter one closely. The man was built like a miniature pincher and looked to have the same personality. He was the leader of the brute squad no doubt so Derian focused his attention on him.

"He knows something about a missing piece of property. My employer would very much like to know where this is before Millard offs it," he answered in a rough voice and as he spoke the men relaxed. Few people truly realized the power of voice and language, but Derian had centuries of practice.

"How do we know you aren't a friend?"

"Milliard? That rat doesn't have any friends. Besides, what kind of idiot try's to rescue a man by walking in the front door?" Derian said.

The larger thugs looked stupidly at the front door. The leader crossed his arms and kept his stare on Derian. With a practiced grin Derian motioned to the door. He was going in; it was their choice whether the exercise included his Colt. The seconds ticked by and his fingers twitched by his side.

A decision was finally made, the door opened and they escorted him inside. Millard lay sprawled out on the hard cement. Dried blood coated his scalp. That explained why the little idiot hadn't jumped to a safer time. Derian kicked him in the side and got a groan in response. "Wake up."

Millard just groaned again and stilled. Derian looked up at the goons and said, "I take it he owes someone a lot of money."

They nodded. It wasn't a big secret. Few things would put a man in the situation Millard found himself. Money was the top contender. Messing with a powerful man's woman was another. Somehow, he couldn't picture Millard attracting the kind of attention from a woman that would get him killed.

"Can I have a moment with him?" Derian asked. The leader opened his mouth to argue, but Derian countered before the man could get a word out, "The information he has is sensitive — got it?"

His tone left no room for argument. Someone that had never been around a dangerous man might have pushed, but this man proved to be no fool. The door shut solidly behind the goons and he turned his attention to his prey. "Wake up you damn fool."

Millard didn't budge. Derian continued, "If you don't start waking up real soon, you are going to wish I had just left you to the three men in the other room." One eye opened then shut quickly. Derian kicked the man in the gut hard enough to make him gasp for air. "Let's try that again."

Both eyes opened wide and a heavy wheeze rattled from his throat. Derian snarled, "Now Millard, I think you know why I am here."

Millard nodded, but a glaze glossed over the man's eyes and his cheeks began to relax. Derian placed his Colt against the weasel's temple. "You can jump, but you'll be dead when you get there."

Millard's neck tensed and his eyes cleared. He wheezed, "I don't know anything."

"That is a load of crap. Where did they take Hailey?"

"I don't know. They never told me. I just did what they needed at the *Domus*."

"What happened to Lucius? Did they take him with her too?"

"The Magister? No, no. He's dead. The man. The man killed him."

Derian's heart stopped. His closest friend, Dead? "You son of a bitch," Derian reached down to grab him by the lapels, "How could you do this? How could you betray the *Domus*? People trusted you! Roderic trusted you!"

Millard looked taken aback and whispered, "Roderic? You don't know?"

"I don't know what?" Before Millard could explain a commotion broke out in the front room. Shouts and shots preceded the door slamming open. A man in black from head to toe stood in the doorjamb with a gun that had no place in the 1960's. Three shots punctured the air and blood spread across Millard's chest. Derian didn't wait to find out who wanted Millard dead. He jumped. The last thing he heard was the shot meant for him.

***

Hailey's eyes flew open. She lay in a bed enveloped in the most luscious bedding she'd ever felt. It was like cotton candy without the stickiness. She could lay here forever, embraced by soft pillows and security. Except, she was hardly secure.

When she sat up her head pounded against her skull and the memories from before flooded back. The last thing she remembered was seeing her father enter the room as the mole-man approached with another damn needle.

Her arm throbbed. It looked like it had met the business end of a meat cleaver. That man had no business being around needles! Then again, when you weren't particularly concerned about your patients, it didn't matter who was messing with the veins. It brought up an interesting question though. Why was she in such an exquisite room? Shouldn't she be back in the cell with Poppi?

She assumed the walls were the same mud brick, but these were plastered and painted a brilliant red. Small tables were intricately decorated with what must have passed as chachkies in Babylon. Luscious textiles hung from the walls and covered the floors. It was a Middle Eastern posh paradise and exactly what she would expect for a harem or palace. Minus the waterfalls and gaggle of giggling girls.

A steaming bath sat at the far end of the room. The sight nearly sent her into a fit of ecstasy. She couldn't remember the last time she took a bath. And she knew without a doubt she stank like three weeks worth of dirty laundry. It was tempting to take advantage of the offering. But there had to be catch. What were they working at? Did they already get what they needed from her or were they trying to butter her up for something they couldn't get on their own?

The table beside the bed was packed with dates, cheeses, and other items she couldn't place. Her stomach growled. Yep. They were trying to butter her up. Well, the way she saw it, as long as she was aware of what they were up to, she could take advantage of what they offered and still refuse to give them what they wanted. After all, it wasn't like they made her sign a contract or anything.

And she congratulated herself on a decision well made an hour later as she sat soaking up the very last of the lukewarm water. Her tummy full, her headache receding, and she was clean. Oh she was so blissfully clean! She sighed and sunk deeper in the water. They might need a crane to pull her out.

The door swung open and Carlo strode in with all his arrogant glory. In another time and place she would have been furious and embarrassed by her nudity. In her current state, she wouldn't care if an entire army marched in. If the situation called for it, she might have the wherewithal to give Carlo the finger— Maybe.

He looked down at her and grinned. The bath had come sans bubbles, so the view must have been excellent. He breathed, "Nice."

Hailey's raised a brow and thinned her lips. His smile widened. How she hated his smile. "Can I help you?" she asked.

"Where would you like to start?" his drawl slithered to her ears, sending a wave of goose bumps across skin.

"Dude. Eww." All the pleasure from the bath fled. Two servants entered the room; at least she assumed they were servants. They wore light linen tunics and had their hair bound up and covered by kerchiefs. Their dark bronzed skin suggested they were from the local population and not part of Nikanuur's *viator* contingent. One carried grooming supplies, the other had a soft linen gown hung over her arm.

Carlo ignored the room's new inhabitants and leaned down to brush his finger across her breast. Hailey jumped out so fast half the water splashed out of the tub. She hurried to the bed and slid under the relative safety of the covers. He'd had an excellent view of her backside, but that was better than waiting to see what he was going to do next. His chuckle followed her retreat. So much for not caring.

Gesturing to the servants, Carlo moved toward the door, "They will assist you in getting dressed. Someone is very eager to meet you."

Then he was gone. Hailey shivered. She really missed Derian. She had never been one for macho displays of manhood, but she would love to see him beat the crap out of Carlo.

20

Derian huddled against the wall in the small shack on the Island of Hokkaido. Never had it served him so well. A bullet meant for him had embedded itself in the soft wood of the shack wall. He pulled the gauze from the wound on his arm. The pain and blood was minimal, but death had been inches away. He had been saved by seconds, his jump reflex triggered well before he was even aware of the threat. The jump had slowed the bullet's trajectory, enough to lessen the impact and give him the extra second to move out of the way. A younger, less experienced *viator* may not have made it.

The image of Millard in the last moments before the jump flashed behind his closed eyes. The humanity had seeped from the data tracker's face as the blood drained onto the hard concrete floor. Sympathy only hung on for a moment; the man betrayed everything that Derian cared for. And the trip had been a waste. There were no answers found in Vegas.

And now there was a new question. What had Millard meant to say about Roderic? Had he meant to suggest that Roderic was a part of the plot they had been fighting so ineffectually? It would serve as a convenient excuse for why they had been so unsuccessful in tracking down any reasonable suspects. Millard couldn't be the only traitor in their midst; he just didn't have the clearance needed to provide everything the enemy had access to.

But Derian was loath to consider his friend as a traitor. Roderic had always been there when it counted. And despite his gruff exterior, he had always been undeniably dedicated to the *Domus* and the *viator*.

Perhaps that was the brilliance of it. Derian put his fist into the wall. Small bits of wood splintered into his hand and the pain brought reality back into focus. He had to move. The threat grew with every moment wasted. The conspiracy found no issue with disposing of their people. And little would stop them from killing those that got in their way. At what point would Hailey become collateral?

Her value could already be exhausted. Derian wouldn't stop to think about that possibility. A piece of him regretted not letting her lead them to Nikanuur's lair. Now he floundered in a sea of infinite possibilities. The thought of failing her hung heavily over his heart. Just as he had finally started thinking seriously of a future with another he risked losing her.

He needed to talk to Lidiya. Perhaps she would have a lead on the old Babylonian's location. And while there he would find out from Roderic just what Millard had been about to tell him. But he needed to rest first. He would be no use to anyone exhausted and wounded. Pulling the old wool blanket over his shoulder he rested his head against the wall. His eyes shut to visions of a sandy blond with terror in her eyes.

Sleep eventually intruded into his dreams providing the much needed reserve to continue on. When he landed in the

Domus it echoed with emptiness. The forest of cubicles outside the entrance to the *castellum* was unusually dark. No heads popped up to check on the intruder. No clicks against keyboards heralded busy fingers.

He punched in his code to the *castellum* and waited as it authorized his credentials. The atmosphere sent unnerving shivers against the back of his neck. Finally the door clicked and granted him access. The halls of the inner sanctum to the *Domus* were equally heavy with silence. Not a single *viator* peeked out of an office to check to see who owned the footsteps passing by.

The first stop was Roderic's laboratory. The door was locked and strips of black and grey tape sealed the cracks. Derian couldn't remember a time when this laboratory was locked.

Derian hustled to Lidiya's command center; the hum of humanity just as absent on that side of the complex. Her door was closed but the knob turned easily in his hand. The blond analyst glanced up furtively when he entered then returned her gaze to the three screens glowing in the dark.

"Did you find him?" she asked.

"I did."

She looked up again and he shook his head. She breathed, "That man was a waste of oxygen."

He couldn't help but agree; though it astonished him how easily Lidiya could disregard him. "What happened to the lab?" he asked. She didn't look up. Her hands flew over the keys and her eyes tracked the data scanning across the screens. "Lidiya. What's going on?"

"They took Roderic away," she responded, her voice tightly controlled.

Shock hit him like oncoming traffic. "What happened?"

"Order came from Council. They sent in team of men I never seen before, hauled him off and sealed the room."

"What about Rusa? Did the order come from him?"

Lidiya giggled, then put her hand to her lips as she blushed. Derian had never seen the Ukrainian woman overcome with the giggles. It seemed an odd time to suddenly develop a sense of humor. "No. I do not think he knew about it. He showed up just as they took Roderic out. He punched hole in wall, then threatened to kill who ever had given order. I think one of guys holding Roderic pissed his pants."

"Did Roderic deny it? Do we know what they say he did?" Derian asked.

"He just let them take him. He didn't say anything and neither did they. I'm not sure what made Rusa angrier." Her brows furrowed.

Derian found a chair and sat heavily, his head resting on his palms and his elbows on his knees. The odds against him grew more debilitating. His resources were limited and the two men he depended on the most during his assignments were both gone. One dead. One might as well be.

The clicking of keys snapped like popcorn in a metal pan. What options did he have? When he worked on a project there would be a time when the pieces would start to fall into place. But that wasn't happening. None of it made sense. All he knew was Nikanuur had a laboratory. That location seemed the most logical place for them to have squirreled Hailey away.

The silence that filled the room was nearly as deafening as a gunshot. Lidiya stared at him, her face filled with obvious indecision. He prompted, "What?"

"I don't know who to trust," she said.

"Neither do I."

Lidiya pressed her palms into her eyes. "Do you believe Roderic is traitor?"

He took a moment to respond. If he showed support for his friend could he lose all the resources of the *Domus*? How would he find Hailey then? Lidiya sat quietly, her head lowered and covered by her hands. Something seemed to hang in the balance, and damned if he knew what it was. But he couldn't betray his friend, no matter the possibilities. "I don't. The *Domus* has been his life. I cannot see him willingly contributing to anything like this."

The moment lengthened and Derian waited for the shoe to drop. She nodded, then started tapping at the keys again. "We know Nikanuur's laboratory is in Babylon," she said with half a smile, "He has always been partial to his homeland. I should find pattern."

Derian leaned toward the screens. "You are amazing."

"I'm not positive on time yet. It has to be politically stable — relatively, it is the Middle East — and time when they could go unnoticed. I do not think it is during Greek occupation, but I could be wrong." The tiredness of her eyes and pinched features showed just how impacted she was by the recent events.

"When did you last sleep? Or eat?" he asked and she gave him a blank stare. "I thought so. I will get you something to eat. You keep working." Telling her to take a nap would meet resistance. It was advice he would be unlikely to take himself, he wouldn't force it on someone else. But food he could take care of and it would keep him active. Hope finally flickered. He wouldn't ruin it by over thinking the situation.

***

Traveling through time was strange. Running from pirates, Nazis, and mad scientists ranked right up there on the weirdness scale. But things just hit surreal and now Hailey wondered about her sanity.

Three strangers sat across the table from her. At her right sat Carlo and his insufferable arrogance. To her left, her father fidgeted like a preschooler at church. Apparently her dear old daddy wasn't any more comfortable at a formal dinner table than she was. And formal was the only word for it. Three plates waited in front of her along with far too many forks for any normal person to use during the course of a meal.

A servant in a long linen tunic and greasy curls that rivaled Nikanuur's offered her a glass of wine. Hailey promptly declined. Imbibing might have helped settle her nerves, but it wouldn't make the three frighteningly gracious hosts disappear.

Evidently in his element, Carlo's slender hands skillfully handled the flatware and delicate wine stems like a seasoned professional. Nikanuur did his best to look inconspicuous. She just hoped the next course had an ingredient she could identify.

"Your father mentioned you only just met," a slender woman with a mouth that seemed to be a cross between Angelina Jolie and Julia Roberts addressed her with the accent of the overtly cultured. Hailey was fascinated by her mouth. The woman could probably fit an entire orange in that ridiculous thing. She cleared her throat and Hailey jerked her eyes away.

"My father is an asshole. I would have preferred we'd never met," Hailey answered, drawing a nasty glare from

Nikanuur, but she kept her expression pleasant and focused across the table. She may have to be involved in the farce, but she wasn't going to be nice about it. One of the men that accompanied The Mouth sniggered. Apparently her father garnered about as much respect from them as he did from her. Interesting.

The next course arrived and thankfully it was soup. Soup was safe. As long as there weren't any eyeballs in it she might actually get something down. Once the room was empty of servants the woman tried again, "It is unfortunate that your introduction to our cause was so inelegant."

Hailey snorted. The woman pursed her lips and Hailey rewarded her with a super star smile. The Mouth laid her spoon gently on the table to reach for her glass and continued, "We had hoped to interest you in working with us. It would be so much more advantageous for all involved."

"Exactly who is Us?" Hailey asked and wondered if slurping her soup would irritate them.

"We are a consortium of sorts. We aim to promote the expansion and development of the *viator*." The rest of the table was busy with their meal. That alone would have told Hailey there was much more to the story than that. Not being an idiot also helped.

"Isn't that a job for the *Domus*?" Hailey asked, if nothing more than to ruffle the feathers in the room.

The Mouth didn't miss a beat. "The *Domus* served its purpose. But it was established under antiquated ideals. They seek to separate us from humanity, not integrate. We deserve to be a part of the world. We deserve to be active participants!"

"Active? Don't you mean running things?"

"We have years of experience and knowledge at our fingertips. Why shouldn't we run things? You see how well humanity has run things for millennia. Why shouldn't we do better when we can?" she answered, her voice quavering with agitation. Oh boy. Someone drank the Kool-Aid. It could be worse, Hailey figured, there could be aliens involved.

"Isn't taking over the world kind of blasé? I mean, it's been done. It never works out for the super villains," Hailey said. That didn't go over well. The woman's hands shook slightly. If she had fangs, they would have sunk into Hailey's neck.

Hailey stopped worrying about her sanity; crazy was clearly sitting right in front of her. But that only encouraged her to poke more. "So, how exactly does torture and kidnapping promote your ideals?"

"We do not torture! The experiments are highly controlled and done as humanly as possible."

"You just happen to forget getting consent. Oh, and the fact that there are people going nutty down in your dungeon." Hailey smiled as the woman gripped her spoon like it was a stress ball. Maybe she could get her to bend it. That would be impressive.

A dark haired man with a moustache only fashionable in the seventies reached over and placed a hand on the Mouth's wrist. The impact was nearly instantaneous. She calmed and put on a sweet smile. It reminded Hailey of Carlo's smile. She didn't like it.

"Your father has made significant advances in *viator* physiology. His work will prevent *viators* from having to wait so long to gain the skills necessary to truly be effective at traveling through time. No longer will *novus* have to flounder through their first hundred years. No longer will they have to travel without protection, not knowing where they might land. It is truly miraculous!"

"Right." Hailey stared into her soup. How much had they figured out she could do? Why were they bothering with the sales pitch? All in all her skills weren't that impressive. She still jumped willy-nilly and she didn't nearly have the control Derian did. She could teleport things, and that was pretty cool, but as far as she knew they had no clue about that party trick. What did they know that she didn't? "So, why me? Why do you care if I join up with you or not?"

If a smile could get sickening sweet, she just saw it. The creepy crawlies skittered up her arm and a sharp pain flashed at her neck where the damn leash was embedded. What she would do for a rare-earth magnet.

"You are the first generation. The only one born with the alterations to your DNA. Everything before you has been unnaturally drug induced and not permanent. You are the culmination of centuries of work." The Mouth took a deep breath to continue, "Had your mother not run off with you we would have raised you under our supportive arm. It is very lucky you found us before it was too late."

"Dude, seriously? Too late for what?"

All heads turned to Nikanuur and he shifted uncomfortably, then cleared his throat. "Any time changes are made to the body unexpected side effects can occur."

"Side effects? What kind of side effects??" Hailey pointed a glare at her father.

"In conjunction with the amplified skills is degeneration in the part of the brain that controls your jumps. This degeneration leads to symptoms of insanity. Each time you jump the risk increases."

"Dude!" Hailey thought back to the two *viators* she'd seen in the cells below. Was she on her way to sitting in the corner rocking herself into a blubbering stupor? What awful luck.

The Mouth spoke again, "With our assistance you can prevent that. And help us find a way to prevent it from happening in the generations to come."

"You haven't done a great job on those people downstairs." She wanted to hurt someone. Like really hurt them. Like grab their neck and shake till the head popped off kind of hurt. These people were evil. And they thought they had her number, that she would go along with anything just because they held all the cards.

"Those test subjects have been instrumental in developing a counteragent to prevent and slow the effects," her father mumbled from behind his fork.

"Test subjects? Test subjects? Those are god damn people! You had no right to do what you did to them!" she shouted. He cringed under her diatribe.

The Mouth interjected before Hailey could continue, "That is not your concern now is it? You have yourself to worry about. And without the counteragent that your father has developed, you have no option but to end up just like them." Her eyes were cold and calculating. Hailey bit into her bottom lip. So they held all the cards—now. But that wouldn't last. And when she got the upper hand…well, she would find some way for them to pay for the terrible things they did. She would find a way.

"What do you say, Hailey? Join us and you will never have to worry that the next jump will send you into a fit of insanity."

Hailey just glared at her.

"An answer, please." The Mouth glared back. Hailey would need to find out the woman's name. Just so she could write her down on the list of people she hated. The woman may have just moved Carlo and her father down from the top two spots.

"Fine." For now. Hailey had no intention of signing up with these assholes. But she needed to buy time and until she could figure out an alternative to the insanity option, she was stuck.

The Mouth and her lackeys were kind enough to talk amongst themselves after they got her acquiescence. Even after the fourth course, Hailey still fumed and desperately wanted to get away. Unfortunately, Carlo decided to push. "You haven't touched your food." He reached over and caressed her arm.

"Seriously. Don't touch me," Hailey growled and he slid a slimy smile at her. Hailey gripped her fork and imagined what she could do with it.

"We will be getting to know each other quite well. You should at the very least get used to it." He trailed a finger up her arm.

"Unless you want a fork stabbed in your face, get your hands off me," she replied. She had to give him a little credit, he didn't argue the point.

21

"Derian!"

The roar ricocheted down the hall. Lidiya didn't bother to look up from her work when she said, "Rusa's back."

"Your powers of observation are astounding," Derian answered. Tired and frustrated, he stretched in the small folding chair that had been his seat for the last several hours. Lidiya had been digging through data for all that time. Nothing in the *Domus* databases gave a hint to when Nikanuur might have established his lab. Now she was scouring the digital archives of historical documents uploaded by museums across the world, hoping to find anything that could give them a lead.

"They are, and you should be happy they are so good. Otherwise we would have no chance at this." Her fingers flew as she entered more search commands. "Go find out what he wants. I can't take you staring at me anymore."

More than happy to comply, he walked out the door to confront the Minoan barreling down the hall. The man was agitated, and more than usual. "There you are! Do you know what they have done??"

Derian pitied whoever ordered Roderic to be detained. Rusa was not one to forgive or forget. Derian replied, "I have heard."

"And not a god damn word to me! There was a time when leadership meant something! When age and experience garnered respect!"

Derian nodded. The old man must have been kept in the dark on quite a few things. He would be interested to know who had found a way to pull the strings behind this force of nature.

"Let's get out of the hall," Derian said as he opened the door to one of the adjacent offices and found it dark and empty. From what he could tell, the three of them were the only ones left in the complex. "Did they shut everything down? Why isn't any one here?"

Rusa sat with a loud exclamation of frustration. "Everyone is terrified to be here. Roderic wasn't the only one they hauled off. Half his staff was taken with him."

That was news. How could an entire department be a part of the conspiracy? Derian asked, "Who's making these decisions? And why aren't you in on it?"

"The Council voted me off. Said I wouldn't be able to keep my decisions unbiased." Rusa slammed his fist on the little end table beside his chair. "I'm not biased! My boy didn't do a damn thing!"

Rusa might be just a little biased, but Derian kept the comment to himself since he happened to agree with the man. He leaned against the small desk that sat in the middle of the room. It belonged to one of the many research specialists that helped maintain the multitude of records kept by the *Domus*. Everything sat as if waiting for its owner to return the next morning. Everything except for the hastily discarded cords tossed out of the way when the computer tower was removed.

"Where did they take them all?"Derian asked.

"Carpathia"

Derian bit back a groan. Carpathia was the *viator* equivalent to Alcatraz. It had a permanently established no jump zone and was located in an ancient stronghold that had stood the test of time. High in the mountains of Eastern Europe, its fortifications could withstand attack from any outside enemy. Legend surrounded the Carpathians long before gypsies and vampire inspired popular culture and fear. They were impenetrable, dark, and it was a place where souls could easily be lost.

But the purpose of the fortress in Carpathia wasn't to keep people out. It kept people in. For millennia it held only the most dangerous rogues.

There was little doubt now. Whoever commanded the force behind this had influence at the highest levels. Levels even beyond those Rusa could touch. Roderic was out of reach.

"I take it you believe there is a conspiracy now," Derian said.

Rusa glared at him. "You've made your point. So what are you doing about it?"

Not much. That was the problem. Derian offered, "We're zeroing in on the laboratory. Once we have a time identified, I'm going in."

"What's the plan? You can't bring anyone back with you. And you can't possibly take on the entire instillation on your own."

"The laboratory is the only lead we have. If I can get in, I can identify persons involved; maybe put a dent in their activities," Derian answered. And he planned to get Hailey the hell out of there.

Rusa grunted, "What use are names going to be? We don't have a force to deal with it. With no Magister, the *venator* are leaderless. They aren't trained for this kind of work. They are loners. We need an assault team!"

"You're a leader. You lead them," Derian said.

"I'm a bureaucrat. I haven't been in the field since before you were born." Based on Rusa's girth, that was more than obvious. It took years of excess and no exercise for a *viator* to gain weight. Considering the paunch on the man, he must have been working at it hard.

"Is there anyone else to lead them?"Derian asked. There wasn't and they both knew it. *Viators*, in general, were independent. *Venator* were to the extreme. They excelled at making decisions on their own in the course of an assignment, but leadership was a rare trait. It took a special personality to lead a contingent of lone wolves. Lucius did it through patience and incomparable competence. Rusa might be able to do it with passion and bluster. It was the best they could hope for.

"You should wait until we have a team to go with you," Rusa said.

That would be the wisest choice, but it would mean leaving Hailey in the hands of her father. The longer he let time pass the more complex the situation became. He could only hope he wouldn't be too late. "I'm leaving as soon as I get an answer from Lidiya."

"This is about that damn girl, isn't it?"Rusa said and flexed his fingers.

Derian didn't respond. Rusa ran an exasperated hand through his hair. "I could never tell your father what to do. Makes sense you'd be the same."

Derian gave a curt nod. His father's stubbornness was legendary. It had made him one of the most effective *venator* in the history of the *Domus*. It was that same stubbornness that had gotten him killed along with Derian's mother. Unwilling to leave her as she lay dying from the mortal wound delivered by a Viking battle axe, he was the only man left in the village when it had been completely overrun. It was a stubbornness that had left his son to tread the road as a *viator* alone.

Was he on a road to relive the same kind of tragedy?

*****

The rest of the evening sucked. They prolonged the agony by bringing out dessert and after dinner drinks. Dark looks and snarky comments did little to speed up the process and when Hailey had finally gotten back to her room her nerves were frazzled and mood irreparably dark. The sumptuous bedding had felt more like a slap than a luxury. Sleep finally stole her away from the angry musings of her mind. Had she woken up to an empty room, she might have actually found a way to be little positive about the coming day.

But Carlo had shocked her from her sleep by sitting on her bed; his irritating smile solidly in place. The man was getting fresh and she was running out of adequate insults to sling. But if he thought he could win her over with persistence, he was mistaken. "I want to see Poppi."

"In time. We have much to do today," he said.

She was not inclined to cooperate. "If I don't see Poppi now, I will make your day a living hell."

Carlo pulled out a small dagger from his belt and began to clean his nails. Hailey closed her eyes and fell back against the pillows. She wondered if her great-grandmother found the fastidious ogre as sexy as she had when they first spied him from the compound window. It was amazing how getting to know a person changed their attractiveness. The more she got to know Derian, the more she wanted to jump his bones. This guy was a totally different story.

Pulling the covers over her head she imagined he wasn't there. How nice it would have been to wake up to Derian beside her. She remembered the conversation from the night before and her heart plummeted. Was she destined to be with these people forever? If she left, would she go crazy and inevitably seek death to cease the agony? Any thought of giving them the finger and spending eternity with Derian was becoming a distant fantasy. It totally sucked.

The blanket flew off her and the cool air sprinkled goose bumps across her four exposed limbs. It was a good thing she'd found a short linen shift to wear to bed. Carlo's lascivious smirk got her moving more than any verbal threat. She ground out in frustration, "Why are you always around? Don't you have better things to do?"

"You are my thing to do." He picked up a simpler version of the linen dress she wore the night before. This one was a soft brown with only the slightest embroidery around the neckline. He rolled it up to help her pull it over her head, but she grabbed it first. The man was so not going to dress her.

"Can I have some privacy?"

"Just put it on. We have things to do."

"I told you, I'm not doing anything until I see Poppi," she demanded, the thought of throwing a full-blown toddler tantrum passed through her mind, but she discarded it. He'd probably enjoy the show.

He seemed to consider his options and then said, "We will stop by on the way."

Hailey sighed at the small victory. He wasn't the only one that could win with persistence. She turned her back on him and pulled the linen over her head. She left on her pajamas. Carlo wasn't about to get the satisfaction of seeing her sans clothing.

When they finally reached her, Poppi was not looking her best. Still in the same stark cell, she sat in a corner, her elbows resting on her knees and her head buried in her hands. Hailey's stomach lurched. Could they have broken the woman so soon?

She knocked against the window. Poppi's head flew up, her eyes flashed with bitterness and Hailey was blissfully relieved. It would take a lot more to keep this woman down.

When Poppi realized it was Hailey, she struggled to her feet and limped over to the window. Her face puffed like an overcooked pastry from the beating the day before and it seemed that Nikanuur had worked her over quite a bit more after Hailey had been dragged from the room.

"I am so sorry Poppi," Hailey shouted through the glass.

Poppi motioned that she couldn't hear, so Hailey went to the door and pulled back the cover to the grate. "The bastard hurt you pretty bad."

"This isn't nothing, baby doll. He just played with me a little. Nothing I haven't bounced back from before." She gave Hailey one of her money-maker grins, then immediately sobered. "What have they done to you, girl? Nothing permanent?"

Permanent? Well, sort of, but that wasn't something she was ready to talk about. "I'm ok. But these people are nuts."

"Certifiable," Poppi agreed.

Hailey glanced over at Carlo who lounged against a small wood table chatting with the guard. She said, "I don't know how to get us out of this."

Her great-grandmother slid her fingers through the grate and curled them around Hailey's hand. "We'll figure it out, baby doll. Derian's looking for you. And with brains like ours, something will come up, I'm sure."

She was right. Derian was probably looking for them. He always came to the rescue. But as the time passed the hope she had that he'd find them faded. But she put on a courageous front and tightened her hand in support. Something would break. It had to. Otherwise...

"Time to go," Carlo said from behind Hailey's back. It seemed that had Poppi been a snake she would have found a way to sink her venom into him; but since that wasn't an option she settled on a nasty glare.

Hailey let Poppi's hand go, then laid her head against the grate. "I really don't like this guy."

"He's a toad. You'll be fine, he can't keep you down baby doll."

Carlo grabbed Hailey by the arm and had her out the door before she could respond. They moved through the hall and up the stairs, then back down to the room with the creepy fat man with terrible needle skills. Her arm throbbed just thinking of what he had done previously. "Don't come near me you fat little butcher!"

The man blushed then looked across the room where her father fussed at a table transferring liquids between bottles. Nikanuur said, "Just put her in the chair Carlo, I will assist in a moment."

Hailey wrenched her arm from Carlo's grasp and stomped over to the chair. When they tried to strap on the restraints, she hissed, "Don't even think about it."

Nikanuur joined them and sat on a small doctor's stool beside her chair. "I am glad you have decided to cooperate."

"It's not like I have a choice," she replied. He rolled a stainless steel table over. On it sat a number of hypodermic needles, vials, swabs, gauze, and a few instruments she couldn't begin to identify. "What are you going to do now?"

He slid a needle into one of the vials and pulled the liquid into the small reservoir. "This is a preventative. It isn't permanent, so we will have to give it to you consistently to prevent the side effects from setting in." He swabbed her arm with alcohol then poked the needle into her vein. It stung for a moment, but the pain subsided quickly.

Memories of sitting beside her Aunt Sue as the resilient old woman endured test after test distracted her from the company. Each test would come back the same, but they kept going, each time hoping that one would be different. Now she was the one in the hot seat and it didn't look like it would be going any differently for her.

"How often is consistently?" Hailey asked.

"We aren't quite sure of that. It is a relatively new discovery. At the very least once a week." Nikanuur said.

Once a week? That more or less chained her to them. "If I weren't to take this, how soon would I go crazy?"

"That depends on the *viator*." Nikanuur motioned for the little mole-man to bring over something from across the room. "What we know of this comes from those artificially adjusted. Unlike you, who was born with the mutation in place."

Mutant? Now she was a mutant? At least she didn't have an eyeball growing out of her underarm, but seriously, things were getting out of hand. It was just another notch on the belt that she wanted to beat him with. "So you have no idea."

Nikanuur shook his head. "No. But some have descended into madness within weeks of the first test. So I wouldn't risk it. This really is your only option."

He was wrong. There were other options. She just hadn't found them yet. The mole-man gave Nikanuur a handful of pills that a horse couldn't swallow. Nikanuur then handed them to her with a small wooden cup that made a shot glass look like a pint.

"You're kidding, right?"

"These will make the nausea less extensive." He walked away and motioned for Carlo to follow while Hailey tried to figure out how to get the damned things down. It wasn't easy and when it was done she felt like they were still lodged in her throat.

Nikanuur returned, this time with a vial filled with blood. He repeated the same procedure as before, and had the needle hovering over her arm before she realized what he was about to do. "Whoa! Hold on. Whose blood is that?"

Two heavy hands pushed down on Hailey's shoulders and Carlo's hot breath tickled against her ear. "It's mine. We don't want you getting lost out there. You never know what kind of trouble you can get into."

Her struggles had about the same effect as her curses. Dread coursed through her as Carlo's blood established a connection between them that would prevent her from ever really being free of the man. Tears stung her eyes as she realized she'd been violated far worse than any person had before. A beating would have been kinder.

"You really are a bastard," she hissed and speared her glare at both Carlo and Nikanuur. "Both of you."

Unaffected, Nikanuur cleaned up and left the room. Carlo let her go and circled to stand in front of her. He smiled. "You will find things go much better for you if you stop resisting. We do not mean you harm and offer many advantages."

He held out a hand to assist her up. She ignored it. He could try to smooth talk her all he wanted, it wouldn't make a bit of difference. "So, what are we going to do now?"

He walked to the door. "We see how talented you truly are."

There wasn't much to do but follow along. They passed back through the same hall and out to the covered porch. The heat of the day had intensified and the bright hands of the sun had shooed the largest of crowds to the cool promise of shade. The soft tan of the buildings matched the ground making it all seem to fade into each other. Squinting against the harsh rays, she strained to see the river that flowed past. The Tigris or the Euphrates, it could be either. She vaguely remembered from history that both had been the life blood that fed the birth of civilization. It was a fitting location for a group hoping to bring their new reality to the forefront of humanity.

Of course she remembered the damn rivers. But heaven help her if she remembered anything else about this time period. Why did they insist on having students remember dates? It would have been far more useful to her if they had insisted she memorize a map of old Babylon. Then she could plan an escape and maybe have half a shot at success. Of course she'd never bothered to study the dates. Why would she have done any different with a map?

He led them down a new set of stairs and into a small courtyard. Here were the first trees and foliage she had seen since landing in Babylon. The temperature dipped dramatically. A small fountain bubbled over glossy blue and purple tiles, the water falling like stars against a night sky. It was the kind of fountain that inspired hours of contemplation. Carlo didn't give it a second look.

They reached a small clearing and she looked up to see the four walls of the building sailing high into the sky. Carlo stopped and pulled out a magnet. He spun her, but she stopped him before he could remove the implanted leash. "Dude, last time one of those came off I jumped without planning to."

He chuckled, "Then control it."

"What? Just control it?" she squeaked as he placed the magnet over her neck. Pain lanced through her temples and shattered her eyesight. Terror seized her. How certain could she be that Nikanuur's injection would work? Would she wake up crazy?

The pain receded and her vision cleared. Carlo grinned down at her in thick condensation. "Good girl."

22

It took three jumps, but now he had her. Derian looked up from behind a fruit seller's booth as Hailey squinted against the sun. A tall dark haired man grabbed her arm and pulled her down the porch and out of sight. So far he'd counted ten guards at various points around the complex. It seemed limited to three buildings; the one large palatial style and two ancillaries that served as stores and barracks. Additional guards were probably stationed throughout. It didn't look good for a solo extraction mission.

He ducked down a small side street and searched for a better vantage point. Just running in and grabbing her wasn't going to be a viable option. He needed a plan, an opportunity — at this point he'd take simple dumb luck.

A two story mud brick building located kitty corner to the complex proved promising. Three children in rags played near the entrance and the high-pitched laughter of chatting women floated from inside the front door. He ducked into a narrow side alley, away from the screams of glee. Ample hand and footholds allowed him to pull his body to the roof. The sun beat heavily on to his back and he thanked the inspiration that had come to Lidiya when she wrapped his head with the soft linen turban.

He pulled the small set of binoculars from the leather pouch tied at his waist. There was little activity across the way. A scan of the complex revealed two doors on either end of the second story porch where he'd seen Hailey and the stranger. Periodically a guard would appear at one end and disappear down the other. The high wall below the porch was windowless, sheer and lacked the convenient handholds that would have assisted an entry. The front gate to the building had giant wood doors guarded by two men that had marked him with heightened suspicion as he passed earlier in the day. Nikanuur may have felt secure in his lab's location but he proved to be no fool.

The hours passed and he kept note of the guard's movements. Seeing Hailey had been a brush with serendipity. Her shoulders had been set with determination and spirit. They hadn't taken that from her and he thanked the heavens. Only a person with a strong sense of self-worth and stubbornness could endure what she had over the last couple weeks and still walk with confidence. He had no doubts she was giving them every bit of hell possible. By the end, they might even thank him for taking her off their hands.

The day grew late and the sun eased toward the desert horizon. The angle of the light ricocheted off the glassy water of the river and the city came alive with the cooling temperature. The complex grew more active as well. The guards patrolled in shorter time intervals and people dressed in various states of formality passed across the porch.

His spine stiffened and his breath caught when he saw the familiar curls of black hair and arrogant stride of Nikanuur. Beside him a rotund man scuttled along chattering with agitation and motioning emphatically. The weight of Derian's Colt 1911 seared into his side. The temptation to attempt a shot at the murderous *viator* gripped him, but it would put the rescue attempt at risk. He didn't make a move and the two men disappeared through the door and into the bowels of the complex.

Night replaced dusk and he planned his next move. As he was about to slide off the side of the building he spied furtive movements in the shadows. He froze and watched as several figures dashed from cover, their costume unmistakably modern.

Derian shifted to get a better look. One of the men moved into the light from a torch outside a small shop and the shine of golden locks brushed over thin shoulders glittered in the night. Derian cursed under his breath.

He crawled down the building in a rush, landing a little harder than intended, but was up and running before his body could complain. Tom Roy was about to put a very large kink in his plans. There was no way he would let that stupid hippy get in his way.

Five guns were drawn on him when he joined them in the shadows. He hissed, "What the hell are you doing here Tom?"

"Damn it Derian, you're going to blow our cover," Tom said, irritation flying off the blond man's tense shoulders.

"You blew your own cover. You're running around like a bunch of teenagers planning to spray paint traffic signs," Derian said.

Tom puffed out his chest and started to argue when a strong hand slapped his shoulder.

"Don't you start, Tom Roy. We're here to get something done, not fight with the past." A heavy set woman with ancient eyes lined in wrinkles that spoke of years of laughter stepped into the light. "You're from the *Domus* aren't you?"

"I am. What are you doing here?"

The old woman looked tired, but resolute. Whatever had brought this ragtag group to Babylon wasn't pleasant. "After you left, we were set on by the group in that building. They took a number of our family; including his pregnant wife."She nodded toward Tom. "We've come to take them back."

"You're out of your league. You can't take on a group like this." He scowled at Tom. "You're a damn fool thinking you can go in there with five men and an old woman. What do you think you can do? This is a job for the *Domus*."

"Damn you. When has the *Domus* ever helped us? What have they done but sit and let this happen?" Tom hissed in reply.

Derian tempered his tongue. The man was right. The *Domus* was ineffective. They hadn't seen this coming and now he was attempting to do the very same thing as these five—alone. The man had a wife and child to save. And he had Hailey. Who would have thought that he and Tom Roy would one day be playing on the same side?

"Perhaps you are right," Derian said. Tom opened his mouth to respond, but promptly shut it. Derian pressed his advantage, "We seem to have the same goal in mind. I think I can help you."

***

Whoever had taken the picture couldn't keep a camera still. Blurred lines and dull colors made it tough to see detail, but it was definitely a plane. Hailey looked up at Carlo.

"Exactly how do you expect me to land on a plane I have never been on?"

"I am sure you will find a way."

He was definitely not helping. She looked back down at the picture. It was a small plane, not like the massive people movers she was used to. Its sleek contours reeked of affluence. Why on Earth did he want her on that plane? "So just land on that plane. Then what? We go for a joy ride?"

There were no more smiles coming from him this time. Whatever he had in mind, he was dead serious. This seemed to be a little more complicated than a simple test of her ability.

"You need to land on this plane on November 3rd in the year 2007. The morning should be general enough," Carlo said.

"Say what? You want me to—" Hailey clamped her mouth shut and squinted at the photograph. "You expect me to do that by just looking at a damn picture?"

He pulled out a second photograph from a manila folder. "This was taken of the plane just before it took off the morning of the third. Focus on this and aim for a little later."

Disbelief was a poor description for how she felt. "If it is so damn easy, you do it and I'll follow."

His face grew pinched and he closed his eyes. She imagined he was counting to ten. When his eyes reopened he was back to his usual jocular self. Oh to permanently wipe that expression from his face, it was a dream to hold on to. He pulled a third photo from the folder. It showed a black metal box with several lights and unmarked switches.

"When you are on the plane you will need to get to this box." He pointed to the switch in the middle. "Turn this off. Then wait for me to arrive."

"Ok, seriously? What is this about?" Whatever he was after she knew she wouldn't like.

"Just do it," he growled.

"And why exactly would I do this? What makes you think I won't just take off to another time and get help?"

He smiled that awful smile again and she knew he had her. "Because not only do we have the key to keeping you sane, but we have your great-grandmother."

The reminder really hadn't been necessary. She wouldn't leave Poppi with the bastards. If there were a chance that she could land somewhere and prevent what had happened she would have jumped on it in an instant. But how could she be certain any of it would work? She could try to find Derian, but she had seen how easily Carlo shot Lucius. The man would have no problem doing the same to her great-grandmother. She was screwed and they both knew it.

"Fine. But if I end up falling to my death because I miss the plane it's your ass."

She closed her eyes and focused on the photograph. There had only been one time she'd successfully landed in a place she intended. And that had been her home. Now she was shooting for a moving target. One that hung thousands of feet in the air. She grimaced. What could possibly go wrong?

The familiar tingle sizzled at the base of her neck. She took a deep breath and hoped for a miracle. She opened her eyes and found herself sitting in a soft leather seat. The small window beside her opened to the vast blue sky over an expanse of landless sea. That jump had been ridiculously easy. Maybe she was getting good at this time travel shit.

Movement to her left brought her attention to a thin man scrunched up in his own seat, his mouth hung open in mid snore. The soft murmur of voices hummed in her ears. She huddled down and debated her next move. How could she possibly explain her sudden appearance on what was quite obviously a private jet? Her last stowaway appearance hadn't been exactly well received.

Ample legroom provided plenty of room for her to crawl through. But then she would have to pick a direction and hope she chose right. A diversion would be nice, but she was at a loss on how to create one.

The voices quieted and the only sound was the soft rumble of the plane. It was hardly loud enough to cover the noise she would make scooting through the cabin. The man beside her shifted again. She had to get moving. As she slid off the cushy seat to the floor a tall man in an Armani suit walked past in the aisle. He didn't bother to check the seats. A shaky breath hissed from between her lips. What was she doing here? She was no super spy.

The plane rattled and shook for several seconds. A voice came over the speaker, "We're hitting some turbulence gentlemen. You may want to take a seat until things settle down."

The well dressed gentleman passed by again, grumbling as he went. Hailey shimmied around the sleeping man's legs and crawled hurriedly down the aisle while the other's back was turned. The cabin was small so she made it just in time to slide out of view. She huddled in the corner of a tiny kitchenette. A cart rattled in its restraints. The two small seats usually reserved for the stewards, remained blissfully unoccupied. A thin door stood closed on the opposite wall. Hailey peeked down the aisle. Based on the way things were set up, she had to be at the back of the plane. She looked at the door. The little black box had to be in there. Otherwise, she was creeping closer to being shit-out-of-luck.

The door opened with a soft click. She stepped in and closed the door, hoping no one would hear it shut over the planes struggling movements through the uncooperative air. The room was pitch-black. Finding anything in the darkness was going to be a serious challenge. With one hand on a wall she tentatively stepped through the room. A stack of luggage sent her sprawling on the floor and she cursed Carlo and his idiotic plan.

Five minutes of floundering around the room rewarded her with success. Her fingers passed over the box and its three switches. She clicked down the center switch and waited. It wasn't long before she felt Carlo appear at her side.

"You didn't bother to find a light switch?" he grumbled.

That would have been far too logical, she thought then answered, "I didn't want to have to see your ugly face."

He growled and stumbled over the same luggage she had earlier. She stifled a giggle. The light blared and her eyes took a moment to grow accustomed to the glare. Carlo had changed out of his usual finely pressed slacks and dress shirt and replaced them with the same type of heavy pants and shirt that Derian wore so well. Carlo, with his thin chest and skinny legs, couldn't hold a candle to Derian in that getup. It made her smile.

He pulled open the door and peered into the cabin. "How many are there?"

"Two and the captain," she said. At least, that's how many she knew of. With any luck there were thirty men in there with a howitzer.

He held out a hand. "Come with me."

"No way dude, this is your deal"

He turned and raised a brow. She sighed in resignation. Forget the howitzer, now she hoped for Nerf guns and padded bats.

Carlo pulled a pistol from a holster at his hip. He pushed Hailey out the door and prodded her down the aisle. It took a moment, but eventually they were noticed. Four heads popped up over the seats. He growled into her ear. "Three?"

"I may have miscounted." The sleeping gentleman hadn't made an appearance yet either, but she decided to keep that to herself.

The men stood, each holding their own weapon of choice. Carlo addressed them, "Gentlemen, I am here to pick up a package, and then I will be on my way."

One of the men took the lead, his gun leveled on the two unexpected guests. "You aren't taking anything. There are five against your two."

"Actually, it is five to one." Carlo pulled Hailey against his chest and put the gun to her head.

"What?? Are you crazy?" she squeaked.

The men didn't seem convinced. Carlo pulled back the hammer. Hailey believed him. It was just her luck. Bullet, insanity—what did it matter? Either way her brain was going to be worthless. "Dude, really? Who brings their own hostage? Was this your big plan? Because I am really not impressed."

"Shut up." His hand tightened around her arm. The number of bruises she was getting from this man's fingers was ridiculous. She wrenched herself out of his grasp and turned to poke her finger into his chest.

"Shut up? Shut up??" Her voice reached an octave even she didn't know she could hit. "I am sick and tired of this shit! I'm leaving!"

Carlo's mouth grew pinched and his nose flared. She may have finally reached his threshold, which suggested a quick retreat was the wisest move. The tingle at the back of her neck started but he slapped her before she could continue. It shocked her out of her jump. "What the hell."

One of the men started forward and Carlo shot him in the chest. Hailey hit the floor then wedged herself between two rows of seats. Shots rang out all around her. "Oh my god, oh my god, oh my god."

The room grew quiet. She desperately wanted to peek out to see who had won the round, but couldn't bring herself to do it. Steps thumped down the aisle away from her. Shouts came from the front of the plane and then two more shots fired. She shook, her head rang and her legs felt like they'd planted roots. She might be dying, but she really didn't want to go this way. She didn't want to die in any way. Did she possibly have enough in her for a final fight?

The footsteps returned and she looked up to Carlo grinning down at her. Not a hair was out of place. His gun was holstered and a black briefcase hung in his hand. The bastard had won. Now what?

"Time to go." He yanked her to her feet.

Hailey put a hand out for balance then swiped her fist at his ridiculously handsome face. He caught it with his free hand and wrenched her around, pulling her arm up into a painful pin.

"You were going to kill me!" she cried.

"The thought has merit." He let go and shoved her forward. "But the need has passed. We have to leave."

"I hate you."

"That was inevitable," he smoothly replied as he brushed his pants where they'd wrinkled.

Hailey looked down the plane. Two bodies hung off their seats, blood dripped from shots to their heads. Another lay twisted in the aisle. "You killed them all. They all had guns, how did you kill them all?"

"I have been doing this quite a bit longer than they have." The ring of truth in the words made the arrogance far more irritating. She couldn't think of anything better than seeing this man fail. Everyone met failure. She wanted to be there when it happened to him.

"The plane is going down. We need to go," Carlo said.

"I am not going with you."

"Then you die either way, with the plane or..." He tapped the side of his head. She growled in frustration and punched the chair beside her. She had no choice in the matter. Not unless she did want to die. If that happened she wouldn't get the pleasure of seeing Carlo meet his end. No. She was going with him. There had to be a way to beat them, she just hadn't found it yet.

23

Locked away in her room again, Hailey paced in front of the window. Outside, the sun sank behind several buildings and people scurried through the streets taking advantage of the cooler temperatures before it became too dark to get anything done. She lifted her hair off the back of her neck and let the cool breeze dry some of the sweat that hadn't yet evaporated. Central air was definitely one of the great inventions of mankind and she missed it terribly. There had to be a good reason they hadn't picked a more modern era to hide their secret lair.

Sticking her head out the window she looked down into the same courtyard where she and Carlo had just left. It was quiet and deceptively beautiful. Looking at it now brought back the vision of death and terror. Somehow she'd grown stupidly sure of herself around Carlo. She lashed out at him like he was a bad puppy. His comfort with killing broke the spell she'd been under and finally the sick sense of fear she'd been running from settled deep in her stomach.

When they'd arrived back he'd been in a hurry to deliver his prize. Thankfully he didn't need her along. It was a sweet little break from the pressure of his presence and she had the time to temper her fear. It irked her to no end that his blood circulated very happily through her veins. She needed to find where they kept the stuff that canceled it from her system.

Escaping Babylon was a priority. But getting any piece of the sadistic bastard out of her was paramount. After all, she couldn't come up with a good plan when she was distracted by the sheer terror of Carlo and her being connected— forever. Her stomach twisted in giant anxiety riddled knots.

She tried the door. It was still locked. She sighed. Only the insane keep trying the same thing expecting a different result. Who said that? Einstein? No wonder they called the man a genius. She wandered over to the window and looked out. Night finally beat back the dusk. A small torch burned in the corner of the courtyard farthest from her room. The guards wouldn't patrol a courtyard inside a building.

Pulling herself up, she balanced on the bottom of the window and felt the outside walls. Her fingers poked and prodded and found the chinks and cracks between each mud brick. They would serve well as handholds. Maintaining these walls had obviously not been a high priority. It was fantastic. It was fortuitous. It was—what was she thinking? She wasn't a gymnast! She was three stories up!

Pacing was a much safer bet, which she kept up for another ten minutes before she found herself leaning out the window again. Waiting was just not something she was willing to do. What could happen? So what if Carlo found her lifeless and broken body on the floor of the courtyard. It would serve him right.

Halfway down the wall she seriously started to question her ability to make sane decisions. Her arms burned and her legs shook from the strain. The fatigue from days on the run had her muscles protesting this new insult. If they could just hold out a little longer, she promised to do everything in her power to escape and find the nearest masseuse. Her leg cramped up and she held on for everything she was worth. Forget the masseuse; her body was acting like a spoiled child. She was going to join a gym.

When she finally made it to the ground she sank below a stand of bushes and let her body rest and nerves settle. When the guards discovered she'd left the room she'd need her reserve back. Perhaps just a few more minutes of rest would be alright.

***

Momma Joe made an impressive fruit seller. Derian peered from the shadows as she waddled up to the front entrance. In her basket sat a number of delicacies to tempt the most vigilant of guards. Beneath those were props for diversion courtesy of Tom Roy.

Before they solidified the plan, the men had filled him in on the events that proceeded Hailey's arrival on the beach. She had failed to mention walking into a force of armed men in an attempt to buy time for Tom Roy's people. Part of him admired her courage, the other part wanted to shake her senseless. But first he had to find her.

Momma Joe slanted a sly grin up at the two guards as she pulled aside the fabric covering her basket. Derian hustled down the side of the building toward the back. He didn't have much time before the diversion distracted the complex's guards from their assigned posts. Three of Tom Roy's men waited for him at the corner. They both fiddled nervously with their weapons making Derian grateful for the cover of darkness. If they were successful this night, it would be by the pure grace of circumstance.

Shouts flooded the night and a large boom punctured the air. Derian waited until he heard running footsteps stomp across the second story porch. Then he waited another few moments to let the last of Nikanuur's men make their way toward the front of the building, before he motioned for his companions to hoist him up. The wood banisters were a beautiful decorative element. With the men grunting beneath him and his boots treading heavily on their shoulders, the round wood became excellent handholds to pull him onto the ledge. He swung over and onto the walkway, then waved the men away.

Only a breath was between him and discovery, so he hurried toward the door and listened for anyone approaching. It seemed fickle fortune was on his side and he followed the stairs down into a hall filled with the soft glow of low powered lights. Nikanuur had obviously been unwilling to give up the benefits of modern invention. Derian listened for the buzz of a generator and was rewarded when he found a small room filled with storage and machinery essential to providing power to the facility.

The discovery did solve the electrical mystery but wasn't what he was looking for. He had to find where Nikanuur kept his prisoners. He continued on. Silence followed as he slipped down the hall, opening and closing doors. The hard mud walls gave way to glass. Flattening himself against the wall he peered into the rooms illuminated only by the little light available from the light fixtures. A figure crouched in the far corner of the cell rocking back and forth, their hands covering their ears as if to shut out the sounds of madness.

Another of Nikanuur's victims and more than likely one of the many missing *viator*.

Derian continued on. He passed several more cells each with *viators* falling into various levels of insanity before he came upon a room with three women. They sat together on the floor leaning against each other for support, each heavy with pregnancy. One had to be Tom Roy's wife. He moved past quietly, not wanting them to be alerted to his presence yet, not while he lacked the ability to free them.

The thought of what Nikanuur intended for the pregnant woman disturbed him. How many newborns had the man already gotten his hands on? How could so many disappearances have happened without the *Domus* being aware? The influence of the conspiracy must have been established well in the past and could explain why there had been so few assignments of merit for the last several decades. The *Domus* had been lulled into a false sense of security and they were paying for it now.

Had Lucius known the extent of the deception his wrath would have been unrestrained. Sadness filled his heart, but he pushed it to the side. He would mourn the death of his friend and teacher when the crisis passed.

The hall ended at a single door. It opened with a soft click and a slight groan of the hinges. He was unprepared to face the guard inside. All the other rooms had been empty beyond the prisoners, but not this one. Derian ran at the guard before the man had a chance to react. They flew across the room, grappling for the upper hand. He had the other man controlled by the shoulders but hadn't gotten the leverage needed to completely incapacitate him.

The guard pistoned his legs up and catapulted them into the glass wall separating the room from another cell. A fist knocked on the other side of the glass by his head and he could hear the muted sounds of Poppi screeching at him, "Do you want to hurry this up?"

Had the guard not been trying to choke him, he might have smiled. A loud boom sounded from the floor above. Plaster fell from the ceiling sending a flurry of dust into the guards face and distracting him from squeezing his fingers around his opponent's neck. Derian pressed his advantage and kneed the man in the kidneys sending him to the ground in a wheeze. He grabbed the keys that hung from the man's belt to release Poppi. She stormed out, went directly to the groaning guard and kicked him in the face.

"Poppi! That wasn't—," Derian said.

"It was absolutely necessary. He's a sick son of a bitch and we're leaving it at that," Poppi growled. Derian put up his hands and let it lay. He was not the man to get between Poppi and her source of fury. They drug the unconscious and bleeding man into the cell and locked him in. Another boom shook through the building, bringing chunks of mud brick down with the plaster.

"I take it those explosions are yours," Poppi said.

Derian walked back into the hall. "Tom Roy actually."

Poppi laughed, "Delicious."

"Where's Hailey?" he asked as he tugged her from the room. The three pregnant women were up and trembling when he reached their cell. He sorted through the keys and finally found one that released the women.

"They have her in another part of the building. I haven't seen her since this morning," Poppi said as she shooed the prisoners toward the exit.

Derian cursed under his breath. It would have been too much to hope for her to be in the first place he looked. He moved down the hall and started opening the other cells. Poppi followed close behind and asked, "Are you sure we want to let them all out? Some look a little cooked in the brain."

Derian kept unlocking doors. At the very least the prisoners would serve as a distraction. At best, they could be taken somewhere safe. He led them up the stairs toward the porch. They were a beat up group, but they moved with an eager step toward freedom. At the rail he looked over and was relieved to see Momma Joe and another of Tom Roy's men waiting for them.

In the time he'd taken releasing the prisoners they'd acquired a rope. The end sailed up to him and he tied it to the thick post holding the ceiling up above the walkway. Derian grabbed Poppi by the arm and said, "Get these people down there. Momma Joe has magnets to get you all ready to jump."

"Where are you going?" she asked.

"To find Hailey." He took off running before she could respond. The woman would want to come with him, but he couldn't afford the help. Time was running out. Tom Roy intended to burn the laboratory to the ground. As soon as he knew his wife was safe there wouldn't be any way to stop him.

At the end of the walkway he had a choice. Stairs led up into the building and another set led down. He chose down. Nikanuur had come from that direction earlier. It had to be the main laboratory; if Hailey was incapacitated, it had to be there.

The explosions knocked out the connections from the lights to the generator, leaving the narrow hall bathed in darkness. He pressed a hand to the cool mud bricks and slowed his step. It wouldn't do any good if he twisted an ankle barreling down the hall. This passage lacked the glass cells but had just as many doors to investigate. After the first few he gave up and assumed the main lab would be at the end just like Poppi's cell.

The gamble paid off when he reached an open door. The darkness prevented him from seeing the room but the air felt freer, as though it had plenty of space to circulate. He entered, but stopped dead when he heard a bang and a muttered curse. The voice was unmistakably female. A second bang was followed by the crash of aluminum and much louder cursing.

"Hailey," Derian whispered, his voice echoing in the vast empty space.

"Shit!" she said. The room grew silent.

"Hailey."

"Derian?"

He started toward her voice and answered, "Yes."

"Oh my god, Dude. You would not believe the crap I have been through," her voice rang with relief. He loved to hear the strength in her voice. Whatever they had done to her, it hadn't taken away her spirit or determination. It also appeared they hadn't been able to control her movements; otherwise she wouldn't be stumbling around alone in their lab.

"We need to go. The building is not going to last long," Derian said.

More clangs trumpeted her rummaging. "Hold on. I have to find something."

"Hailey."

The sound of a cart being moved heralded her next comment, "Seriously, just a minute."

Another explosion went off and Derian knew more would follow in quick succession. By this time Tom had to know his wife was safe. If they didn't leave they would be buried under three stories of rubble. He followed the sounds she made and grabbed her by the arm. "There isn't time."

She snatched his shirt, pulled him down and kissed him. His lips sizzled like water over a hot griddle. His body reacted swiftly to her touch despite the very dire situation they were in. She pulled back and breathed, "Sorry. I missed you. We can go now."

They hurried through the hall and two more explosions went off. Luckily these were in different parts of the complex. He tugged her up the stairs and out onto the porch. His first look at her was breathtaking. In the shadows he could just make out her features — her eyes were shining.

The rope still hung to the street below. Hailey looked down and grumbled under her breath, "Again?"

"What?"

"Never mind, let's go." She swung one leg over the rail just as Momma Joe stepped out of the shadows.

"Do y'all have Poppi with you?" Momma Joe asked.

"She was supposed to be with you," he said. Hailey looked down at the large woman holding the rope below. She looked back up at Derian with a frown.

"She was, but said she had to go back to find her granddaughter," Momma Joe said.

Her granddaughter? Poppi knew he had come back for Hailey. Frustration flung itself full force back into his chest. Momma Joe spoke in the false shout used when trying to cross a distance and not be overheard, "We didn't get to take out the implant before she went back in!"

Hailey swung her leg back over the rail. Derian said, "No. Get down the rope."

"She went looking for Moina, Derian. I have to find her." She started toward the stairs leading up into the building.

"There are fires all over this building! I'll go get her, just get out of here." He grabbed her and pushed her back toward the rope. She pushed against his chest.

"No Derian! I am going. I am not leaving without you or Poppi," she argued. He resisted the urge to throw her down to Momma Joe. If he thought she would stay down there it would have been a viable option. She realized her advantage. "I'm sorry Derian. They're family."

He growled out a curse. Then pulled out his Glock and gave it to her. "If things get bad in there and I tell you to leave, you listen to me."

She nodded, her lips set thin with determination. They went up the stairs and then hid behind a large pillar as three guards ran past. Once the way was empty they continued on, Hailey led them through halls she'd only just discovered while searching for the lab. The smell of burning wood filled their noses. The deeper they searched the thicker the air became, stinging their eyes and making it harder to see.

Derian was close to calling the mission over when they found them. But not alone. The dark haired man that had accompanied Hailey earlier had Moina by the hair; tears streaked her face, as he yanked her roughly to her knees. Nikanuur stood beside them, his face covered in soot and twisted with anger. Poppi was braced for action, facing both men.

Hailey raised her arm and pointed her gun at the men. "Let her go, Carlo."

"Ah, there you are. We were wondering." Carlo lifted his lips in a derisive smile, then looked squarely at Derian. "So this is the man you ladies were so certain would come to your rescue."

Nikanuur giggled beside him. Clearly the ancient scientist was not pulling the strings in this situation. Lucius would have been happy to know his interpretation had been the correct one. Carlo was a stranger, not someone that had spent time at the *Domus*, or Derian would have known him.

"Let her go," Hailey repeated.

"I think I will keep her actually. Unless you would like to come with us instead?" Hailey started forward just as another explosion struck. This one blew out the side of the room closest to the door sending rubble flying through the air. Dust and smoke billowed. Hailey hit the ground at the deafening sound. Her instinct, as always, was spot on. Derian reached down to lift her to her feet.

In the depth of the shadows Derian could see the others moving through the dust. Coughing, Poppi came toward them, her arms around Moina. Blood poured from the blond woman's forehead.

"We have to get out of here. A wood beam landed on Carlo. But he's awake and pissed," Poppi said.

Derian nodded and turned toward their exit. It was gone, covered in debris. "We have to jump."

Hailey looked worried. "Poppi still has the implant."

Poppi grinned and said, "No problem. You three jump. I'll just crawl out of here and meet you somewhere later."

Hailey scowled at her. "Whatever. We're not leaving you." She ran toward the back of the room. "Carlo had a magnet. I'll go see if he still does."

Derian spied a shadow moving through the dust. "Hailey! Wait!"

The warning was late, but not for Hailey. Derian felt a piercing pain lance through is chest. The sound of several more shots and shouting accompanied him as he fell to the ground. Then Hailey was by his side. "Shit. Derian."

She pressed her hand against the wound and white sparks flashed in his eyes.

"Hailey, I..." He coughed.

"Don't you dare tell me you love me now. You are going to tell me that later, when you're not dying and there is a big bed waiting for us. This always happens in the movies. The guy says he loves her when he thinks he's dying and then he wakes up in a hospital with her smiling down at her. Won't you feel stupid when that happens." Hailey was babbling. She looked up as Poppi came over to join her great-granddaughter. Both women were breathing heavy, their chests fluttering in deep emotion. He must look really bad if they were working that hard to put on a brave front. His hands curled around hers.

"You have to go Hailey," he told her but she shook her head. He pulled her hand to his lips and kissed it. "Please."

Darkness enveloped his head and he had to let himself go into oblivion.

24

His eyes shut. He was leaving her. "Oh hell no."

Hailey looked up at her great-grandmother. The woman stood wringing her hands and whispered, "That's a lot of blood baby doll."

"No shit. Get your ass down here and put pressure on the wound," Hailey said.

Poppi complied and Hailey lurched to her feet to run to the area where the blast had come into the room. Debris lay scattered everywhere blocking the door. The room had one entrance, no windows, and smoke poured into all available space. She turned back to shout at Poppi, "Where's Moina?"

"Gone. Jumped." Poppi shrugged, but sadness welled up behind her eyes. Given the chance, Hailey would strangle Moina for abandoning her great-grandmother. But, if she didn't get them all out of there, it wouldn't happen.

Nikanuur was gone as well. The weasel probably jumped as soon as things got too exciting. She pulled the gun from her waistband. Something told her Carlo hadn't quite given up on her yet. The bastard had found a way out from under the beam that had nailed him earlier. Hailey moved to the wall and watched the shadows. Poppi's coughs betrayed her location. He would expect to find her beside her great-grandmother. The bastard would shoot them in the back if it suited his purpose. That they were both still alive suggested they still had value.

Movement to her left drew her eye. "There you are you asshole," Hailey whispered. Pointing the gun, she pulled the trigger. It jumped in her hand and she blinked. A muffled thud sounded as he hit the floor. She let out a shaky breath, somehow she'd hit him. When she approached blood seeped from his wound onto the floor, his eyes closed. She kicked him and he didn't move. She kicked him again, just to be sure. His chest still lifted with breath, but she was satisfied with him being unconscious. The magnet gave itself up after a few seconds of rifling. She kicked him again for good measure.

Poppi let out a whoosh of relief when Hailey ran back, holding the magnet in her hand. "Girl, I thought he'd got you."

"Oh please, he's an amateur," Hailey said as she lifted Poppi's tangled hair and placed the magnet on her neck. The pain darkened her eyes, but she held solid and smiled at Hailey when it finally came lose.

A red glow pierced the smoke. They were running out of time. She looked to Poppi and said, "You need to jump."

"But Derian."

"Don't worry. I am going to try something." Hailey was pretty certain it wouldn't work. After all, Derian had said it couldn't be done. But then again...

"I'm not leaving you." Poppi coughed and Hailey joined her on the ground to where the smoke had yet to grasp all the breathable air.

She put a hand on her great-grandmother's leg. "Trust me, please"

They stared at each other in silence while Poppi decided her move. She had been taking care of herself for millennia and the self-preservation instinct was incredibly high. Hailey grew impatient. There wasn't time for internal battles of conscience. "Please, I can't worry about you and Derian. I'm going to try and jump with him."

"That's not possible," Poppi said.

"It's worth a shot. You can stay and watch or you can leave before it gets so bad in here that none of us gets out."

Tears filled Poppi's eyes. She lunged at Hailey and wrapped her in a desperate embrace. "Ok baby doll. I'll catch up with you later."

Both women knew as Poppi faded from view that they might very well never see each other again. But Hailey didn't dwell. This would work, or it wouldn't. Either way she wasn't leaving him behind.

The blood still oozed, but not like it had. She placed two fingers against his neck. Encouraged by a faint pulse she brushed his hair away from his face. His complexion had grayed and his breath was labored. If only he hadn't lost consciousness. He might have actually been able to get himself out of here himself. Ah well, no time for what-ifs.

She wrapped her arms around his shoulders and laid her head over his heart. The coppery tang of blood filled her nostrils. Her experience with gunshot wounds was limited — limited as in non-existent. She needed to get him somewhere safe. Now.

If she pulled this off it could mean big trouble for her. Playing Russian Roulette with her sanity could make for a very unhappy ending. She took solace in the bag tied about her waist filled with samples from the lab. There was no way to know which held the drug she needed to prevent insanity. With luck she would have time after the jump to figure it out.

The tingle warmed her neck and she focused intently on holding on to him. The smoke in the air made her dizzy and if she put this off any longer they would both be unconscious — and dead. But she was terrified to discover she couldn't do it. What if she jumped and couldn't hold on to him? Could she really live without him?

His soft breath rose in his chest and she felt her heart stir. She had to try.

***

"Girlfriend, is that man bleeding on my new couch?"

Hailey came awake with a jerk, sending shock waves of pain through her head. She hadn't died. Death couldn't hurt this much. She must be dying.

"Jesus, Hailey. You look like crap." Jason stood above her, a cup of tea in one hand his remote in the other. "How did you get on my couch? I just left the room."

She grinned at him. He flinched, so it must not have been pleasant. But she was so stoked that it worked. Another super power to add to her list and this one was welcome.

Derian's breath came steady and in the light the blood didn't look that bad. Well, that wasn't true. It looked awful, but it wasn't the giant gaping wound she thought it had been in Babylon. And the blood had stopped flowing. It was just the left over from the shirt that had soaked into the couch.

Granted, Jason would still have a hell of a time getting it out of his new purple suede couch. Hailey breathed, "We, uh, kind of need some help," her voice ground out like a fifty year smoker.

Jason put down his drink and remote to help her stand. He said, "You don't sound good."

"It's been a rough couple weeks."

He looked down at Derian and raised both brows. "I bet. Who's the sweet piece of ass?"

Hailey's laugh nearly came out as a gurgle and she slapped at his arm. "That's Derian. Can we use your guest room? I need to get him cleaned up. It's not as bad as it looks."

"It looks like he's been shot."

"Ok, so it is as bad as it looks. But he's not dying. Help me move him?"

Jason nodded, then slid his arms under Derian's and locked his fingers against his chest. Hailey grabbed the legs and they shuffled toward the guest bedroom. Once they had the bulky *viator* settled in the bed, Jason took off to find clean towels, boil water and collect the first aid kit.

Hailey rolled Derian on his side. The bullet had gone straight through the muscle in his chest, but thankfully hadn't lodged itself there. The back of his shirt was wet with blood and he groaned as she poked at the puffy flesh. She should consider taking him to a hospital, but how would she explain this?

Getting up on the bed, she straddled his legs and kept him on his side, then leaned in to examine where the bullet entered. It was so red with blood she couldn't see how bad it was. She needed to clean it up. If worry hadn't been so prevalent she might be queasy about the whole thing.

"Girl, don't you think you should wait until he's healed?" Hailey swung her head around to find Jason laughing at the door.

"Just shut up and help me get his shirt off."

He put down the bowl of steaming water and handful of towels, then hurried over to help hoist the ruined shirt over Derian's shoulders. The hard sinewy muscle revealed when his clothes slithered over his abdomen teased her senses. Jason moved out of the way and Derian groaned as they eased him back against the pillow.

"Those are some stellar abs babe," Jason whispered in awe.

Tell her about it. She wrenched her gaze away and squashed the urge to punch Jason in the gut. This was her hot stud. "I get it, he's hot. Can we move on please?"

Jason had the good sense to look sheepish. Hailey wet a towel and started to clean the entry wound. Jason sat quietly at the end of the bed and watched. The blood came away with relative ease, but the soot seemed to have ground permanently into his pores. Hailey looked at her hands and grimaced at her own blackened skin. "I will be right back. I should clean up first."

She closed the door to the bathroom and braced her hands against the counter. The face that looked back at her was unfamiliar. Soot formed a thick mask over her fading bruises. Her fingers shook as she ran the water over the grime. Jason was right. She did look like crap and no amount of conditioner would untangle the rat's nest of hair that sat on her head.

Scrubbing away the last of the nastiness from under her fingernails she pushed thoughts of worry about Derian's condition from her mind. They would approach it one step at a time. If she had to take him to the hospital, she would and worry about how to explain it then.

The water that she splashed in her eyes helped to sooth the thudding headache. She needed to get Derian back up and running before she ended up in the hospital herself. Was the headache indication that she was on the verge of going nuts? Nikanuur said she should take the counteragent once a week. It had only been one day. She should be fine. Right?

She ran a worried hand over her face. Now that she had Derian back, she was even more determined to find a solution. Perhaps conventional medicine would have an answer for her. With a final grimace at her reflection, she returned to Derian's side.

Jason pulled the blankets up over Derian's hips and added a second pillow. He then wrapped her in his arms and settled his chin on the crown of her head. His chest rumbled against her back as he said, "Well, it's clean. I have some bandages we can use. But he really should go see a doctor."

"I know. I just don't know how to explain what happened," she said in a whisper. He hugged her tight and let her go. They finished dressing the wound, checked him for fever several times, and turned out the lights to let him sleep. If he would just wake up, she would feel much better. But he had only groaned under their ministrations.

She slumped onto couch. Somehow she would find a way to pay for the couch to be shampooed. Later. After she was done making a mess of it. Jason handed her a beer. And she took a grateful gulp. It hit her stomach like ice on a warm back, the shock welcome. Jason sat on the bright purple ottoman bought especially to coordinate with his couch.

"So what is going on? You get shot at. You disappear. You show up again, have me help you get your car, then you disappear again. And now you show up in my living room with a hot guy with a bullet in his chest."

"It's a little complicated."

"That's what you said last time." He leaned forward. "Who's the dude?"

Hailey paused. Jason had always been pretty open-minded. Even he would find the truth a little out of the comfort zone. But lies would never fly; no one knew a smoke screen better than Jason. "He's my body guard."

"Girl! What do you need a body guard for?" His hands reached out and enveloped hers. It would be so easy to confide everything. It all piled so deep inside it was coming out her ears. But—no, she really couldn't tell him everything.

"I've gotten caught up in some freaky stuff. But I can't tell you more than that. Can you trust me?"

He pulled her off the couch and into his arms. "Of course."

"Can we stay a little while? Just until he's healed and we can figure out where to go next?" She looked up into his soft green eyes. They did nothing for her, even if he had been available to the ladies of Southern California.

"Sure, baby. Anything for you." He grinned and waggled his eyebrows.

"Get your hands off her," a gravelly voice ordered from across the room.

Jason dumped her onto the floor and threw his hands in the air. Once she had her legs untangled she peered up over the ottoman to find Derian leaning against the hall doorjamb and pointing a gun at Jason's chest.

"Dude!" Hailey struggled to get to her feet. Her body protested, but she ordered it silent. Now she had to prevent one of the heroes in her life from killing the other.

***

Sweat threatened to give away his fatigue. It had taken nearly everything he had to lug his body out of the bed at the sound of voices. His gun hung lightly in his hand until he found the blond man oozing his charm all over Hailey. Thought hadn't come to mind when he pointed the gun at the man. It came in a flurry now that the stage was set.

"Dude. It's cool," the blond man said as he held his hands up in surrender.

"Derian. Please put the gun down. This is my friend, Jason," Hailey said. He lowered the gun and leaned his head against the doorframe. Her friend. It was a relief that he wouldn't be fighting for her life again. But his stomach felt hollow. It had never occurred to him that she might have had a love left behind when she first jumped. She had been so tentative about his advances. He should have known.

Hailey stood and came toward him and pointed behind him. "Back to bed. We're safe for now. Jason's letting us crash here for a little bit."

She looped his arm around her shoulder and encouraged him to lean against her as she led him to the bedroom. He welcomed the soft cushion of the mattress. The pain in his chest was intense and moving took his breath away. But the wound was clean and he'd had worse. A day of rest and he would be able to function. His gaze took in her worried expression.

"Should I take you to a hospital?" she asked.

"No, I just need to rest."

"Are you sure? I think you need stitches. Don't you need stitches? And what about pain? Because we don't have any pain meds, except maybe Advil. Do you want some Advil?"

She reached out three times to touch him, each time pulling back before making contact.

"I don't need Advil. I'm sorry about pulling the gun on your friend. I didn't realize who he was."

"Don't apologize. There's no reason you should have known," she said.

"It's obvious by the way he looks at you."

"By the way he looks at me...what are you talking about?" her forehead wrinkled as she asked.

Derian lay quietly. He should just be happy she was safe. For the moment. No matter that she loved another man. It wasn't her fault that he had fallen so completely for her.

He would do everything he could to keep her safe and leave it at that—though so far he hadn't done a particularly good job of it. His memory flashed to the smoke filled room in Babylon and the unexpected gunshot. How had they gotten out?

"Earth to Derian. What did you mean?" Hailey asked.

He shook his head. "How did we get here? I don't remember jumping."

Hailey gave a tentative smile. "Well, you know how we keep finding little things I can do that other *viators* can't?"

His raised brow encouraged her to continue. Her eyes flashed with triumph and said, "I did it."

"Did what?"

"I jumped us both. I was totally freaked that I wouldn't be able to do it, but I did!" She was so excited by her exclamation that she actually touched him. Her hand felt warm against his leg and it took all his self control not to groan out loud. The pain was a welcome distraction, without it he wouldn't be able to hide the effect she had on him.

"That isn't possible," he said. At least it hadn't been. "How did you do it?"

"Just like everything else." She thought for moment then continued, "I had to focus a little more and I think it took a little longer to fade out, but it wasn't that hard."

She was amazing. A feat like that wasn't even possible for the oldest *viator*. She couldn't know how valuable such a gift would be. "Does your father know?"

Her expression lost its glow. "No. Everyone left before I tried it."

"What if it hadn't worked?" he asked.

She cocked her head at him. "It did."

"Hailey..."

Jason popped his head into the room. "Hey babe. I need to head out to run some errands, meet some friends." He nodded his head at Derian. "Are you two going to be alright? Need anything?"

She turned, keeping her hand on his leg. "Maybe some more gauze. Oh! And some Mountain Dew! I haven't had caffeine in like two weeks!"

When Jason left she turned back to Derian, the smallest hint of yellowing bruise sat on her cheekbone. A bit of soot smudged at the hairline above her ear. She hadn't had a shower yet then; he must not have been out very long. Her fingers tightened on his leg. "Are you ok?" she asked.

He stared at the fingers as they pinched absently at the fabric of his pants. "Won't Jason mind you touching me?" The words came out harsher than planned and he cringed.

She lifted her hand and crossed her arms over her chest. Her shoulders squared and chin tipped in challenge. He was being ridiculous. There hadn't been any promises made. No declarations. But she should have told him! Should have told him her affections weren't available.

"Why would he care if I were touching you?" she asked.

"He must be a very open minded gentleman. If you were mine I wouldn't want anyone else touching you."

Her eyebrows shot up. "Is that right?"

She stood and looked down at him, wary and silent like a cowboy in a shootout. Hailey was never silent. He shifted uncomfortably. He should have kept his mouth shut. What business of his had it been? Turning her back she walked to the other side of the room, then spun around, as though a thought had just occurred to her. "Are you jealous?"

"No," he replied, but of course he was.

She slinked up to the bed and warnings went off in his mind like bomb raid sirens. "That is really too bad." She leaned down and braced herself on the bed; her face swooped in to within inches of his face. "Because, if I thought that you were jealous, then I might think you had feelings for me."

His heart thumped erratically and his head grew dizzy from lack of oxygen. When had he stopped breathing?

"And if I thought you had feelings for me, then I might just be overcome with the desire to kiss you. And we both know that wouldn't be good after you've just been shot."

"Hailey...," his voice rattled over strained vocal cords. She wasn't touching him, but every piece of him responded as if she were pressing her soft body against his.

She smiled with mischief when she said, "Jason likes boys."

25

Hailey pushed herself away from Derian. His face had lost all its color and now he looked like he would pass out if she blew on him. She probably needed to lay-off. It had been far too tempting to tease him, even if he were injured. Hailey hadn't had much luck with men in the last several years, but she knew what jealously looked like. She'd seen it enough times in the eyes of Jason's paramours when he paid too much attention to someone across the bar.

It felt great though; knowing that he liked her enough to be jealous. She frowned. She shouldn't read too much into it. Just because he liked her didn't mean he loved her. Pulling away from him she sat on the side of the bed. "I know you don't want to go to the hospital, but we need to get it stitched up."

She felt tired. He looked tired. If her father and his cronies showed up they were so screwed.

"About what I said," he started but she cut him off before he could get started. It was not a conversation she felt ready to have.

"Chill. We're good. I'm more worried about you getting an infection than whether we're miscommunicating. I've never dealt with gunshot wounds before. It's not really my thing."

He laughed. The deep rumble intoxicated her senses. It was such a rare thing for him to laugh it helped to distract her from how terribly weak he looked. She settled onto the bed beside him and felt his forehead.

"I have," he said, his smile fading.

"Have what?"

"Dealt with gunshot wounds. This is not my first war wound and definitely not the worst. We'll keep it clean and I'll have you sew it up. I will be fine."

She felt the color drain from her face. He actually expected her to sew up the wound? She couldn't sew a button on a shirt let alone poke needles through skin. "I don't think that's a great idea. That's what doctors are for."

"And doctors ask questions and we don't have answers. If things were different we could go to the *Domus* for help." A shadowed expression flickered across his face. Apparently things had gotten worse at the *Domus*. No big surprise. Lucius was dead.

"Derian. Your friend, Lucius. He's dead," she said.

His eyes closed and he tightened the grip on her hand. "I know."

"He meant a lot to you."

"Like a father. No — more like an older brother."

Hailey recognized the feeling of loss. Family was a rare commodity for the two of them. Losing Sue had been a tragedy she still hadn't recovered from. Perhaps she never would. Both Sue and Lucius proved that family wasn't determined by blood. It was determined by love and commitment, compassion and constancy. She wanted to take the pain away, but no one could do that. It would live with him until death.

They sat quietly like that for a while. She didn't want to break into his thoughts and didn't want to share hers. He was so beaten up. Soot darkened his eyebrows and his eyes were glassy from the pain. The man was amazing. No matter the crazy situation she ended up in, he still came running to her rescue. She never really thought she would fall for the heroic type. Most of the men she dated wouldn't pull a cat down from a tree let alone run into a burning building gun drawn. Maybe that had been the problem.

His eyes drifted closed and he fell into a deep sleep. But she didn't let go of his hand. Ever since they'd met it had been like two cars passing on the freeway. They would be together for a few fleeting moments and then be thrown in different directions. Now she had him by her side and she didn't want to let go. How had he gotten so solidly in her heart that she couldn't imagine a life without him?

A life that was now significantly more complicated than before. She could time travel, live for thousands of years, and teleport stuff. And who knew what else they would discover.

Of course, insanity waited just around the corner, and just when things were beginning to fall her way. She had a hot guy, new job opportunities. Granted she had bad guys chasing her and no idea how to work her new talents, but at least it was an adventure and better than spending eternity looking at the grey walls of her cubicle. It was too bad Nikanuur hadn't stuck around. She would have liked to have shot him along with Carlo.

She spun around at the soft sound of rustling clothing. Poppi stood across the room, her hair frizzy and her face still covered in soot.

"You didn't even get a shower?" Hailey said.

"I was worried."

Hailey smiled and went over to embrace her great-grandmother. Poppi smelled like a fire pit. She imagined she must stink about the same. With Derian resting it was time to get herself figured out. She pushed Poppi out the door and said, "Come on, you get the shower first. But don't take too long. I want some hot water for myself."

***

The sticky dampness of his sweat soaked pillow was the first sensation he felt. Hot, agonizing pain was the second. Derian pulled himself up and leaned against the headboard. He would need stitches and antibiotics. An infected wound would wreck havoc on their situation.

Pulling the bandage away he peered at the wound. The entry was pretty small; he wasn't eager to see where the bullet had exited. The caliber hadn't been large enough to mangle him, but it still hurt like hell.

Hailey hadn't looked eager to help. It wasn't an unusual reaction and he certainly didn't take it personally. He needed someone to do it. Perhaps her friend would be less squeamish around blood. A doctor had to be the last resort. It wasn't that he expected trouble, but fielding questions from local authorities was a nuisance and they didn't have the time.

The night rose out of the dusk, blanketing the room in shadow. The clock indicated it had been early afternoon when Hailey helped him back into the room. He must have only slept a few hours, though he felt like it had been much longer than that. Pushing off the mattress he shuffled to the door. A drink would do much to help soothe the low grade fever he could feel behind his eyes. Nothing too hot to worry over, but it reminded him again of the threat of infection.

Voices filtered into the hall as he made his way toward the living room. When he finally moved into the light Hailey was smiling and on her way toward him.

"Hey sleepy head. How are you feeling?" She reached a hand out to touch his forehead and frowned.

"It is only a low fever." He looked over to the kitchen table where Jason and Poppi sat, with mirrored expressions of worry. "I could use some water."

She helped him to the table and into a chair. Then she went to the freezer for ice. Poppi looked tired. Her eyes squinted at him like she had just pulled herself out of a deep haze. Jason sat uncomfortably at the table, his expression confused. It seemed Hailey hadn't told her friend quite enough to make him understand. Though thankfully he didn't look terrified.

A tall glass of ice water plunked in front of him and he let the liquid slide down his throat. The rawness from smoke inhalation made it painful, but the cool wetness was welcomed by the rest of his body.

"I think you and Poppi tie for the most sleep. She just woke up too. I think it was close to thirty hours," Hailey said and pulled a chair up next to him.

Thirty hours? His body must have shut down. He couldn't remember the last time he'd slept so long. Poppi smiled at him then laid her head on her arms. How Hailey looked fresh and ready to take on the next adventure was beyond him. She never seemed to stop. Each challenge she faced was dealt with and discarded so she could move on to the next.

"So, we need to do something about your wound. And you won't go to the hospital. So we worked it out." Hailey laid a hand on his arm. It was warm and strong, sending sizzles of pleasure to counteract the pain. If she would run those hands over his body, maybe she could make all the pain go away. "Poppi said she can get some supplies. Antibiotics, stuff like that. "

He raised a brow at Poppi. A sparkling eye peaked out from over her arm. They both knew she would steal the supplies. Having jumped at a very young age, she had to learn how to survive by any means necessary. Unfortunately, she continued her methods even when more ethically sound options were available. It wouldn't do any good to let Hailey know that; he really did want the supplies. Perhaps someday her great-grandmother could explain how she was always able to procure the things they needed.

Derian nodded. A timer went off and Jason sprung up to run to the oven. Hailey rose to help and returned with several plates and a steaming hot pizza. His stomach clenched, letting him know just how hungry he was.

Poppi inhaled several pieces before rising to her feet. She stretched, winked at Jason and then said, "I'll be back in a few. Thanks for dinner."

"Uh, Poppi, you can use the front door," Hailey said. She shifted nervously in her seat. It was an apartment, and likely only had one door to the outside. Jason looked at Hailey like she'd lost a marble. Derian hid his smile. It was better for the man to be confused then to really know how Poppi would have left the room.

The ancient *viator* flipped her hair and strutted to the door. "Now, don't go running off you two. I'm getting tired of hopping all over the place looking for you.

She swooped out and slammed the door. Jason opened his mouth and Hailey held up a hand. "Don't ask. She's a little nutty."

The poor man just shook his head and started cleaning up the dinner plates. Derian watched Hailey. Very little of the past two weeks showed. She was vibrant, alive, and in control of the situation. What place could he have in her life? What place could she have in his? If they were able to get past the current crisis, things would change. Life would settle down and he would, as always, go back to his solitary life.

His body ached for hers. With the imminent threat gone and her an arm's length away, he could feel himself pulling her into his lap. Taking her face into his hands and kissing her, tasting her. Her shirt gaped a little at her breast and his hands tingled in unconscious anticipation.

He shifted his shoulders triggering a sharp pain. It distracted him from his fantasy very well. He couldn't afford to think of sleeping with her. Not if there wasn't a future for them. She couldn't possibly understand what life was like as a *viator*. Forever was a very long time. And forever was what he wanted from her.

"Are you alright? You look a little stressed." Hailey had returned to his side, her hands moved toward his forehead.

"Are you going to keep checking my vital signs every ten minutes like a good nurse?"

She patted his cheek. "There are other vital signs I would like to check, but not with Jason here."

He blanched and she immediately sobered. "I'm sorry. I shouldn't tease like that. Not while you're hurt."

"It's not..."

She stood up and said, "Not very ladylike, I know. I'm just a little stressed. My mouth runs away from me when I get stressed out. I start saying really stupid stuff."

If she only knew the things he wanted her to do with her run away mouth. She went to the hall and looked back. "Poppi said she'd be back pretty quick. I'm going to go get things set up in the bedroom."

When she disappeared into the hall Jason peeked in from the kitchen then jumped into the chair beside Derian and said, "Listen up. I'm heading over to a friend's for a couple of days." He nodded his head toward the hall. "I don't know what is going on here. I know you're into some pretty heavy stuff. But she says you're the real deal. That you've taken good care of her so far." He leaned in and dropped his voice, "She's an awesome chick. Better than most people deserve. Don't screw this up."

Derian nodded. "I know better than you think. Nothing will happen to her."

Jason leaned back in his chair and grinned. "That I'm not worried about. With the two of you? I pity the bad guys. I'm talking about your thing for her."

"I beg your pardon?" Derian asked.

"Please dude, I see how you watch her. You look like a starved puppy in front of a hot dog cart."

Derian blanched. He didn't think it had been that obvious. "I'm not..."

Jason waved him off. "Whatever dude. There are condoms in my dresser. If you feel up to it, give it a shot. She likes you. A lot. Treat her good and she'll be the best thing that's ever happened to you."Jason stood and called toward the hall, "Hailey!"

She popped her head back into the room. "You heading out?"

"Yep. I'll see you in a couple days." Jason picked up a duffle bag and headed to the front door. "I told your boyfriend where to find the condoms, have fun."

"You what?? Dude!" she screeched.

Jason laughed and shut the door behind him. Hailey looked over at Derian, her cheeks rosy with embarrassment. "I am so sorry about him."

She disappeared into the hall again and he smiled to himself. The only thing she seemed to run away from was the thought of sleeping with him. He didn't know if that was encouraging, but it was funny.

A startled yell came from the hall and Derian nearly passed out getting to his feet. His gun wasn't at his side. At some point it had been moved and he had been too fuzzy headed to find it before joining everyone at the table. Cursing his ineptitude he stumbled toward the hall.

Hailey had her finger up and shaking at Poppi. He leaned heavily against the wall in relief. Adrenaline would be enough to react to a crisis, but not enough to keep up an enduring battle. He needed at least another day before he really could react effectively. Hopefully their luck would hold out.

Poppi sauntered up to him and put her arm around his waist. "Come on hero man. Let's get this over with. It's no good having you waddle around like an old lady."

Hailey stood at the entrance to the guest bedroom her arms propped on her hips. "You know what woman, if you weren't family."

"You know you love me. I add excitement to your life," Poppi said then giggled.

"I don't need more excitement in my life." Hailey added another pillow to the pile at the head of the bed. Towels were piled on the side table and hot water had been set out in a large stock pot. Derian slid onto the bed as Hailey fiddled with each towel, unfolding then refolding, making sure each corner matched up with the other.

Poppi grabbed the towels from her hands. "Go sit on the other side and hold his hand."

"I want to help."

"You're spastic. Hold his hand and don't look at the needle." Poppi said and Hailey blanched.

"Do you have issues with needles?" Derian asked.

She settled onto the side of the bed and crushed his fingers in her palm. She hadn't regained any color. "Kind of."

Her nose flared. Kind of was not the word for it. She looked terrified. Derian said, "If you want to wait in the other room..."

She snorted. Then loosened her grip to a less painful pressure. "I'm sorry. I'm a little nervous."

"It will be fine," he said.

And it did turn out fine. It hadn't been nearly as bad as it could have. That's not to say it didn't hurt like hell, but they all got through it alright—mostly. By the end Hailey looked like she'd just had twenty bullets pulled from her gut. She'd jumped each time the needle touched his skin until Poppi told her she was making things more complicated by moving. He spent the rest of the time entertained by her efforts at staying still.

The two women helped him up as they switched out the bedding. Poppi gathered up the wet and bloody towels, then headed out to clean up and call it a night. She winked at Derian as she closed the door. Hailey, with her back to the door, didn't notice. Did everyone think he could make a move on Hailey while recovering from a gunshot wound?

He watched as her fingers gripped the blankets and pulled them up over his abdomen. She tucked and patted but kept her eyes away from his face and his wound.

"Is something wrong?" he asked.

She froze in the middle of readjusting the blankets a third time. When she looked up there was a vulnerability that he'd never seen before. She grabbed his hand and sat, stilling her nervous fidgeting. "I... you keep coming to my rescue. I don't even know what to say." She stood, then started to pace the room, "Every time I need you, you show up. It's amazing. Awesome."

Then she stopped and pursed her lips in a thin line. "You have to stop. I can't take this." Confused, he braced his elbow on the mattress and tried to sit up, but she ran back to the bed and pushed him down. "No, don't get up. See you keep doing that." With a frustrated exclamation she threw up her arms. "You don't pay any attention to yourself; you just go and save me. Then you get shot."

She ran a finger over the wound and he hissed. Her finger pulled back in surprise. "I don't know why I did that. I'm sorry. It's like bruises, you see them and you touch them, and you know it will hurt but you still touch them."

Derian grabbed her hand before she could vault off the bed again. "You're babbling," he said as he pulled her down beside him and tucked her under the arm of his uninjured side. She trembled so slightly he would never have noticed if she weren't pressed up against his body. "We're ok *léof.*"

A tear dripped from her face onto his chest. He held her tight. Eventually she relaxed and her body became heavy against his in a deep sleep. His fingers combed through her hair and he kissed the top of her head.

"I will never stop coming to your rescue," he whispered into her hair.

26

Waking up was like clawing through a bucket of marbles. As consciousness would appear sleep would fall back in around her. Eventually she made it into the daylight to find herself tucked up against Derian. The fingers of one of her hands were splayed across his belly; the other arm was dead asleep between them. She adjusted to bring blood back to it and waited for the inevitable prickly pins.

Her headache had dulled and that was encouraging. Concern ate at her, and she wondered if the constant headaches were one of the wonderful side effects of her father's tampering. But she would worry about that later. At the moment she just wanted to be happily snuggled next to Derian. She shifted her head so she could get a good look at him.

The pallor in his cheeks looked brighter. She reached up and touched his forehead. It was warm, but not any different than the rest of him. He gave off a lot of heat. It was nice, like having a personal furnace through the night. He would come in handy on cold winter nights in Siberia. Maybe they could make a trip to Siberia to test it out.

She grimaced. Maybe not. Siberia had never been high on her travel list, but perhaps Italy during the height of the renaissance. How cool would it be to see the people that created the art and architecture that culture had worshiped for so many years? Her mind reeled at the opportunities. She could spend the rest of her life as a time traveling tourist. If she didn't go crazy before then.

She shook away the dark thoughts. She had never been the type to whine about fate. Everybody had some illness or problem they had to look forward too. Cancer, Alzheimer's, heart disease. Shoot, she was lucky to be around this long. There were so many things that could have gone wrong, like being killed by pirates or Nazis. Or shot by psycho time travelers with obsessive compulsions to rule the world. She could walk out today and get hit by a bus. There wasn't a thing she could do about it. So why worry?

She sighed and wondered if Aunt Sue had given herself the same pep talk. Maybe minus the pirates and Nazis. Derian shifted and tightened his arm around her. A tiny moan escaped her lips. It felt so good to be held in his arms. Sure, they'd hugged a few times and had some crazy hot kisses, but this was seriously the best of all. She could lie here all day.

The wound on his chest looked ok, as far as she could tell. It wasn't puffy or angry looking and he didn't have a fever. She would have to get up and look at his back to see if that one was doing alright, but she just couldn't make herself slide out from under his arm. So she stayed there, content to listen to his heart beat against her ear.

Eventually, the worry grew enough to encourage her to take a look and she lifted his arm to allow her to duck under. A growl made her stop. "Um, Derian?"

"Don't go."

"I need to check your back."

He pulled her back against his side. "It's fine."

"I really just want to check."

"Please, just stay where you are for a few minutes," he asked. Hailey lay quietly for a few minutes. His breathing was deep and strong. He didn't say anything or move and curiosity finally claimed victory. She heaved up and shifted so she sat cross-legged. The reason for him wanting her to stay at his side stood rigid amongst the soft folds of the blanket. She blushed then looked up at his face. His arm was thrown over his eyes. She giggled.

"Jesus, Hailey."

"Dude, don't be embarrassed. Sometimes I wish I had a flag that I could wave when I wanted to get laid," she said, her eyes couldn't stop roving over his body. It was such a yummy body. He groaned in mortification, but she just couldn't help herself. Teasing was fun.

Then again, it wasn't nearly as fun as doing. The two of them had done a silly dance around sex since they'd met. What if this was her last day of sanity? Could she imagine spending it in any better way than with the man she loved?

"So, have you ever seen Indiana Jones?" she asked. He moved his arm to give her a wary glare. "Do you know that scene in the first one where Marion and Indy are on the ship?"

Recognition flashed in his eyes. She widened her lips into a giant Cheshire grin. "Ah, so *viators* do watch movies."

"Of course we watch movies," he grumbled but a light of humor flickered in his eyes.

She laughed. Then leaned toward him to whisper into his ear, "Tell me where it doesn't hurt."

Derian chuckled and pointed at his forehead. Hailey gave him a quick kiss. He pointed to his nose. She responded with another. He pointed to his neck and when she opened her mouth to suck slightly he shivered beneath her touch. Hailey loved kisses on her neck, but had never found a guy that liked it nearly as much as she did. It seemed that finally she had.

Trailing her lips up she found the soft spot beneath the ear where the jaw connected. His good arm came up and his fingers threaded into her hair. Her legs clenched and she wiggled to release the tension building up like a tempest. It had only been a few kisses. How seductive could she be if she got this worked up after just a couple kisses?

She sat up to catch her breath and hopefully gain a little control. He watched her, soundlessly inquiring. He was waiting for her move. She glanced at his wound. "I don't want to hurt you, so maybe we should…"

He pointed to his lips. "These don't hurt." His arm reached up and pulled her down, his mouth hungry and insistent. It tightened her insides like a rubber band aimed at the back of a classmate's head. Her hands strained to run all over his body, but she held back, not wanting to brush against his wound.

Figuring she could at least control one hand she slid it down his chest. The hairs felt soft yet wiry against her palm. He groaned into her mouth, his tongue danced with hers as their lips moved along a current that had them both rushing toward something inevitable. Something that really felt right. She pulled back and looked at him. Both of their chests heaved to pull enough oxygen to survive their desire. "How is this going to work?" she breathed.

"Sit up," he said.

She moved off of him. When he started to push himself up she murmured with concern. He just smiled and leaned his torso against the headboard. Then reached out and pulled her toward him, having her straddle his legs. His erection pushed hard against her and she reached down to rub her hands down its length. They definitely needed to get out of their clothes.

Her shirt flew off a second later. Then she reached back to unhook her bra. Why make him struggle with the contraption when all she really wanted was his hands on her breasts? He complied without direction. Each hand took a breast and his thumbs stroked over her nipples. She nearly surged up off his lap at the bolts of desire that ran from her breasts to between her legs.

His head dipped and he took one taut peak into his mouth. She groaned and let the sheer frustration for release echo through the room. He snaked his strong arm around her waist and pulled her hard against his hips. She responded by circling her hips against him and it was his turn to groan with frustration.

"Can we stop messing around and get your pants off?" she asked.

He chuckled against her breast and it sent a new shiver of anticipation through her skin.

"I'm serious." She pulled back and reached down to unbutton her jeans. It was going to take some acrobatics to get them off. Swinging a leg over, she stumbled off the bed and shimmied out of her pants. She threw her underwear off as well and then jumped back on the bed to help him off with his pants.

When she was finally able to press her naked body against his she sighed in ecstasy. He nuzzled her neck and sent the banked fire roaring back into a blaze. "Oh my god, Derian. Please don't stop."

His hand cupped the soft mound between her legs. A finger slid against the wet slit and grazed against the pert nub that centered her desire. "You, *léof*, are the most amazing thing I have ever found in my life."

The finger slid into her wet entrance and she arched her spine to press harder against his hand. She pleaded, "Please, I want you inside me."

He added a second finger and moved them slowly in then out. Hailey growled and wrapped her hands around his hard length. "I want this in me, now."

His thumb circled around the nub and she shuddered at the intensity. If he didn't stop she would fall apart like an overcooked turkey. She'd never had to beg for it before. Most of the time they were more than happy to get to the big finale. Leave it to Derian to once again prove the exception. His second hand wrapped around and grabbed her ass, kneading into the skin and adding to the build up that warmed from the center of her body.

At one point she'd assumed she was in control of this adventure. But that was lost somewhere along the line. He demanded she lose it before she got what she wanted. She looked into his eyes and saw the challenge, the encouragement. He was determined to make her orgasm like this. Why was she fighting it?

She let go. All her focus turned inward to the sensation of his hands playing against her body. It built so high she felt anxiety like one felt just as they reached the apex of a roller coaster. But it didn't last long as he hit the final button that sent her plummeting down into release.

Her body still shook from the intensity when he slid into her. The nerve endings inside her were super-sensitized and the feel of him made the tiny hairs on her arm stand on end.

He pushed slowly until their bodies met. His fingers tucked a tendril of hair behind her ear and he took her mouth with a gentle kiss.

They moved against each other and with each other. Her hips rose and fell as his arms guided her. Their tongues mimicked the lower halves of their bodies, thrusting and retreating. The crazy anticipation from before was different now, less frantic, but no less intense. It built up with the friction, sending her gasping for air.

They pulled away from the kiss and she watched the desire in his eyes flood toward his release. She cupped the back of his head with one hand, then swooped down to kiss his neck. Sucking and scraping her teeth against his skin. He bucked in response finally reaching his release. Her second followed close behind as he ground his hips against her pelvis sending them both into a shared oblivion.

***

Her head rested on his shoulder, her soft breath puffed against his neck. Thankfully she stopped nuzzling. He couldn't handle her lips in that tender spot. Not for a little while at least. She snuggled in and he wrapped his arm around her waist to pull her closer. She fit so perfectly pressed against him.

The chest wound hurt. It had been a risk, making love when the stitches were so new. He'd been lucky nothing had yanked free in their excitement. But there wasn't an injury that could have kept his hands off of her.

She stirred and started to pull away. He held her tighter and she giggled. He grabbed her hip and said, "Don't laugh. Please."

She wiggled her hips in a little circle. He growled and nuzzled her neck. Two could play at that game. Now she giggled in hyperventilative spasms. "Stop! Derian, please!"

She pushed against him, her finger grazed his wound and he gasped. "Oh my god! I am so sorry!" Pulling off of him she wobbled to find her balance on the hardwood floor. Then searched the room for her clothes.

"Poppi brought some pain medication. Would you like some pain meds? I can go find them for you. Maybe some water. I'm sure you're thirsty, I mean…" She blushed.

"Why do you run away from me?"

She shifted back and forth on her toes, the thoughts streamed across her face at an incredible pace. She cocked her head and asked, "Do I really run away from you?"

"Yes."

"I don't usually run from things."

"No, you don't."

"Hunh." She sat back down, but kept to the foot of the bed and pulled her underwear and bra back on before sitting cross-legged. She wasn't embarrassed by her near nakedness. In fact, she was one of the rare people that seemed completely comfortable in their skin, her self-worth evident in all she did. And she didn't shrink from anything. Except him.

Determination squared her shoulders and her eyes hardened with purpose. "Alright. Here's the thing." She took a fortifying breath. "I'm a little nuts about you. And it freaks me out."

"Nuts?"

Her cheek sunk in where her teeth bit the inside. "You aren't going to make this easy for me are you?" He held a hand out and beckoned her into his arms. She shook her head. "No, I can't think straight when you're touching me."

That boded well for him. Her fingers picked at the feather-stuffed blanket.

"Hailey."

"No, I'm serious."

"So am I. Come here," he said and waved her over with his hand. Despite her wary look she complied and he tucked her beside him, their backs against the headboard. She tensed. It was a vast contrast to the pliant limbs that had wrapped around him only a few minutes before. He leaned down, his lips beside her ear. "I'm nuts about you too."

Her breath surged out of her, "Serious?"

"Yes."

"Well. What exactly does that mean?"

"I don't know. But I am sure we'll figure it out in time," he answered. She tensed again. He thought back over his words and wondered what he had said wrong. He hadn't exactly told her he loved her. Was she worried about hearing the words? "Hailey, you understand, I've never felt like this. And I've never been in love before. But I am positive that is what I feel for you."

She buried her head into his shoulder. He nudged her and said, "Hailey?" Her response was muffled. "Hailey, I can't hear you."

Lifting her head she sighed, "I love you too."

His heart lifted at the proclamation, but a small piece of him worried. Sadness filled her eyes. Sadness wasn't exactly what he expected with a declaration of love. "Hailey, what's wrong?"

"It sucks —," she started.

A knock pounded at the door. Poppi hollered for them to hurry and join her in the living room. Something very important required their attention. Hailey skittered out of the room, but he had to move a little slower. He grinned when he found his pants. Hailey had thrown them across the room in her eagerness to get back into his arms.

"Dude!" He heard her surprised exclamation when he entered the hall. It sounded of surprise, not fear. Nonetheless he hurried to see what had elicited the response.

Lucius sat at the kitchen table and turned to Derian as he entered the room. He looked tired but definitely not dead. Derian wasn't sure how to react at first. He hadn't yet come to terms with his friend's death. Having him show up alive was a twist he hadn't been prepared for. Lucius smiled, but he looked troubled. "Derian."

"Lucius," he replied. So many things were conveyed with those two words. They didn't need to say more. Both men were extremely relieved to see the other alive.

"How did you? But I saw you...," Hailey stuttered, her brows creased and lips set in a frown.

Lucius cracked his neck, his expression maintaining a stern darkness. "It's a long story. We don't have time for it right now."

Poppi rolled her eyes. "He's been a little impatient. But I told him he had to give you two a little more time. Nearly had to tie him down."

Hailey blushed. Sensitivity to the finer skills in human interaction was lost on her great-grandmother. But he was grateful for Poppi's consideration. It had given him those extra few moments with Hailey in his arms.

Lucius glared at Poppi. "Does *she* really need to be here?"

Hailey recovered from her embarrassment and came to her great-grandmother's defense. "Yes she does. She's been a bigger help then you have."

Lucius raised a skeptical brow, but kept his thoughts internal. From experience, Derian knew it had been a wise decision. He sat down at the table and looked to Lucius. "Tell me. What's going on?"

"The *Domus* is shut down," Lucius said.

"Yes, I know. A good portion of Roderic's staff were relocated to Carpathia." The old centurion stiffened his shoulders and his neck strained under the tension. Derian continued, "How much do you know about what happened after you were shot?"

"Not much. I was only able to jump again a few hours ago. I went to the *Domus* and it was completely locked down. No one was in the building. All the records were either missing or destroyed. I couldn't find a single thing that could tell me where everyone went or exactly what happened."

Something big must have gone down while he was in Babylon. Who could have completely shut down the *Domus*? With Rusa removed from power anyone in the Council could be running things. They had no contacts and it seemed the entire staff had been dispersed. The *Domus* was out of commission and it had been accomplished far too easily.

Lucius shook his head, then pressed his palms into his eyes. Whatever he had been through since the confrontation in the *castellum*, it wore on him. Derian took over the story and filled the Magister in on what he'd missed.

Hailey's eyes widened with surprise when he mentioned that Roderic had been removed under suspicion of treason.

She asked, "Do you think it's true?"

Lucius responded, "No. Whoever is manipulating the situation needed him gone. It gave them the excuse to get rid of Rusa as well."

"Rusa can't possibly be the only one on the Council that wasn't corrupt," she said.

"There are several good *viator* on the Council. But we don't know what has become of them. They may have been removed like Rusa, or worse. We can't know," Derian said

Lucius stood, stretching out his tall frame that couldn't stay seated comfortably for long. He began to pace the room. "With Nikanuur's lab destroyed and the *Domus* empty we are low on avenues to pursue." He stopped and looked directly at Hailey. "We need to get Roderic out of Carpathia."

"No." Derian was adamant. Hailey had put herself at risk too many times. She would have to go in alone. And it was too far away for them to be of any help. He wouldn't allow it. Not again. Poppi's crossed arms established her opinion on the matter. For once the woman stood on his side and he appreciated it.

"Is this place protected by a no jump zone?" Hailey asked.

Lucius nodded. He hadn't taken his eyes off her, despite Derian's response. Hailey considered him and Derian knew she was seriously thinking of going in. He said, "It's too dangerous."

"Oh I know it is, but not for the reasons you think." She switched her gaze to Derian. His heart thumped with trepidation at her expression. She drew in a deep breath and said, "There are some unexpected side effects from what my father did to me before I was born. The next time I jump I could turn into a raving lunatic."

27

Hailey filled them in on the side effect of her father's tampering. Once it was all explained Poppi stormed around the apartment yelling in a language Hailey couldn't place. It was typical but heartwarming to know her great-grandmother cared enough to throw one of her tantrums. Derian, on the other hand sat silent. Granted he looked sick, but he hadn't said a thing. What did she expect? They'd just declared their love for each other and then she drops this little black bomb of joy. She regretted not telling him sooner — like, as soon as he was conscious, but there wasn't a damn thing she could do about it now.

Lucius took it a little less personally. "That is inconvenient."

"Dude, you have no idea," she replied.

A slight smile touched his lips and squeezed her shoulder. "You have the most interesting way of describing how you feel." She gave a wry twist to her lips and shrugged.

Poppi finished her tirade and turn it onto Hailey. "You knew about this and you still tried to jump with him?"

"Yes," she said. It hadn't ever been a question really.

"You're an idiot," Poppi spat out.

"You would have done the same. And we don't know whether that would have mattered anyway. Who knows if jumping makes it worse or if it just happens over time? Nikanuur wasn't exactly forthcoming with information."

She crossed her arms and looked pointedly at Derian. By the way he glared back at her it was pretty obvious he thought she was an idiot too. Good thing she didn't care what either of them thought of her. Well, at least in this case.

She glanced up at a very confused Lucius and explained, "Derian was unconscious in a burning building. They're mad at me for saving his life."

"How exactly did you save his life?" Lucius asked.

"I jumped him."

"Not possible," he countered.

"You know, when it comes to me, let's just throw all those assumptions out. Ok? I did it. Period." She stood up from the chair and started toward the hall. "It doesn't matter. So let's drop it. I have some stuff for you guys to look at."

Poppi started to yell again, but Hailey just let it go. She retrieved the bag of vials tucked in a drawer in the guest bedroom. When Derian found her in the lab she hadn't had the time or ability to go through the stash left by Nikanuur and his mole-like assistant. She had no idea if they were what she needed.

She pulled out a vial and watched the clear liquid slide within the cool glass as it tipped. She brought out the rest. They all looked the same. Maybe they *were* all the same. Now *that* would be inconvenient.

She needed the stuff that erased Carlo's ability to track her and whatever Nikanuur developed to stem the side effects. She placed them on the dresser. As far as she knew it could be a rat poison or a something to prevent zits. It was a crap shoot. There wasn't a chemist among them, and the only one they knew was locked up in some dank dungeon.

"Was it too much to ask for you to label them?" Hailey huffed.

"Hailey," a voice said from behind her, startling her from her thoughts. She swung around to find Derian leaning against the shut door.

"I found them." She held up a vial. "You and Lucius will probably want to look at these."

He crossed his arms against his chest, his stony expression unreadable. Was he pissed or just concerned? Hailey said, "I'm sorry I didn't tell you sooner. I meant to. I'm still kind of coming to terms with it myself."

"You shouldn't have tried to jump with me."

"Seriously? Come on. I wasn't going to leave you to die. There wasn't any other way." She crossed her arms too. He wanted a confrontation, fine. She would give him one.

"You could have died."

"We don't know that. And anyway, how exactly is this different from what you do when you're trying to protect me? You even got shot!"

His face lost its color. "You're right. I haven't protected you very well."

"What? Where the hell did you get that from — what from saying trying? You got that from me saying trying? Are we seriously going to argue semantics?" She advanced on him and poked him in the shoulder. He winced. It hadn't been the injured shoulder, but it had been a little hard. She took a step back.

"First off, you have done an excellent job of protecting me. I'm still alive aren't I? I don't exactly make it easy." She grabbed his hand. Everything that filled her heart came up from her chest. Her voice caught in her throat, but he had to hear what she had to say, even if it came out a little soggy. "Second, there is nothing you can say that will ever make me regret what I did. I love you."

"I—, *leof* I can't…"

"Can't stand the thought of a woman saving you?" She smirked as she cut him off.

He grabbed her and pulled her into his arms. "No, I can't stand the thought of losing you. And now…" He frowned down at her so she laid her head against his chest—the uninjured side of course.

Walking into a dangerous situation was one thing. Knowing that your body was a walking time bomb was entirely different. It wasn't like she didn't understand how he felt. She'd experienced it first hand with her Aunt Sue and it sucked royally. Honestly, there wasn't much to say. Except that she loved him. Loved him with everything piece of her heart.

"Derian, I…"

He silenced her with a finger to her lips. Heavy lidded eyes took in each part of her face. His thumb traced her jaw, his fingers tickled her cheek bone. Her lips parted from the soft pleasure of his touch. It wasn't frantic or wildly passionate. But it yanked harder on her soul than the other ever did. This was what it felt like to be loved. How long had she been looking for it? Yet it happened now? She wanted to stomp her feet like a pigtailed brat and scream.

He dropped his head and touched his lips to hers. It was so achingly sweet. She melted against the arm wrapped across her back. Their tongues touched, tentative and playful. The taste sweet and warm, like honey and tea. Her senses filled with his presence. Each slight movement seared a memory of sound, each touch branded her. His teeth nipped her bottom lip and her skin practically flayed itself from her bones.

The kiss went deep to a place where souls danced and the heart ruled. And then the tears fell. The memory of the past few weeks filled her mind. Each moment shared with him was a diamond of joy. Every moment apart a dark shadow. She realized that despite the insanity and danger, she'd never had a better time. Twenty days of adventure with him were worth two thousand years alive and alone.

"Please don't cry," he said his voice a harsh whisper.

She tried to pull away, but his hold gripped her like a vice. Raising her hand she knuckled the tears from her eyes. A soft cough helped to swipe the emotion from her throat. "I'm sorry. It's been crazy. It all just caught up to me."

He pulled her into an embrace and kissed her temple. Then let her step away. Neither of them was eager to put their feelings into words so she retrieved the vials and followed him back to Lucius and Poppi.

The two ancient *viator* sat at the table, eyeing each other like two gamblers at a poker table. Hailey settled into the chair beside her great-grandmother and placed the vials in the center of the table. There were six. Each looked exactly the same.

Lucius picked one up, rolling the glass between his fingers, watching the liquid flow. "From the lab?"

She nodded, not quite sure of her voice. He removed the small rubber stopper and put his nose to the opening. He frowned. Then picked up a second vial and did the same. Everyone watched, silently waiting for him to describe his reaction. He repeated the process for each vial, then set them all down and folded his hands.

Poppi looked like she was going to burst into a nervous attack. Her patience clearly at an end. "Well?"

"I'm not certain," Lucius replied.

"Did they all smell the same?" Hailey asked.

"No. There were three distinct scents," he answered. She hadn't realized she had been holding her breath until it came out in a whoosh. One of those vials could hold the key to hiding from Carlo and another could keep her sane—for a little while at least. Perhaps they could even reproduce them.

Poppi grabbed one and sniffed. "What are they?"

"One took away Derian's connection to me. Another is supposed to help prevent the brain degeneration," Hailey said. Both men looked up at her in surprise.

"That's great! We could figure what is in it and make more!" Poppi replied. "But there are three. What is the third?"

Hailey shrugged. It really could be anything.

"Poison." Three heads snapped to look at Lucius. He leaned back in the chair, his arms crossed. "The same poison they have been using on the *venators*."

Now that was inconvenient. She had a two-thirds chance of getting what she needed. But the risk was immediate death. The odds were in her favor. Perhaps there were tests.

"It seems there is now more reason to free Roderic from his prison," Hailey sighed. It was a frustrating mess.

"We will have to take the traditional route." Lucius stood, his gaze directed at Derian. Hailey's heart skipped. There was little chance he would want her to come along. It meant she and Derian would be separated again. That was completely out of the question.

"I'm going too." Her hands were clenched, her response vehement.

"No," both Derian and Lucius answered.

Poppi laughed and said, "Do you really think you can stop her? She'll just jump and beat you there."

A knock sounded at the door before either man could respond. Hailey ran to answer it, thankful for the excuse to leave the conversation. A small woman with eyes just like a Campbell's Soup kid stood at the door. A smooth black braid hung over her shoulder and to her waist. Her hands wrapped around a large duffle bag that had to be two-thirds her size. When she saw Hailey her smile grew but stopped before it lost its charmingly shy quality. "Hello. I am looking for Lucius. Is he here?"

"Uh. Yes," Hailey answered, not quite sure how to take the visitor.

"Oh! Wonderful. I was worried. It was such a long trip, I did not know if I would make it in time or not. But you look quite well. So I must have." She stepped through the door before Hailey had a chance to invite her in. Her big brown eyes scanned the room.

"Oh yes, this is exactly it." The strange little woman looked down at the couch and frowned. "I do hope you aren't attached to this couch."

"Excuse me?" Who the hell was this woman?

"Grace?" Lucius walked into the room, his voice gruff. The woman threw her bag on the couch and ran to Lucius, launching herself into his arms. He stumbled back and for a moment a smile touched his face. It disappeared, to be replaced with thin lips of disapproval. His arms took her by the shoulders and held her away. "What are you doing here?"

"I told you something terrible was going to happen," Grace said.

"And I told you to stay home," he replied.

Grace propped her arms on her hips and leaned back to look him in the eye. Hailey couldn't help but grin. Something told her this was not a battle the old *viator* would win. Lucius didn't take his eyes off Grace to say, "Hailey, would you mind giving me a moment?"

Hailey snorted. In other words, he didn't want her witnessing his defeat at the hands of a pint-sized woman. Nonetheless, she returned to the kitchen. Derian watched the interchange through the small walkway between the two rooms; his curiosity anything but constrained. Poppi was up and ready to confront the newcomer.

"Sit down Poppi. They need a moment," Hailey ordered.

"Who is she? What is she doing here? Is she a spy?" Poppi didn't sit. Hailey rolled her eyes.

"I don't know, but she and Lucius seem close." Hailey looked back at the couple. The space between the two could be measured in millimeters; the conversation hushed but agitated. "Where do you think he's been all this time?"

Hailey had addressed Derian, but that didn't' stop Poppi from responding, "If he's been shacking up with that chick while we've been battling the bad guys I am going to be so pissed."

"Chill out," Hailey said as she sat down beside Derian and rested her head on his good shoulder. The day was starting to wear her down. Another nap next to Derian would be just the thing. They waited quietly for Lucius to return. The temptation to bring up Roderic's rescue was strong, but she kept her mouth shut. She was tired and confused. So much had happened. So much was unanswered.

In the matter of a few weeks she'd gone from being a bored marketing specialist to a time travelling super hero. Well, skip the hero part, but something was super. She'd been chased, beat up, knocked out, and manipulated. And in all that she'd managed to meet the man of her dreams and fall in love. Who would believe it?

Derian leaned to the side and placed a kiss on her brow. She rested her hand on his leg. The touch warm, the connection electric. Whether he liked it or not, she was going with them. Wasting time hiding when she could be with him was out of the question.

A frustrated shout came from the living room. "Damn it woman!"

All attention swung back on Lucius and Grace. She was smiling up at him. He scowled and Hailey suppressed a giggle. Score one for Grace. Hailey felt quite impressed with her powers of prediction.

When the two joined them in the kitchen Grace extended her hand to Hailey. "I am sorry. I did not properly introduce myself. I am called Grace."

She was young, but her formal speech pattern threw Hailey. "Do you mind me asking when you first jumped?"

Grace blushed, then looked up at Lucius. "Oh, I am not a *viator*."

Before Hailey could ask for more Poppi approached the girl, her face scrunched in suspicion. "You aren't a normal human either, are you?"

Grace's hand fluttered to her chest. Hailey imagined the woman even knew how to do a proper swoon. Lucius put his arm around Grace's shoulders and puffed out his chest. Poppi poked her finger at Grace and he nearly growled.

"What are you?"Poppi asked.

"Poppi, don't be rude." Eager to reduce the tension Hailey stood to put a restraining hand on her great-grandmother's arm.

"No. That is quite alright. She is correct." Grace smiled at Lucius then moved from his arms and took a seat at the table and looked up at Hailey. "I am a *tiresian*."

Poppi threw her arms in the air to exclaim, "I knew it! You people always look like possessed dolls!"

"Poppi!" Hailey smacked her great-grandmother on the shoulder. "Seriously, chill."

Derian sat stiff, curiously watching the women, then addressed the Lucius. "How exactly, did you find yourself a *tiresian*?"

Lucius pulled out a chair and positioned himself between Grace and where Poppi stood. "I fell into the situation. It isn't pertinent."

"How exactly did you find him? You put a spell on him didn't you? You have him mystified as your love slave, right?" Poppi continued. Hailey's mouth flopped open, then she swung another fist into her great-grandmother's shoulder to silence the tirade. What had gotten into her?

Grace rolled her eyes. "That is all silly superstition. Lucius simply looked at some of Hailey's mail. That is all."

Poppi rubbed her shoulder as she glared at Lucius. He raised a brow, then looked away. The confusion was too much. Hailey asked, "Ok, seriously people. What is a *tiresian*?"

"Oh dear." Grace turned to Lucius. "She is a new *viator* then? I thought with what she did that she was much older."

"With what I did? What?" Could this really get any more annoying? Derian reached up and grabbed her hand.

Grace smiled. "No matter. I can read the future. All of my kind can. Your friends are shocked to meet me because it has been rumored that we are all dead."

"Dead?"Hailey breathed. Great. Pirates, Nazis, time travel, mad scientists and a chick that could see the future, could it get any more ridiculous?

"It is a long story," Grace said.

"I'm sure." It always was, though Hailey found it a rather convenient excuse most of the time. Every once in a while she would like someone to say it was a short story and actually tell it. "So you're here why?"

"Perhaps she saw something quite alarming." The air from the room rushed out as they all swung around. Carlo stood in the living room. Beside him Nikanuur held one of the bulbous pole weapons. Hailey still wasn't quite sure what the thing could do, though with the way things were going, lasers were not out of the question.

Carlo favored a more traditional weapon. He held a menacing black Glock on Hailey and sneered.

"Are you fricking serious?" she said.

"You have something of ours." Carlo used the gun to motion toward the vials lying on the table. Lucius and Derian moved to stand between the two men and the women. Carlo cleared his throat to say, "Quite chivalrous gentlemen. I still want those vials."

"No," Derian's voice carried strong across the space.

Carlo sighed and aimed the gun at his chest. "Do I really need to shoot you a second time?"

Hailey stepped forward. "No. I'll get them for you."

"Please do, and don't keep us waiting." Carlo's snakey smile slipped across his lips. Her skin crawled. Oh she hated that smile. Hailey turned her back on the weapons and walked around Derian and Lucius. Poppi was gone. So were the vials.

28

What the hell was she supposed to do? Shooting her great-grandmother was wrong, right? She glanced back. Not a weapon on them. The whole group demonstrated a definite lack of planning. Now, with Derian in the line of fire—again—she needed to think. Think of something, anything.

Carlo's patience was limited, as in limited to two seconds. "What is the problem?"

"Um," she stalled. They were so screwed.

A buzz sounded and Grace gasped, her fingers put to her lips in fright. Hailey craned her neck around Lucius to see her father brandishing his weapon, its bulbous top glowing red, waves emanated from it like heat off asphalt. Grabbing her guts she stepped back in front of the men and walked toward Carlo.

"So, listen, we have a bit of an issue. Poppi, sort of ran off with the vials and…"

Apparently Carlo lost his smooth character in the few moments she spent at the table. His skin flushed with frustration and lips curled. The gun never wavered from Derian as he said, "I suggest you find them."

"Seriously? I doubt she's hiding in a closet. She's long gone and you know it," she barked back. The hand on his gun tightened. He could shoot her just for being the bearer of bad news. It wouldn't be out of character. The guy was a class-A bastard.

"Then I will have to leave you with your father. I believe he is in need of releasing his frustrations." He dismissed them with a turn of his head and addressed Nikanuur, "Do not walk away from here unsuccessful."

Then he faded from view. Nikanuur shook with fury. Hailey wracked her brain for options. She needed to come up with something pretty spectacular if they were going to make it through the next couple minutes.

***

Damn the woman. Poppi once again proved true to form and left them in a lurch. Nikanuur failed to impress his superiors with the handling of the last several weeks and the light to prove himself shone dangerously in his eyes. Derian reached forward and grabbed Hailey's arm to shove her behind him, but she wrenched it clear of his grasp. "So what's it gonna be Daddy? Are you going to kill us all with your fancy toy gun?"

As she spoke her hands moved behind her hips. Derian watched in surprise as his Glock materialized in her fingers. Nikanuur sneered and Hailey raised her hand, the gun cocked and ready to fire. "How about I make it a fair fight?"

The Babylonian barked in surprise just as the gun erupted in her hands. Nikanuur's weapon discharged wide and the combination of the kickback and the impact of the bullet spiraled him onto the couch.

Derian hurried to Hailey's side and pulled her into his arms. She stood silent, shaking as she stared at her dead father. Blood darkened the purple suede cushions. Her voice harsh with emotion broke the silence that had descended on the room. Hailey looked dejectedly at her dead father. "Jason is going to be so pissed about the couch. He just got your blood off of it."

A thud sounded behind them. They whipped around to see Lucius bending down to help Grace who had fainted from the shock.

"Dude. Does she do that a lot?" Hailey asked.

Lucius sat and cradled Grace's head on his lap, smoothing away the soft tendrils of hair that fell across her face. "She has led a rather sheltered existence."

"Right on." Hailey leaned against Derian. "Can we take a nap? I have a splitting headache."

***

They didn't get to the nap right away. Derian and Lucius left to dispose of Nikanuur's body and she had no intention of asking them how. As a father, he sucked. But a dead body was a freaky thing; especially a dead body that had been very much alive only an hour before. A dead body she'd made dead. Shivers ran up her spine and she wondered if she were cut out for this kind of action.

She walked out onto the second story patio and looked out across the complex's pool. The water sat still and the bright blue paint from the bottom made her think of smurfs. Why didn't they ever paint pools pink or red? Why did they always have to be that same blue? A mother approached the pool gate two toddlers in tow, each holding towels covered

326

in cartoon characters and blow up toys. Hailey's gut clenched.

Poppi was gone. It didn't make sense. Everything she had done and said had made Hailey trust her. For a few days she had actually felt like family meant something. Had it all been a lie? Frustration bubbled over as she kicked at a glass coffee table. Why? Why had Poppi taken the vials?

Her toe kicked something and it rattled across the floor and stopped against the rail. She stooped down and lifted one of the vials up to the light; its contents sparkled in the sunlight. Her great-grandmother must have dropped it during her escape. She peered deeply into the clear depths. There was a two-thirds shot that what it contained could help her. The fact that there was a one in three chance she would die an instant poison induced death made her sigh in resignation.

The vial's smooth surface slid against her skin as she tucked it into her pocket. They definitely needed to rescue Roderic from his mountain prison. At least now she had something to give him.

Hailey returned to the kitchen and looked to the living room. Derian and Lucius had the couch wedged halfway through the door. She grimaced. Jason was definitely going to be pissed about the couch.

Grace sat at the table, her hands cupping a mug in an attempt to pull solace from the warm ceramic. Her quiet voice barely registered over the grunting of the two men in the next room, "I am sorry you had to shoot your father."

"He was an asshole," Hailey replied.

Grace looked wide-eyed in shock, her lips trembling. No doubt the two of them had vastly different familial experiences. There wasn't a single person in her bloodline she liked. Not even Poppi. Not now.

Hailey rubbed her eyes with her knuckles. Her brain pounded against her skull and she tentatively reached behind her neck to rub at the base. Once again she wondered if her sanity was preparing its escape plan. The bastard that did this to her was dead. It was a relief of sorts, not having to worry about him coming after her anymore. And Carlo made it more or less clear that his interest in her had waned. Maybe he didn't like being shot. She snorted at the thought and fresh pain pierced the back of her eyes.

Grace looked on in concern. "Is there anything I can do?"

She shook her head. The man with the knowledge to help her died ten feet from where she stood. Hailey looked on as the men finally pushed the couch out the door. Derian rested against the bright purple arm, his head hung with exhaustion. He really shouldn't be doing such activities with the stitches so fresh and the wound barely healed. But that was an argument she lost before a word got out.

"Do you want to go to a doctor?" Grace asked.

The thought had merit. Perhaps modern medicine had an answer but it would take too much time. She had seen that in the years Aunt Sue suffered while battling cancer. The glass vial sat heavy in her pocket. The answer could very well lie in the unlabeled liquid.

Derian picked up his side of the couch and moved out of view. Hopefully they could get the couch down the stairs and into the dumpster before Jason got back.

"Hailey?" Grace asked and she realized she hadn't responded to the woman's last question.

"No. I should feel better after some rest," Hailey replied. Grace held out her tiny hand for Hailey's. They waited for the men, hands clasped in companionable silence.

When Derian and Lucius returned exhaustion sunk its iron grip into them all, leaving discussion a distant priority. Hailey pointed Lucius and Grace toward Jason's bedroom. They'd already destroyed the couch; he could hardly be pissed if they used his room to nap. Derian and she drifted off to sleep in each other's arms in the guest room. Heavy and dreamless, the sleep did much to overcome her anxiety and exhaustion.

Her eyes fluttered open and her first thought zeroed in on the vial she'd transferred to her purse. She would tell the others about it. But not right now. Right now she just wanted to relish being held in strong arms again. She snuggled into Derian. He shifted and pulled her tight against his side.

"Are you awake?" he asked.

"Yes."

"How did you teleport my Glock? I don't remember it disappearing."

Hailey blushed. "I meant to tell you. I forgot it in Babylon when I jumped us."

He pressed a kiss against her temple. "Amazing."

"Yeh. I guess I never have to worry about losing anything anymore. I just have to remember the last time I had it and voila, it's in my hands." His chest rumbled as he chuckled. He was in a good mood, so she figured now was the time to ask the burning question. "When did you and Lucius want to leave for Carpathia?"

He stilled. She didn't care that he didn't want to talk about it. She wasn't being left behind. He said, "Lucius and I are going alone. We will jump as soon as we have the two of you settled somewhere safe."

"Right. And you see how well that worked for Lucius. If you leave us, we'll just find a way to follow you, probably get into trouble and then you'll have to come to our rescue again. It would just be easier if you took us along." She braced her weight on her elbow and pressed her hand against his heart. "To keep an eye on us, you know."

Derian grabbed her hand and stilled it from sliding down his belly. "You are trying to manipulate me."

"Of course I am. Is it working?"

"No."

"Then let's be direct. You aren't leaving me behind, period. And I can guarantee Grace is saying the exact same thing to Lucius,"

Derian swept his eyes to the ceiling. She could see him counting to ten in his head. He replied, "This is foolish,"

She laid her head on his chest, the tiny hairs tickled her cheek. "Sure. But we can be foolish together."

His arm came around her waist and crushed her against him. She lifted her head and his mouth sought hers in a sweet trembling sensation far beyond faint affection. Love could fly so quickly into the stars and she had no intention of letting this one go.

A giant shout boomed from down the hall, "The hell you will woman!"

Hailey grinned as she deepened the kiss. From what she saw of Grace already, the shy little woman could take down the stern centurion with a tip of smile. The four of them were going on an adventure.

29

Hailey eyed the gangly sky hop as he swung her bag onto the belt leading into the airport. He didn't even look to see if it landed. She wondered at the likelihood of it waiting for her when they arrived in Kiev, luck was not looking like her friend when it came to the baggage claim.

Grace stood next to her hugging the giant duffle bag in a death grip. "Are you sure it's safe? Can't I just take it on the plane with me?"

"It'll be fine." She lied. She'd feel like crap if the damn thing ended up mangled or worse, detoured to Timbuktu. But something about Grace made her want to soothe and coddle her. "Besides, they won't let you take it on the plane. It's way too big. What do you have in there anyway?"

Grace dropped the bag to the ground and pulled open the long zipper. She dug her hands deep into its bowels and pulled out two leather bound books that looked like the years had eaten their share of its contents. Pulling the sides back together she struggled to zip it back up. Hailey took pity and bent down to help.

Inside she glimpsed heaps of mix matched clothes and piles of books, but none of the base necessities for the average woman. She looked up at Grace. There wasn't a lick of makeup on the girl and her hair hung straight as a cowboy on stilts. A mystery stood right in front of her. The woman might tug at the sympathy strings but Hailey had enough of mysteries.

But Lucius trusted Grace and Derian trusted Lucius. That left her only one option. She'd trust Grace. But with both eyes wide open and a hand on her gun.

Well, the gun was figurative. They couldn't bring them on the plane and there was a little trouble regarding registration. Apparently guns that time travel aren't always on the up and up with the authorities. Hailey shrugged it off. She could just pop it back in her hand should she need it.

Her new powers were still pretty foreign and unwieldy, but she was slowly getting used to it. Kind of like watching a lot of British television. Eventually the accents and slang start to make sense. Grace thanked Hailey for the help then hauled the bag over to the check-in kiosk. Her tiny hands held on a little too long and the young sky hop had to wrench it from her grasp.

"Come on, it will be fine. We need to catch up with the guys," Hailey said. Both Derian and Lucius had gone ahead since neither carried luggage. When they stopped by her apartment she thought to do the same, but then again, one never knew what one might need in the middle of the Carpathian Mountains.

And again the surreal hit home. So she was off on a rescue mission with two hot time traveling dudes, one that happened to be her own personal hot time traveling dude, and a chick that could read the future. Nothing strange about that.

Grace fell in beside her and they navigated the tightly knit crowds on the way to the departure gates. Hailey asked, "So where did they say we were going again?"

"Transcarpathia. It's a region of the Carpathian Mountains in the west Ukraine," Grace said.

"Transcarpathia? Is that anything like Transylvania?" The names invoked thoughts of vampires and creepy bat infested castles. Just the kind of place she would expect an evil plot to be hatched.

"Not precisely. Transylvania is south of this area in Romania. They aren't too far apart, but definitely different regions." Grace could spout off facts like a contestant on jeopardy. It unnerved Hailey a little, she never really knew what to expect.

"Have you been there?" Hailey asked.

Grace cocked her head. "Oh no. This is the first time I have ever been away from home. I've dreamt about it though."

"You've dreamt about going to Transcarpathia?" Hailey asked. People dreamt about going to Hawaii, maybe Egypt. Not Eastern Europe. At least not people she knew.

Grace giggled and said, "No. Not there specifically. I've dreamt of just being able to go anywhere. This is all quite wonderful."

They reached the escalators that led up to departures. Grace stepped gingerly onto the moving belt, her bottom lip pulled into her mouth by bright white teeth. Hailey looked at the young woman and said, "So, you've not been around much have you?"

Grace shook her head. "No. My people have lived a hidden life for centuries. Going out among the mundane is considered taboo." She looked at Hailey with sadness filled eyes but there was something more there. Something that spoke of strength and determination, "But some things are more important than cultural mores and taboos. Sometimes you have to join in the fight even if it does not come directly for you. Sometimes you have to stand up for what you believe in and love."

The speech sounded practiced. Who was she trying to convince? They reached the top and Grace skipped off the belt and shuffled away from the crowd. Hailey sauntered up to her then nodded toward the line of people waiting to be inspected. "Well let's get in line. I am dying for a beer before we get on the plane and that mass of people is in our way.

Grace's eyes grew wide. "Beer? Oh, do you think I could have a taste? Do you like hops in your beer or do you only drink light beer? I have heard so much about it, but we never had alcohol around. I've always wanted to know what it was like. Do you think I would like it?"

Hailey raised her eyes to the ceiling. Lucius had better take her off her hands when they got to the gate. It was his turn to show the sheltered tourist around.

It took thirty minutes for them to make it through the line and past the security point. Grace nearly decked one of the TSA agents when they pulled her aside for a random pat down. The tiny woman actually cursed, though Hailey was pretty sure she was just testing out the words to see how they worked.

Derian and Lucius waited at Gate A17. Both let out sighs of relief as she and Grace approached. Hailey grinned up at Derian. It wasn't like she would get lost in an airport. She'd already made it through Nazi infested France; evil scientist created torture chambers and walked away from a gun fight with her father. This was cake in comparison.

He pulled her under the crook of his arm and they walked toward the nearest eatery that served beer. "So why don't we just pop out of here and meet them there? It would be so much nicer." She ran her hand around his waist and splayed her fingers over his hip. "Just think, in less than two seconds you and I could be in a hotel, under the covers and enjoying life instead of waiting for a plane and sitting with stinky tourists."

He moved his hand to cup the back of her neck and leaned down to kiss her. When they came up for air several waiting passengers sent censoring glares in her direction. She glared back. Just because they didn't have a hot guy to smooch with was no reason to be rude. Kissing wasn't illegal.

Derian steered her into the restaurant and found them a seat. After they ordered from the overworked waitress he grabbed her hands from across the table. "There is nothing more I would like than to spend the day exploring your body." His eyes sparkled with mischief but then grew serious. "But too much can happen between here and Kiev. We need to stay with Lucius and Grace. If for nothing more than safety in numbers."

It wasn't what she wanted to hear. But he was right. Too much rode on this mission and the last thing they needed was to get separated before they made it to the mountains. "I still don't understand who or what she is. Half the time I think she's just an overprotected naive little girl. The rest of the time she scares the shit out of me with her knowledge and what she can see."

"Well, she's definitely overprotected. But the other comes from her talent and her age." The waitress dropped off the beer and Derian took a long swallow. Hailey rested her hands around the cool bottle and let the sweet promise of what the first taste would bring settle in her mouth. Anticipation of a good beer was almost as good as the genuine article.

"What do you mean her age? She can't be more than twenty- five," Hailey said before she let the first sip slide down her throat. Oh man that was a great beer.

"She's probably closer to three or four hundred years," he said.

The answer surprised her enough that a few drops of beer dribbled from her lip and onto the shiny finished table top. She swiped her hand across her chin and hoped no one noticed. "Three or four hundred? Are you serious? How is that possible? She can't jump time like us."

"No. No she can't. I don't know how it works. I only met a *tiresian* once. The meeting was short and over eight hundred years ago. We just don't know that much about them. And no one really worried about it because they were supposed to have all died."

Hailey looked down at her beer. How was it possible that things could get even more confusing? Grace was a mystery. But then, so was she. Lucius seemed pretty smitten with Grace, when he didn't look like he wanted to strangle her. Whatever happened between those two would be an interesting story. Maybe she could get it out of one of them on the plane.

In the meantime, she had a good beer and a good man in front of her. No need to worry right now. There was plenty of time for that in the future. "So, did I mention you have the most incredible sexy eyes?"

Derian coughed into his beer. "Is that some kind of pick up line, *léof?*"

"I don't know. Did it work?"

He leaned over and pressed his lips to hers. Apparently it did work.

About the Author:

Erin Lausten is a woman of many talents and seemingly varied hobbies. Her life is as busy and fast paced as her books. Working as an archeologist and research librarian in the recent past, Erin has a unique view of the world. She sees all possibilities and doesn't accept the limited scope accepted by society. Her favorite question is "Why not?" Join her, if only for a story or two, in her flights of fancy and 'what if' scenarios.

The Saga continues

Join Grace and Lucius in **Unforeseen**, the second book in the Viator Series, to be released Summer of 2012. Discover their story and more from Hailey, Derian, Poppi, and the rest of the *viators* in another fast-paced adventure romance.

Books by Erin Lausten:

<u>Viator series:</u>
Unexpected
Unforeseen
Shadows and Intrigue

<u>Steampunk:</u>
Cibola's Promise
Cibola's Revenge

<u>Other:</u>
Love Uncommon

Discover Erin Lausten titles at
http://erinlausten.com

Find Erin on the Web:
https://www.facebook.com/erinlausten
http://erinlausten.wordpress.com/
https://twitter.com/erinlausten

www.ingramcontent.com/pod-product-compliance
Lightning Source LLC
Chambersburg PA
CBHW050920250626
47155CB00001B/315